"So, you're finally going to eat lunch with me," Nathan said, giving Charlotte a mischievous glance. **"After all these years."**

A vision of him laughing at her while she flailed wildly in the schoolyard trying to free a frog he'd put on her head from her tangled braids came rushing to the front of her mind. The next week he'd asked her to eat her lunch with him. An invitation she'd flatly refused.

"Only for work, and you'll be dismissed instantly if I get so much as a glimpse or hint of a frog." She smiled at his chuckle.

"No teasing." He met her gaze with his clear blue eyes. Eyes so intense they invited her to trust. "I promise."

"I have not agreed to hire you yet, Mr. Taylor."

"You must call me Nathan. I fear I'll never be able to think of you as Miss Green."

"Nathan." The name rolled off her tongue with ease. She liked the sound of it. It was a strong and manly name. "I don't see how I can offer you the job. Not with our history."

Angel Moore fell in love with romance in elementary school when she read the story of Robin Hood and Maid Marian. Who doesn't want to escape to a happily-ever-after world? Married to her best friend, she has two wonderful sons, a lovely daughter-in-law and three grandkids. She loves sharing her faith and the hope she knows is real because of God's goodness to her. Find her at www.angelmoorebooks.com.

Books by Angel Moore

Love Inspired Historical

Conveniently Wed
The Marriage Bargain
The Rightful Heir
Husband by Arrangement
A Ready-Made Texas Family

ANGEL MOORE

A Ready-Made Texas Family

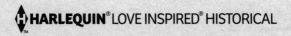

HARLEQUIN® LOVE INSPIRED® HISTORICAL

Recycling programs
for this product may
not exist in your area.

LOVE INSPIRED BOOKS

ISBN-13: 978-1-335-00523-6

A Ready-Made Texas Family

Copyright © 2019 by Angelissa J. Moore

All rights reserved. Except for use in any review, the reproduction
or utilization of this work in whole or in part in any form by any
electronic, mechanical or other means, now known or hereafter
invented, including xerography, photocopying and recording, or in
any information storage or retrieval system, is forbidden without
the written permission of the editorial office, Love Inspired Books,
195 Broadway, New York, NY 10007 U.S.A.

This is a work of fiction. Names, characters, places and incidents are
either the product of the author's imagination or are used fictitiously, and
any resemblance to actual persons, living or dead, business establishments,
events or locales is entirely coincidental.

This edition published by arrangement with Love Inspired Books.

® and TM are trademarks of Love Inspired Books, used under license.
Trademarks indicated with ® are registered in the United States Patent
and Trademark Office, the Canadian Intellectual Property Office and in
other countries.

www.Harlequin.com

Printed in U.S.A.

Strength and honour are her clothing;
and she shall rejoice in time to come.
—*Proverbs* 31:25

Chapter One

"No. No. No." Charlotte Green held up her hands and took a step back from the registration desk. "I will not—cannot—work with him." She felt her face twist in denial as she pointed at the man who'd followed the town banker into her lobby. Nathan Taylor had tormented her through much of their childhood. The fact that he'd grown into a handsome man did not escape her notice. His black suit jacket fit his broad shoulders as though it were hand tailored. The blue eyes dancing with mischief taunted her without saying a word.

"Miss Green, you have no choice." Thomas Freeman refused to listen to her. "Your father borrowed from my bank to run this hotel. The only way for you to repay my money is for Green's Grand Hotel to remain a successful business. My alternative will be to sell the property to another hotelier." He smirked. An actual smirk. Thomas Freeman wanted his money.

Charlotte knew that whatever happened to her and her younger siblings did not matter to the man.

She refused to allow him to bully her. "I will find a way. I'll find someone else, but I will not work with him. He is incorrigible."

Nathan stepped around Mr. Freeman. "Miss Green, please accept my condolences on the loss of your parents. I know this is a terrible time for you and your family." Sympathy? It was unlike any trait she'd ever seen in him. She would not be caught off guard by the charm he'd acquired in the years since he'd left Gran Colina.

Charlotte schooled her features into what she hoped was politeness. "Thank you, Mr. Taylor." She picked up her pencil and looked across the desk at both men. "If you will excuse me, I have work to do." She turned her attention to the registration book but was unable to focus as the entries swam before her eyes. She blinked quickly. No one would see her cry. Any sign of weakness in front of Mr. Freeman could cause an increase in the scrutiny he'd fixed on her Monday morning after her father and his wife, the woman she'd grown to accept and love as her mother, were killed in a train wreck.

The banker persisted. "Mr. Taylor will be here to make certain the work is done in a timely and proficient manner. He comes highly recommended by his uncle."

She tossed the pencil onto the book. "What qualifications for running a hotel does the nephew of our town doctor have? I grew up in this hotel. There's not a person alive who knows more about this business than I do."

Charlotte gasped as the truth of her words sank in. It was Friday morning. Four days since her parents had died.

Michael and Sarah bolted through the door that led to the family residence and wrapped themselves around her legs.

"Michael took my doll!" Sarah reached around Charlotte and tried to snatch the handkerchief doll from the boy.

Charlotte held out her hand to Michael. "Give me the doll."

He hid the doll behind his back. "I won't. She took Pa's hat. I'm keeping her doll till she gives me my hat. Pa woulda wanted me to have his hat."

Charlotte knelt between her young sister and brother. At five and six years old, they had resorted to bickering as a way to cope with their grief. "Sarah, you can't take things from Michael and not expect him to be upset."

Sarah sniveled against Charlotte's shoulder. "But I only wanted to hold it. It smells like Pa."

"It's mine. You said so, Charlotte. She can't have it!" Michael's bottom lip quivered as he fought against tears.

She wrapped them both in a hug. "Shush now." She rocked them in her arms and sent up a silent prayer for wisdom. "Let me take care of these gentlemen, and I'll come find something for each of you to have."

"Can I have Momma's shawl?" Sarah whimpered. "It's the same color as her eyes."

"We'll all choose together." Charlotte stood and held them both by the hand. "For now, Sarah, you give Michael the hat, and, Michael, you hand the doll to

Sarah." She turned them toward the door they'd come through. "Both of you go to the kitchen and wait for me. We'll have milk and cookies when I'm done."

They scurried through the door, and Charlotte turned back to the men. "Excuse the interruption."

Mr. Freeman nodded in the direction of the kids. "Those two are the reason you need help. You can't take care of the hotel. You have woman's work to do."

Charlotte bristled like the gray mouser who stood guard on the back porch of the hotel. "Michael and Sarah are not work. They are my brother and sister, and the very reason I will not relinquish this business to you or anyone else."

The banker snapped at her. "I won't sit idly by while my investment in this property wastes away under your childish attempts to run it. Mr. Taylor is here and will remain on staff as the hotel manager until such time as I say differently or the note is paid in full."

The front door of the hotel opened, and a family who'd checked in the day before entered. The mother smiled at the father, and the children bounded up the stairway toward their rooms.

Nathan cleared his throat. "If I may?" He looked at Charlotte. "Miss Green, is there somewhere you and I could speak in private? The lobby isn't really the best place to discuss your personal business."

At least he acknowledged that it was indeed her business. Unlike Mr. Freeman.

"We could step into my parlor."

Mr. Freeman balked. "I don't have time for more discussion. Mr. Taylor, this hotel cannot survive under the oversight of Miss Green. If you refuse to accept this position or if she refuses to allow you to stay, I will have no choice but to call the note due and sell the hotel."

"You can't do that! This hotel is mine. It belongs to me and the children." He couldn't take away their home.

"I can, and I will. The note was signed by your father. At his death, I have a responsibility to protect the holdings of the bank. This hotel was put up as surety. I can't sit idly by and let it lose value."

"Give us the rest of the morning to discuss the matter between us." Mr. Taylor seemed determined to take matters in hand.

Charlotte wouldn't stand idly by and listen to them. "The two of you may discuss matters until your heart is content, but this hotel is mine. I won't concede that fact to anyone. For any reason." She closed the registration book and went into the residence.

Nathan convinced Thomas Freeman to give him an opportunity to prove his skills at problem solving by allowing him to speak to Charlotte alone. In mere moments he took a seat in a straight-backed chair in Charlotte's parlor. She sat across from him, perched on the edge of the settee like a bird ready to take flight.

"I'm sorry to have met again under these circumstances." He knew the pain of loss was fresh for her.

She turned at the sound of something falling to the floor in the kitchen and called out to the kids. "Be careful in there. I'll only be a few more minutes." Her blue eyes trained on him the instant she turned back to face him. "I'm surprised to see you here at all."

Charlotte Green had lost none of her feistiness. It was one of the things that had intrigued him about her when they were in school. All the older girls were looking for husbands and planning on babies and farms. Not Charlotte. Her vivid imagination filled her with stories of adventures she wanted to take and how exciting her life was in the moment. He knew no man would conquer her strong will. He could see that strength of character had stayed with her.

"I had no intention of returning to Gran Colina, though I did love living here. My father did, too."

"I'm sorry you made the trip at Mr. Freeman's invitation to work here, but you must understand that the position is not available to you. I would not take on anyone if not for the loan at the bank." She clasped her hands together and settled them in the lap of her black dress. It was harsh against her milky skin. The beauty he'd seen years ago had blossomed. Her dark brown tresses were twisted into a bun, but he remembered the way they had fallen in shiny waves around her shoulders. The tendrils that danced by her ears would be a major distraction if he wasn't so focused on the reason he was in Gran Colina.

"Miss Green—Charlotte, if I may—you are in a most precarious situation. If you do not allow me to stay, you will lose your home. Your livelihood."

Sarah burst into the room. "You said you were coming, and we're hungry."

Charlotte lifted a finger to silence her interruption, but the child would not be deterred.

"If you don't come now, we're gonna eat the cookies without you." Sarah stood at Charlotte's knee and stared at Nathan. The doll from the earlier argument was tucked under her arm. "You should leave my sister alone. She has to take care of us, not talk to you."

Nathan smiled at Sarah. "That's what we're discussing. I'm here to help her, so she can have time to care for you."

"I don't need—"

Sarah cut off Charlotte's protest and tugged on her hand. "Then you can come in the kitchen and give us cookies."

"You mustn't interrupt." Charlotte cupped Sarah's cheek. "I have to finish speaking to Mr. Taylor. Five more minutes." She nudged her young sister in the direction of the kitchen.

To Nathan she said, "As you can see, I have things to do, so if you'll just accept that your coming here was mistake, we can say our goodbyes."

"How old is she?" Nathan pointed toward the door Sarah had gone through.

"Five, but that has nothing to do with this."

"It has everything to do with this. Your brother is a bit older? Maybe a year or two?"

"He's six."

"How will you provide for them when Mr. Freeman takes the hotel from you?"

She stiffened, and her eyes narrowed. "He will not take the hotel. You may think you're my only solution, but I assure you that you are not."

"I have no doubt of your determination, Charlotte. We both know how stubborn you can be."

"What does that mean?" Indignation dripped from her words.

"It means I know you."

"You do not. We haven't seen each other in six years."

"I do. Maybe not everything about you now that

you are a young lady of what? Nineteen. If I remember right, you're three years younger than me. I realize you're no longer a schoolgirl, but I guarantee that I know more about you than any stranger you could hope to hire for help." The bell on the registration desk rang. "And you need help."

Michael came into the room. "Sarah spilled the milk. I told her to wait, but it's all over the floor and on her dress. She's gonna smell something awful if you don't make her change her clothes. I know, 'cause it happened to me once when I was a little kid."

The bell rang again, and Nathan stood. "I'll take care of the desk, and you take care of Sarah. We'll meet back here in ten minutes."

"Ten minutes." As much as her face rebuffed Nathan, she stood and followed Michael into the kitchen.

Nathan was handing over a room key to a new guest when Charlotte joined him behind the registration desk.

"I wasn't expecting a new guest this morning." She pulled the registration book closer to read the name.

"Mr. Eaton arrived on the train with me. He mentioned that he hadn't booked a room, so I suggested he come here. He had business to attend to this morning and has just finished." He pulled the book back in front of him and notated the estimated end date of the man's stay. "I have convinced him to stay until the train on Monday morning. In the best room available and at a good rate. For the hotel and for him."

Charlotte took the pen from his hand. "I could have taken over the desk. Sarah would have been fine for a few minutes."

"But you didn't need to." He faced her and leaned

against the desk with his back to the front door. "And if I hadn't been on the train, Mr. Eaton might have gone to Martha's Boarding House instead."

She almost smiled. A slight lifting of the corner of her full lips that didn't reach her eyes, but it was a start. "Martha closed that place down three years ago and moved to live with her daughter in Albuquerque."

"So things have changed a bit since I left."

"A lot has changed." She put the pen away. "Especially in the last few days." The sorrow washed over her anew.

He hated to see her pain. A pain he knew too well. "When my mother passed away, I didn't know how my father and I would get along without her."

"I didn't know." Her gaze met his. "I'm sorry."

"It was five years ago." He pushed away from the desk. "That's when I went to work at the Turner Hotel in Dallas." The pain of the loss stirred in him. If they hadn't moved away from Gran Colina in pursuit of financial stability, his mother might still be alive. Her death drove him to succeed.

"I've heard of them. Pa used to say that we might not be as fancy as a Turner Hotel, but we owed it to our guests to do as fine a job as they did."

"When I met with your parents in Dallas, your father told me how hard all of you worked to make Green's Grand Hotel the success it is. He wanted to expand and grow the business in order to provide a living for all of his children when they became adults."

Charlotte's face lost some of its color. "You met with Pa? When?"

"I thought you knew. He and your mother were in Dallas to see how Turner Hotels are managed. He was hoping to learn something that could be implemented here. They refused him on the spot. No one from the Turner family would help him. They never share trade secrets with someone outside of their business. I was the only person in Dallas your parents knew. They invited me to share a meal with them. That's when your father told me about his plans to make improvements here. I offered to share anything I'd learned with them. I saw it as a neighborly thing to do. After all, they weren't in competition with the Turner Hotel. We met on several occasions during their time in Dallas."

She leaned against the desk. "I didn't know. They told me they were going to celebrate their anniversary. They were on their way home when the train wrecked. Someone didn't throw a switch on the tracks is the only explanation I've heard. I'm still not sure what happened. Only that they're gone."

"Charlotte, I know you're grieving, but please consider taking me on to manage the hotel. I gave up my job in Dallas because Mr. Freeman assured me that he was in ownership of the hotel due to your parents' passing." The offer had come with the promise of bettering himself financially. He'd made his decision based on a strong suggestion that the position could develop into a partnership in the future. "In my five years at Turner Hotels, I rose as far as I could for someone who is not part of the family. The higher positions were saved for Turners. I can't go back now." He pointed into the private residence. "You have your hands full here. Your father shared his vision with me. I know how he intended to grow this business. Let me help you."

"He borrowed money, but I don't know where it is.

If I had the money for renovations, I could just give it back to the bank."

Her dilemma was tragic, but he could help her. If she didn't have the will of a wild horse, they could both benefit from this arrangement. And, according to Mr. Freeman, she didn't have a choice in the matter. Whether she believed it or not.

He looked around to ensure that no one would overhear. "Your father ordered new furnishings with that money. Everything should arrive in six to eight weeks."

She shook her head. "How do you know that?"

"I helped him find the suppliers and place the orders."

"Why would you do that? If you worked for Turner Hotels, weren't you putting your job at risk?"

"It was the right thing to do. I grew up here. I couldn't turn my back on him or anyone else in town."

"But if you hadn't helped him, maybe I could have paid back that money and saved the hotel. Can I cancel the orders?"

"No. The money cannot be refunded." He tapped his knuckles on the registration book. "Your father knew Gran Colina was growing so fast that he had to make changes to compete with other hotels that are sure to open in town. He didn't want to lose everything he'd worked so hard for just because this place was older."

"It's too much. I can't think right now. I have to make sure everything is on track in the kitchen for the lunch crowd."

"Let me share the details of it with you. I feel certain you'll see the wisdom in your father's plans."

She glared at him. "What's in it for you, Nathan

Taylor? What difference does it make to you? After all these years in Dallas, why do you want to be in Gran Colina?"

"Have lunch with me, and I'll answer all of your questions." He hoped what he knew would be enough to satisfy her. He could tell her all the things he had discussed with her father and mother about the hotel. He hoped his experience would turn the small hotel into something he could be proud of—something that would give him the security he'd lost when his family had moved away. Gran Colina was the last place where he'd felt like he belonged. He didn't want to end up like his father, roaming from one job and town to another.

The blue eyes that stared at him couldn't be part of the reason he returned. Charlotte Green had made it plain years ago that he was not someone she wanted for a friend. Her reaction to his arrival today confirmed that her feelings had not changed.

Charlotte carried two plates to the table by the window where Nathan had waited for over an hour. Every time she'd looked at him, he was writing notes in a small book that he closed as she approached. "I'm sorry. I hired more help for the kitchen earlier this week, but she's still learning how to manage the lunch rush."

He stood and pulled out her chair. "Those are the type of problems that I'm trained to handle." He returned to his seat.

"I've worked in the kitchen here since I was a little girl. I know exactly how to handle that."

"Shall I say grace?" At her nod he offered thanks for their food. When he looked up she caught a glimpse of mischievousness. "So," he said, "you're finally going to eat lunch with me. After all these years."

A vision of Nathan laughing at her came rushing to the front of her mind. He had put a frog on her head, and she'd flailed wildly in the schoolyard trying to free the slimy creature from her tangled braids. The next week he'd asked her to eat her lunch with him. An invitation she'd flatly refused, and one that had not been repeated.

"Only for work, and you'll be dismissed instantly if I get so much as a glimpse or hint of a frog." She smiled at his chuckle.

"No teasing." He met her gaze with his clear blue eyes. Eyes so intense they invited her to trust. "I promise."

Then he blinked, picked up his glass of water and changed the subject back to the hotel. "Your experience here will make your training much easier, but there is a lot about the business side of running a hotel and restaurant that most people never consider."

"You do realize that I only need someone to train me. I won't be hiring a manager; I will manage the hotel myself."

"I assume you've handled the registration desk many times."

She nodded. "Yes, and I've worked in the restaurant. The staff has been here for years. The cook worked with Momma for the last several months, so it seemed natural to move her up to that responsibility. I had to take on a new assistant for her, so I hired her daughter. She peels potatoes and washes up. Things that Momma and I used to do together." The memories of laughing over the worktable while she made a piecrust and her mother cut up potatoes came flooding back with the force of a river.

Her father had remarried when Charlotte was seven. His bride, Nancy, had loved and treated Charlotte as her own child. So much so, that Charlotte had decided to call her Momma. In Charlotte's childish mind, it had seemed right to give her father's wife a maternal name, but it had to be different than Ma. Ma had nurtured Charlotte until she passed when Charlotte was five. Two years later, Nancy had stepped into their lives, and Charlotte would never forget the love she and her father received from such a fine Christian woman. But now was not a time for fond remembrances.

She refused to succumb to her emotions. No savvy businesswoman cried in a business meeting. It hadn't been a week since they'd passed, and her carefree days were over. The details of the work must be done. She finished reciting her list of the hotel workers to Nathan. "There are two maids who make up the rooms, do all the cleaning and manage the laundry. Pa always carried the guests' cases up to their rooms."

"Did your mother order the food for the restaurant?"

"Yes. She also cooked, but I did most of the baking."

"Do you intend to continue baking?"

"I do. Most of it can be done in the evenings after the children are in bed. I worked hard to master Momma's recipes. It's what I do best, and I find it helps me to relax."

He held up slice of bread. "Did you make this?"

"Yes. Last night."

"It's very good." He spread fresh butter on the slice. "What time did you retire for the evening?"

Up to this point, his questions had been businesslike. She had no problems answering, but this seemed personal. "What difference does that make?"

"If you went to bed before midnight, I would be most surprised. How long do you think you can keep up that pace?"

"I'll do what needs to be done. Pa and Momma did."

He shook his head. "Your pa didn't intend for you to run this hotel by yourself."

"No, he didn't. According to you, he intended to build it into a much larger and more successful business. But, in the same way he didn't count on a train wreck, I can't count on going to bed early anymore. There are some things about which we get no choice." She pushed aside the sandwich she'd barely touched. Her appetite was completely gone. It had disappeared on Monday with the news of the death of her parents. She wasn't sure if, or when, it would return.

Nathan reached across the table and put his hand on top of hers. The unexpectedness of his touch startled her, but the comfort of its warmth kept her from pulling away. "You've suffered a great shock. You're making the best decisions you can at the moment, but you'll have time to think back on them later. Do you really want to be exhausted all the time? Your brother and sister need more than the money you'll make in this hotel. They need you."

"My heart is so broken. I am doing my best, but it's hard to breathe." Was he right? She looked up at him, not expecting to pour out her heart, but it happened. "Learning about the train wreck on Monday was more of a shock than Ma's death when I was a child. Pa never expected to marry again, but then Nancy came along and won his heart. And mine. She was as much my mother as the one who gave me birth. I owe it to the two of them to make sure Michael and Sarah are taken care of. And I know how Michael and Sarah feel, because my mother died when I was young. I can't believe it's happening again." Charlotte put her elbows on the table and dropped her face into her hands.

Nathan didn't say anything. She hadn't expected him to. No one knew what to say to her. Almost everyone in town had tried, but she was beyond receiving comfort. No words would heal the aching in her chest or take away the mind-numbing grief.

Brown boots appeared on the floor to her right, and she heard the wearer clear his throat.

"Miss Green, I'd like a moment of your time."

She looked up to see Gilbert Jefferson standing beside her. "What is it, Mr. Jefferson?"

The former sheriff stood over her with his hat in his hands. He was shaved and dressed in what must be his best suit. She was surprised, given the unkempt state that was his recent form. His reputation had suffered greatly in recent months after he'd tried to sway the town elections for sheriff and mayor. If not for the mercy of the traveling judge, he might have been sent to jail.

Jefferson looked from her to Nathan and back. "I'd like to speak to you privately about a matter of some importance."

Nathan seemed to sit a bit taller in his chair at the words. "If you have business with Miss Green about the hotel, then, as the hotel manager, I must insist you speak in my presence."

Charlotte cut her eyes to Nathan. How dare he make

such a statement? The warning he conveyed to her without a word gave her reason for concern.

"Mr. Jefferson, you may speak freely in front of Mr. Taylor. You may remember him from his time in Gran Colina. He is Doc Taylor's nephew."

A huff and the way Mr. Jefferson tortured the brim of his hat in his fists let Charlotte know she would not agree with anything he shared. "It's about you, Miss Green. Not the hotel."

She couldn't imagine what business he had with her. "I am engaged in a meeting with Mr. Taylor at the moment. You'll understand that there are many things I must attend to at this time. Please forgive that I am unable to speak to you now."

"Fine. I'll just come out with it." Mr. Jefferson looked over both shoulders and lowered his voice. "I'm here to ask permission to come calling."

Charlotte choked. A sputtering fit of coughing over-took her at the preposterous words. Nathan put a glass of water in her hand and came to stand beside her and thump her on the back.

"Try to catch your breath, Charlotte." Nathan ceased his pounding, but when he returned to his seat, she could see the laughter in his eyes.

She took a long drink of water and set the glass on the table. "Please forgive me, Mr. Jefferson."

"I'd like your answer today." The man hadn't moved an inch. "I think now would be best. I'll be needing to arrange for courting you in the proper ways of a woman of your standing and means."

Her standing and means? She felt her face flare hot and her eyes grow wide. Nathan, ignored by Mr. Jefferson, gave a slight shake of his head. It had been years since she'd been around Nathan. He'd always irritated her beyond words, but his signals to her were as clear as if they'd been the dearest of friends. For some unknown reason, he wanted her to refuse with grace instead of the indignation that boiled to the surface on her insides. Caught unawares as she was by the request she considered to be ludicrous, Charlotte heeded his silent warning.

"I'm sorry, Mr. Jefferson. Please understand that I'm in mourning for my parents and cannot at this time entertain a suitor."

"Well, sure, you're still prob'ly crying over your folks, but that'll end soon enough. I was thinking that spending time with me would help you over it."

She opened her mouth but saw the slight lift of Nathan's finger on the tablecloth.

Michael and Sarah came through the kitchen door at that moment. Charlotte had left them at the kitchen table to eat their lunch while she talked to Nathan.

Michael interrupted without excusing himself. "Charlotte, Sarah needs a nap. She's snapping at me like a turtle."

"I didn't snap. I just told you to quit pulling my pigtails." Tears clung to Sarah's blond lashes. Her green eyes were heavy with fatigue.

Mr. Jefferson looked at the kids. "You two need to head back into the kitchen. It ain't good manners to talk when adults are talking."

Charlotte saw Nathan shrug his shoulders. If she wasn't so perturbed at Mr. Jefferson's interference with her siblings, she'd have laughed at Nathan's abdication from his earlier cautions to guard her tongue with the man. Somehow, knowing that Nathan no longer objected made it easier to ignore Mr. Jefferson.

"Okay, you two." She held out a hand to each of the children. "I think we've earned an hour or two of time at home. You run along to the parlor, and I'll be right behind you. I just have to answer a question for Mr. Jefferson first." She nudged them toward their residence.

Nathan smiled at her calm tone, but she knew he wasn't fooled by it. Mr. Jefferson, on the other hand, misinterpreted her to the fullest extent.

Mr. Jefferson smiled. "I'm glad to see you understand the need for us to make our courtship official today. In spite of the young ones."

She stood and took a step toward the man. "I am giving you my official answer now." She took another step, and Mr. Jefferson leaned back a bit. "I do not do things in spite of my siblings." She stepped forward again, and this time he moved away from her. "From this very moment, everything I do will be for those two." She couldn't help herself. She lifted her hand and would have poked a finger into his chest if Nathan hadn't hummed a negative note. "My answer to your offer of courtship is a resounding no. Not now. Not tomorrow. Not ever." She stepped forward, and Mr. Jefferson stumbled backward. "You may always remember that I reached this decision because of you. Thank you for raising the keen awareness of my responsibilities to my siblings to a new height." She stopped and took a breath. "Good day to you, Mr. Jefferson. You're welcome to stay for a piece of complimentary pie if you like."

She brushed her hands together as if she were wiping the garden dirt from her palms and left the restaurant.

Charlotte was almost to her residence when the sound of Nathan's laughter made her aware that he'd followed her.

"Wait a minute." Nathan caught her before she closed the door to the residence.

"I'm busy at the moment, Mr. Taylor." In truth, she was trembling. Anger had risen in her with a lightning speed she'd never experienced.

"I want to offer a word of caution." His serious tone made her stop to listen.

"What is it?"

Nathan paused as if choosing his words with great care. "That incident may be the first of many."

"With Gilbert Jefferson? I think I made myself plain. He won't be coming back around."

"He may not be back, but others will come."

"There have not been a steady stream of gentleman callers at my door, Mr. Taylor. I don't expect that to change. Mother took great pains to shoo away anyone she thought unsuitable."

"Things are different now. What he said is true. You have a station in life that makes you attractive." He lifted his hand to indicate their surroundings. "This hotel is quite a prize for a man. And a young wife in the bargain sweetens the deal."

"Bargain? A sweet deal?" She glared at him. "Is that what you think of me?"

He shook his head. "Not me. I have no intention of marrying."

"So you're saying you don't think I'm attractive or a good prospect for marriage?" She didn't know what bothered her more. The thought of being pursued for her worldly goods or the thought that Nathan didn't consider her worthy of marrying.

"No. I'm not saying that. I'm saying that you need to use caution. Men who would never have come around if your parents were here will approach you now. They won't all have pure motives. As to whether or not you are a good prospect for marriage, that is not for me to say. I have no intention of marrying anyone. I have committed myself to a successful career. I won't be caught in want again. I've seen the damage that can do to a person's health and even their life."

No man had ever pursued her with diligence. "I'm sure you're mistaken."

"Time will prove which of us is right." He shrugged and changed the subject. "If you'll show me where to find the journals for the hotel, I'll sit at the desk while you spend time with Michael and Sarah. You can comfort them, and I'll familiarize myself with the state of the hotel finances and such."

"I have not agreed to hire you, Mr. Taylor."

"Nathan. You must call me Nathan. I fear I'll never be able to think of you as Miss Green. Not after all the years of calling you Charlotte."

"Nathan." The name rolled of her tongue with ease. She liked the sound of it. It was a strong and manly name. "I don't see how I can offer you the job. Not with our history."

He leaned over and lowered his voice. "Our history is that we were children together. Surely, as adults, we can overlook the things we did to one another in school. Maybe you could even find it in your heart to forgive

me for tormenting you with my incessant teasing—
and a frog."

Michael's voice drifted from the settee. "It'll be fun,
Sarah. You'll see. Charlotte will take care of us. We
won't be orphans. Not like the ones who came through
on the train last month."

Nathan's face blanched. "Go to them. Let me help
you."

She nodded and pointed to the corner of the parlor.
"The journals are in the cabinet under the window. You
may take everything except the black ledger on the top
of the pile. That one contains our personal finances."

He opened the cabinet door, and the journals tumbled onto the floor. He cut his eyes at her as he knelt
and stacked them in some semblance of order.

"Sorry. I was in a hurry to find something and
shoved them back into the cabinet when the registration desk bell rang." Let him disapprove of her methods all he wanted. She didn't have time to make the
inside of her cabinets look like a museum of orderli-
ness. She pointed to the lobby door. "You can leave
that ajar and call me if you need anything."

He picked up the journals and went through the
doorway. "I'll close it. You need some time with your
family."

The door closed, and she sank onto the settee with
her sad brother and sister.

After hearing Gilbert Jefferson's proposal, she was
grateful anew for Momma's constant protection from
various suitors. She'd refused many young men who'd
come to call on Charlotte. Anger had been Charlotte's
response on most of those occasions. Now that she
had the responsibility for her siblings, she wondered

if God had prompted her mother to issue those rejections. For so long, Charlotte had longed for a man to capture her heart and whisk her away to a romantic life filled with adventure.

Death and responsibility for two small children had turned her focus. She had no time for anything but Michael and Sarah and the hotel. Nothing would distract her. Nothing—and no one.

Sarah climbed into her lap, and Michael snuggled close to her side. They were a family. Even though their parents were gone, Charlotte wouldn't let these two ever want for love and protection.

She'd protect the kids. And their future. Even if it meant letting Nathan Taylor manage Green's Grand Hotel. But only long enough to teach her how to run the place on her own.

Chapter Two

"**Y**ou look exhausted." Nathan said the first thing that came to mind when Charlotte entered the lobby—and immediately regretted it. The afternoon had turned to evening while he'd studied the hotel records. He closed the last journal and added it to the stack on the shelf under the registration desk.

"Thank you." She sidled up beside him and looked at the registration book.

"I'm sorry. I plead fatigue as the excuse for my lack of manners."

"You're forgiven because I don't have the energy to argue with you tonight."

"Are the kids asleep?" He didn't see how she'd be able to handle the business and the children. His mother had always cared for him while his father worked. If Charlotte insisted on being both mother and father to the kids and keeping the hotel in top-notch order, he didn't know how she'd manage.

"Finally. Poor Sarah cried herself to sleep. Again." She closed the book and drew in a deep breath that echoed out as a sigh. "Michael is angry. He goes to sleep with the edge of the blanket clutched in his hands. Tension fills his little body. I think I'm more concerned for him than her."

"It's been a tough week. They're young. They'll adjust in time."

"If only they didn't have to." Her brow furrowed in an expression she was much too young to wear. "Pa wanted the hotel to provide for us, but we'd give it all to have him back."

He didn't have an answer for her. He'd missed his mother terribly for months. Even after five years the scent of lilacs or hearing her favorite hymn in church brought back the pain of losing her.

He checked his pocket watch. Ten thirty. He snapped the cover shut and slid it into his vest pocket. "So, are we settled?"

"Huh?" She frowned. "Settled on what?"

"On my position as hotel manager."

"I've been thinking about it all evening. I don't like it." She walked around the desk in the direction of the kitchen and turned back to face him. "After praying over it, I don't know that I have a choice. Mr. Freeman apparently has the power to take possession of the hotel. My father wouldn't be pleased if I gave away what he worked so hard to build." She pulled her bottom lip inward. "Since you helped Pa make the arrangements for the changes, you'll have a leg up on anyone else I could hire."

"I know my business, Charlotte. You won't regret it." He knew she didn't like him—in fact, could barely tolerate him. He wouldn't let that keep him from helping her. "Your parents were excited about the changes they planned and the furnishings they ordered. I thought about how rewarding it would be for them to come back to Gran Colina and realize their dreams. I had no idea I'd be on hand to oversee it." He knew as soon as the words left his mouth that he'd provoked her.

She bristled. "You will be here as the manager. I will have oversight of any changes."

"Of course, I only meant—"

She held up one hand. "It doesn't matter. As long as we understand each other."

He swallowed his apology and tried to attribute her shortness to grief. "We do, as long as you realize that I know the hotel business better than anyone else you could hire. I commit to you that I'll use all my knowledge and experience to help you fulfill your parents' plans."

"Fine." Her curt nod was in time with the single-word response.

"Fine." He lifted his jacket from the back of a chair near the desk. He'd removed it after the restaurant had closed and all the guests had returned to their rooms for the night. He slid his arms into the sleeves, hating the warmth of it on the hot August night.

Charlotte pointed over her shoulder at the kitchen door. "I've got some baking to do."

"I have a question before you go." Nathan came from behind the desk. "I'll need to make living arrangements. Would you be interested in a suggestion that would save money for you?"

She clasped her hands together in front of her. "I would."

"After looking over the journals and knowing the amount of the banknote—" Her breath caught on this revelation. "I only know the exact amount because your father noted it in the journal as a liability. He had shared much of the information with me when we were working on the orders."

"I see. I hadn't fully reviewed the journals. Every time I started to read them something distracted me." She shrugged. "You probably already had an idea of the amount because of helping him order everything. I'm just not accustomed to anyone knowing our private business. It's not the sort of thing Pa shared."

"I promise you have my full confidence and discretion."

"Thank you." She twisted her hands. "What is your idea for saving money?"

"If there is a space in the hotel that could be allocated as my lodging, the amount I will need to earn can be greatly reduced." He held up one finger. "On the provision that as the income increases my salary will move up incrementally. An event I expect to occur within two months of the renovations."

"What are the amounts that you have in mind?"

He took out his notebook, opened it to the page where he'd done his figures and passed it to her. "I would like the first amount to be my starting salary." He pointed to a number on the next page. "This is the first raise in pay I propose." She nodded, and he turned the page. "This is the salary I received at Turner Hotels. I'd like to reach that amount within the first four months of my employment." Telling her everything up front was his preferred way, so he pointed at the final figure on the page. "This is my goal by the end of the first year."

"That amount would be considered by most to be excessive." She looked up from the notebook. "I can agree to the first amount. Maybe even the second, but these last two numbers are not justified for a place the size of our establishment."

"You are correct. But by the time these later numbers would go into effect the hotel will be on a more stable, and profitable, footing."

"I don't want you to misunderstand, Nathan. I'm agreeing to let you manage and teach me the business, but I've made no commitment about a long-term arrangement."

"Look at this." He turned the page of his notebook to another section. "This profit is wholly achievable by the end of the first quarter after the changes I will propose are implemented." Near the middle of the next page was another number. "This should be the profit at the end of the first year."

Her eyes grew wide. Their blue color shone with the first glimmer of hope he'd seen in her. "How certain are you of this?"

Nathan nodded. "This is my field of expertise. When the hotel has grown this much, you'll need me to stay."

"That's not a decision I can make right now."

"I'll make you a guarantee. If we are not within fifteen percent of these figures by the estimated dates, I'll leave without contest."

"And all I need to do is give you a room?"

"Yes. And agree to these amounts for my compensation." He tapped the notebook and slipped it back into his pocket.

She leaned her head back and looked up the staircase. "Hmm… There's a room at the top of the second staircase. It's in the corner of the hotel. It's part of the attic." She pointed in the general direction. "Pa cleared it out a few weeks ago. Said he had something in mind for it, but he wouldn't tell me what. It's not much, but you're welcome to it."

"I'm sure it will do." He reached behind the desk and retrieved his valise. "The rest of my things are at the train station. Not knowing where I'd be staying, I arranged for them to be stored. I can have them delivered tomorrow." He began to climb the stairs.

"Wait." Charlotte called him back. "The room is empty. You can't stay there tonight. We'll have to make arrangements for a bed and other furnishings tomorrow. I daresay we'll find everything you need in the attic." She pulled a key from the board behind the registration desk. "Stay in room eight for a couple of nights. It's not our biggest room, but it's one of our best. It will give you a sense of the lodgings through the eyes of a guest."

He raised his brows. "That is the kind of thinking that can turn you into a successful hotelier, Charlotte Green."

"If I don't get to the baking, there'll be no bread for tomorrow." She handed him the key and let her hand rest on the post at the bottom of the stairs. "Please remember that I'm not making any promises about the future."

"I won't forget."

"Good night, Nathan."

"Good night, Charlotte." He tossed the key into the air and caught it. "I hope you rest well. I know the happenings of today did not go as you expected, but I trust you won't be sorry in the months and years to come."

He watched her walk into the kitchen, and then he headed up the stairs. Room eight was nice. Not fancy or new like the rooms at Turner Hotels, but well cared for and clean.

Green's Grand Hotel had the foundations of a good business. A lot of hard work and some savvy changes could make it into a fine establishment capable of holding its own against any competition that could choose to make Gran Colina its home.

As difficult as the changes would be to implement, he knew the hardest part of his new job would be working with Charlotte. She'd intrigued him when they'd sat near each other in school, but the Charlotte he'd encountered today carried the weight of newfound responsibilities. And he'd grown out of his boyish ways that teased a girl to get her attention.

All his time and concentration had to be spent on his job. Women were a distraction that could keep a man from attaining his goals. His feeble attempts to court the Turners' granddaughter had left him without a deserved promotion and stuck in a job surrounded by people who no longer wanted him there.

He wouldn't make the mistake of mixing work and his personal feelings again. No. He was convinced God didn't want him to marry. And he was fine with that. Love was painful. He wasn't willing to expose himself to the inevitable hurt and shame that he'd experienced by pursuing a woman. Any woman.

Not even one with blue eyes as clear as the noon sky in summer.

The gentle babbling of the river that ran beside the cemetery faded away. The shadowy stranger who held her hand and walked with her disappeared into the morning mist. The sounds of hammering that nailed tight the lid on her father's coffin pounded into her brain. She clutched her ears and screamed. Relentless knocking dragged Charlotte from her dream.

Sarah ran into her room. "Charlotte!" she cried, and climbed onto the bed.

Charlotte pushed her hair out of her face and shushed her little sister. "It's okay, Sarah. I'm sorry I frightened you. It was just an old dream."

The knocking started again. Nathan's muffled voice sounded in the distance. Charlotte jumped out of bed and tied on her robe as she sailed across the parlor to the door connecting to the hotel. She eased it open only enough to see him.

"Is everything okay? I heard screaming."

"Yes. I'm sorry. It was a bad dream." Sarah came up beside her, thumb in her mouth, and tugged on Charlotte's robe.

Nathan bent at the waist and eyed the girl through the narrow opening. "Are you okay, Sarah?"

Her sister didn't speak but nodded her head.

"I'm glad. Dreams can be scary, but I always feel better when I wake up." Nathan was being kind. Charlotte had no intention of telling him that the screams he'd heard were hers.

Sarah shook her head from side to side in an exaggerated motion. "I didn't have a dream." She pointed up at Charlotte. "Sissy did."

Nathan tilted his head up to her and then back down to Sarah. "Did you go to her room and make sure she was okay?"

She nodded, the thumb back in her mouth.

He looked back at Charlotte and stood without losing her gaze. "I'm glad to see you're in such good hands." He lifted one hand to the middle of his chest and pointed in a way that only she could see. "Do you think you could get dressed and help me with this crowd?"

One glance over his shoulder revealed a large group of people in the lobby. Her eyes closed. "Oh, no. That's the group of mayors that Oscar Livingston invited to town. I'm sorry I overslept. I'll be ready in a jiffy."

"Um..." He pointed up at her head with the same hand. "You might want to do something with your hair."

"Oh! You!" She gasped and closed the door in his face. The sound of his laughter echoed through the door.

Fifteen minutes later the kids were sitting at the table in the hotel kitchen with a stack of pancakes to share. Charlotte left them with Inez Atkins, the cook, and her daughter.

"You children listen to Mrs. Atkins and Bertha. I need you both to be dears today."

Sarah swirled her bite of pancake through a lake of cane syrup. "Will you let us have candy today?" She lifted her fork, and syrup dripped down the front of her dress as she tried to poke the oversize bite into her mouth.

"No promises." Charlotte wiped the child's mouth, laughed and left the room.

Several of the mayors were seated in groups around the lobby. Nathan stood behind the desk listening to a rather stocky man with a loud voice who held a fat cigar between two fingers.

"I'm sorry, sir. The room you requested is occupied. I'm happy to put you in a similar accommodation and guarantee no dissatisfaction to you." Nathan's voice was measured and professional. None of the emotion she imagined he felt carried into his tone.

"I don't want a similar room. I want that room. I've stayed in that very room on every visit to Gran Colina since this hotel opened twenty years ago. Charles always gave me room eight."

Charlotte recognized the guest's voice. "Mr. Thornhill, it's so good to have you back with us." She smiled at the man when he turned to her. Nathan looked over the guest's shoulder and mouthed an apology. "Please forgive me for not having your room ready. I gave out the key to that room just last evening. I will personally see that things are moved around and your room is ready within the hour." She tucked her hand into his arm and turned him toward the restaurant. "Won't you come and enjoy a late breakfast while you wait? Our treat for the inconvenience."

Mr. Thornhill patted her hand. "That sounds wonderful. Does your mother still make the lightest pancakes a man ever could eat?"

His question was innocent, and sweet, but her pain was deep and sharp. "I'm sorry to have to tell you that my parents were killed in a train wreck on Monday."

He stopped in the middle of the lobby. "Oh, my dear. How dreadful for your family. Is there anything I can do for you or the young ones?"

She smiled at him. "No, but thank you kindly. We'll get through."

"So that's why that new fella didn't know about my room." He nodded in understanding. "Is he the new owner?"

He wasn't the first person to assume that she would

not retain ownership of the hotel. "No. It's Green's Grand Hotel. It will stay in our family."

Mr. Thornhill leaned in and lowered his voice. "Are you sure that's the smartest course of action for you? A woman in business isn't attractive to men. And it's awfully taxing on a young lady to learn all that has to be learned to be successful."

"I haven't found that to be the situation at all, Mr. Thornhill." She almost laughed. "And while I appreciate your concern, the matters of business as it relates to the hotel are well in hand. Now let's get you that breakfast so I can get room eight ready for you."

Charlotte left Mr. Thornhill at a table by the window with a cup of hot coffee and a plate of pancakes ordered from the kitchen.

Nathan was making notes in the registration book and looked up when she neared the desk. He looked around as if confirming that he would not be overheard. "I did not require your help with that guest. You've given away a meal that he would have gladly paid for and promised that I will relocate my things, though I don't have any time to spare this morning."

"The cost of a meal is nothing in comparison to the amount of money Mr. Thornhill brings to the hotel every year." She took the pen from his hand and moved behind the desk, effectively forcing him to withdraw. "It will take only a few minutes for you to move your things. Ask the maid to clean the room. I think Nora is working in the rooms on that wing this morning. Tell her that I said it's for Mr. Thornhill." She smiled as another one of the visiting mayors approached the desk. Under her breath she added, "It will help her tremendously if you strip the linens from the bed."

He glowered at her. "I am not—"

"Good morning, sir. Welcome to Green's Grand Hotel. We're pleased to have you staying with us." From behind the desk, she made a shooing motion at Nathan. It was probably unkind, and her father would have scolded her for doing it, but his arrogance had annoyed her.

It was a full half hour before she saw Nathan again. He was on the landing at the top of the stairs and greeted Mr. Thornhill. She overheard him say, "I'm so sorry for the delay. You must forgive me for not realizing that the room is always reserved for you when you are in Gran Colina." Nathan took the man's valise and walked down the hall with him.

When Nathan came back to the desk, she chuckled. "Thank you for your cooperation."

"You are welcome." He picked up a notepad. "I'll be in the kitchen with Mrs. Atkins, going over the menu for the next two weeks."

"I will do that."

"I've studied the books and have a good idea of what and when your mother ordered things. Are you familiar with that information?"

She wondered why he seemed so detached and professional. "No, but it can't be that difficult. Momma did her ordering every Friday morning. I can do that."

He raised his eyebrows and tapped a pencil against the edge of the notebook. "You do know that today is Saturday?"

"Yes, why?" It dawned on her that she hadn't placed the order the day before. Her mind had been distracted by Nathan's arrival and the children's sadness. "Oh, no. Did Mrs. Atkins say something to you?"

"When I stopped into the kitchen for breakfast this morning, she asked if the order would be arriving before lunch. She said the menu she prepared for the mayors who are here was based on the notes she found in your mother's journals in the kitchen. She doesn't have all the ingredients she needs for supper." He slid the pencil behind his ear. "I thought it best to rectify that immediately."

"That's why you didn't want to move your things." Another deep breath helped her swallow her pride. "I'm sorry, Nathan."

"I accept your apology, but we must get these details handled. If you'll let me get through today, we can talk this evening. There are some things that can't wait until then, but I won't do anything without your knowledge that would require your input."

She nodded, and he left her. There was so much to do. How had her parents made it look so easy? Greeting the guests and baking had been her contribution. She needed to pay close attention to learn every aspect of the hotel business.

The bell over the front door rang, and Alfred Murray entered the lobby. He looked around until he caught sight of her. She went to meet him.

"What can I do for you, Mr. Murray?"

He glanced at his shoes and then at her. "I'd like to…" He paused, as he often did when he was nervous. Words didn't come quickly to the town barber, but everyone knew that to press him would make the words even slower. "I'd like to ask if you'd…"

Michael came out of the restaurant and marched up to her. "Charlotte, me and Sarah are ready for you to help us."

Mr. Murray looked at Michael and waited. Charlotte knew he'd start his request again at the beginning.

"Michael, you must not interrupt." She put her hand on his shoulder. "You may wait quietly while I speak to Mr. Murray."

The deflated look that crossed the man's face was sad. "Miss Green, I want to ask if you would, if you and I, if—"

Michael broke in again. "Charlotte, I can't wait. Sarah already went outside."

Charlotte looked at Michael. "Where did she go?"

"To the cemetery. You said we could put flowers on the grave today. She went to pick flowers and put them on the grave. She said you wouldn't come 'cause you're so busy."

"How long has she been gone?" She tightened her hold on Michael's shoulder.

"I don't know. She finished eating before me. I had more pancakes."

"Mr. Murray, I'm sorry, but I have to find Sarah. I can't let her go there by herself." The barber looked stunned but only nodded.

Nathan walked through the restaurant door and retrieved a ledger from the registration desk. He would have walked by her without comment, but she grabbed his arm.

"Will you help Mr. Murray? Sarah has gone to the cemetery alone. I have to catch up to her." She didn't wait for an answer, but grabbed Michael's hand and raced out the door with him.

Charlotte took off at a run down the porch steps. Michael was a fast runner, so she hoisted the hem of her dress and cut through the alley beside the bank.

They ran by trash bins and empty crates. Twice she stumbled and thought she would fall, but with Michael's help to catch her balance, she was able to keep moving.

"Don't go so fast, Charlotte." Michael was slowing now. "Sarah knows the way to the cemetery." He stopped running and walked. With each step his gait slowed.

She finally stopped with a stitch in her side and leaned over to be at eye level with him. "We have to get to her. She could be very sad if she is there alone."

"I don't want to go. I told her I didn't want to go." His bottom lip slid out in a pout. "We don't need to go there. Momma and Pa aren't there."

"Oh, Michael, I'm so sorry, but I have to find her." She looked over his shoulder at the way they'd come. "You can go home if you want. I'll find Sarah and bring her back."

"Really? I don't have to go?"

"No, you don't." She stood straight again. "I want you to head home and wait for me. I'll be there as soon as I can."

He sniffed. "I will." He turned and bolted at full speed.

Her sorrow for him was as strong as the fear she held for Sarah being in the cemetery alone. Perhaps she shouldn't have allowed them to attend the funeral for their parents. Maybe it was too much for Sarah's young mind to absorb.

Charlotte lifted her skirt in both hands to keep from tripping and ran the rest of the way to the cemetery. The gate was open, and she pushed it wide. She stopped still inside the fence. She looked in every direction at once, but Sarah was nowhere to be found.

"Sarah! Sarah!" She made herself wait to see if her sister would answer. After a few seconds she called again. This time she tried to sound calm. "Sarah, where are you? Sarah, honey, I can't see you. Are you here?"

On feet as heavy as lead, Charlotte began to walk toward the fresh graves of her parents. "Sarah." She used the singsong voice that Sarah loved so well. "Sarah. Where are you?"

She stopped again to listen and heard nothing. A few more steps and she would arrive at the end of the row where her parents were buried.

"Sarah, I'm not upset with you for coming. Please tell me where you are. I want to be here with you." She eased herself closer to the grave. "Michael said you brought flowers. Are they your favorite? I know they're pretty."

Charlotte walked as lightly as she could, listening for her sister after every step. Almost imperceptible at first, she heard whimpering.

"Sarah, I'm here. Show me where you are."

Sarah broke out in earnest sobs, and Charlotte saw her behind a large gravestone.

"I couldn't find any pretty flowers." Sarah sat with her knees up and her head buried in her crossed arms. "Momma loves pretty flowers. I want her to have pretty flowers."

Charlotte crumpled to her knees beside her sister. "I can help you find flowers."

Sarah reached down and picked up the wildflowers she had brought. "These were the only ones I saw. They're purple. Momma loves pink."

Charlotte reached out and tugged at the tendrils of Sarah's blond hair. "You know Momma always loved every flower you ever brought her." She slid her hand under Sarah's chin and lifted the child's wet face to look into her eyes. "These flowers are beautiful. God made all the flowers. I promise Momma would love these, too."

"But I can't find Momma. I looked everywhere, but I'm too little. I can't see over the tall rocks." Sarah pointed at the grave marker that blocked her view.

Oh, how she wanted to take away Sarah's pain. "I'll help you. Next time, ask me to come with you and you won't be lost." She stood and held her hand out for Sarah.

Sarah rubbed the sleeve of her dress across her wet face and slid her hand into Charlotte's. "You were busy. Michael said you were busy."

Charlotte pulled Sarah to her feet. "I'm never too busy for either of you."

They walked together in silence to the end of the row. Charlotte stood hand in hand with her young sister, and they wept at the foot of their mother's grave. She didn't know if her heart would ever heal. The pain of Ma's death flooded over Charlotte in a wave of sorrow as it joined her fresh loss. She'd been a little older than Sarah when Ma had passed. She knew that pain all too well. How could this young child understand when Charlotte was grown and couldn't?

Chapter Three

Nathan dragged the bed frame he'd found in the attic into the small room Charlotte had given him. He set it up against the far wall of the room and added the mattress to it. He was pleased with the items he'd gathered to make the place into a home. A table and chair in the corner by the window gave him somewhere to work or have a quiet meal. When the owner of the mercantile had made a delivery in the afternoon, Nathan had pressed him to help move a wardrobe into the room. The stationmaster had delivered the trunk filled with his belongings. All that remained was to clean everything and put his things away.

He would do that after his planning meeting with Charlotte. A cloud of dust floated to the floor as he brushed his hands together. A quick check of the time showed that he needed to arrive at Charlotte's door in three minutes. He slid his arms into the sleeves of his jacket and grabbed his notes.

At the bottom of the attic stairs he encountered Mr. Thornhill. "Good evening, sir. I hope you will enjoy your dinner with Mayor Livingston tonight."

"I always do. The food here is always excellent, though I told Miss Green how sad I am that the Greens were in such a horrible accident."

"I'm sure she appreciated your condolences." Nathan descended the final steps and said, "I hope your room is satisfactory."

"Yes. Just as I expected. You being new means you don't know my story. My wife and I traveled to Gran Colina after we were married. This is the first hotel we ever stayed in, and room eight was our room. We returned at least once every year until she passed, and Mr. Green always made sure we had room eight. When the Good Lord called her home, I just kept coming. We visited here so often that it became a part of our lives."

"Thank you for sharing with me, Mr. Thornhill. I apologize for your wait, but I am glad Miss Green was aware of the situation."

The lobby was buzzing with the noise of several mayors talking at the same time. Nathan smiled as he watched the skilled politicians trying to convince each other of one thing or another.

He joined Charlotte behind the desk. "Did you get some rest this afternoon?"

She nodded. "I was able to spend time with the children and share an early supper. That is restful to my soul if not my body. They're at a very active age. Thank you for covering the desk. I hope it didn't hinder you from placing the order for Mrs. Atkins."

"No. We were able to work here in the lobby."

"Poor Sarah was so upset that it took several hours for her to relax."

"I understand that they are grieving. I hope you're

thinking of a way to help them through this time so you can focus on the future of the hotel."

She put down the pen. "You don't have to remind me of my responsibilities for my siblings or the hotel. I'm fully aware of the workload I must carry."

It was difficult to see her under so much pressure that every statement was greeted as a challenge. He lowered his tone in an attempt to calm her. "I know you are, but it is imperative that we prioritize and schedule the things that must be done in a timely manner."

Charlotte closed the registration book with more force than was necessary. "That is why we are meeting now. Shall we?"

She put the bell in a prominent place on the registration desk and held out her hand for him to precede her into her parlor. He waited until she was seated on the settee to take his place across from her.

"Since you are aware of my father's plans, I'd like you to lay out what you think should be done and in what order. We can discuss the benefits and possible problems. Then I'll choose the course of action that I feel is best."

Nathan looked down at the notes in his lap. "Well, first I'd like to explain what has been ordered."

Charlotte sat a bit straighter and poised her pencil over the paper she had brought with her from the registration desk. "Okay. I gather from what you said that the bulk of the orders will be furniture for the hotel."

"There is a lot of furniture. There are also several items for the restaurant and the kitchen."

For the next hour and a half he explained in great detail all that her father and mother had decided to do.

Charlotte rose from the settee. "Would you like

a cup of tea? You've given me so much information that I need to think about. I want to ponder all of it before I decide."

He stood with her. "What if we have that tea in the kitchen of the hotel? Do you think the supper crowd has thinned out enough for you to do your baking?"

"It may have. Just let me check on the children." She returned a few minutes later. "They are sound asleep. I'm hoping they'll rest well. The events of the week have kept them from sleeping. It's a bit early, but I knew that their little bodies would take over and insist on rest soon enough."

They left the door ajar and went through the lobby to the empty restaurant.

He looked around at the bare tables. The cloths had been stripped off and the chairs moved in preparation for the floors to be mopped.

"The kitchen staff and maids work with great efficiency. Your parents established some excellent work habits here."

Charlotte pushed open the door to the kitchen. "Momma was one for cleanliness. She said even though she'd never found the verse in the Bible, she still believed cleanliness was next to godliness."

Nathan smiled at her. "It is a good way to live." He put the kettle on to boil while she gathered cups.

"Cream?"

"Just sugar. And some of that pie from supper if there's any left."

She opened the pie safe and pulled out the remnants of a buttermilk pie she'd made the night before. "I'm surprised. Usually it's all gone before the supper crowd leaves."

"Well, I may have asked Mrs. Atkins to hold me a piece or two when I had a sandwich during a lull this afternoon." He took the pie from her and sliced it. "I'm willing to share."

They sat at the table with their tea and pie and enjoyed the quiet after the busy day.

She drained the last of her tea from the cup and set it on the table. "So you think the best thing we can do is deep clean the hotel from top to bottom and eliminate things in the weeks before the new furnishings arrive?"

"Yes. The place is clean." He brushed some lint from the knee of his pants. "Well, maybe not the attic. We'll need to get rid of anything that will be replaced. Even if we can't take it out of the room until the new furnishings arrive, I'd like to do a detailed inventory. Then we can go into each room and move quickly on the day the furniture arrives."

"What about the lobby and the restaurant?"

"I noticed a lot of personal things in the lobby. Those will need to go."

"Personal items?" Charlotte used her finger to capture the last crumb of pie off her plate. She closed her eyes and savored the morsel.

"Pictures. There is a portrait of Charles and Nancy over the fireplace, some figurines on the tables between the chairs. I noticed a couple of hats on the hall tree that weren't taken by any of the guests today. Those sorts of things."

She leaned forward with her elbows on the table and rested her chin on her fisted hands. "But those are the things that make the hotel like home. Momma liked people to know they were like family when they were here."

He pushed his plate to the side and flipped to a page in his notes. "While I appreciate her sentiment, a hotel is not a home. People don't come to a hotel to feel at home. They come to experience life unlike what they do every day."

"I don't agree." She held out one hand, palm up. "Take Mr. Thornhill. He stays in the same room. I'd like to suggest we leave that room as it is. He may not want anything there to be removed."

"Then I suggest you give it to him before he leaves. We cannot keep a room as it has been for twenty years to satisfy someone who visits on occasion."

"But I like that room. Ma decorated that room. It hasn't changed since the hotel opened."

He knew she wasn't talking about the woman she'd grown to love and referred to as her mother. This time she meant the mother who had brought her into the world. The mother who'd died when she was a young girl.

"Please take anything you feel strongly about and put it in your residence. I have no objection to that."

"No objection? You have no objection to me keeping something my mother made or purchased for this hotel?" The chair scraped across the floor as she stood. "I can assure you that nothing will be discarded without my express permission." She flapped her napkin onto the table. "And that includes everything. Not one dish or doily." She left the room, and the kitchen door swung back and forth on its hinges.

He had managed to upset her several times in just two days. How would they ever get the hotel ready for the shipment of furnishings in less than eight weeks if she insisted on overseeing everything herself?

The next morning Charlotte kneaded the bread again, knowing it would be too tough for anything but toast if she didn't stop. She dropped the dough back into the wooden bowl and covered it with a towel. Then she sprinkled flour onto the table and rolled the dough she'd prepared earlier onto the surface.

She was greasing a loaf pan when Mrs. Atkins entered the kitchen.

"You are working early today." The cook put her reticule on a shelf in the pantry and tied on her apron.

"I didn't finish the baking last night." She put the rolled dough into the loaf pan and set it aside. "I hope I'm not in your way."

"You won't be." Mrs. Atkins pulled a large iron pan onto the front of the stove. "Why don't you let me make you some biscuits and gravy before you head to church this morning?"

"You're a dear." Charlotte finished the last of her preparations for the bread and began to wash the dishes she'd used. "I couldn't eat a bite, but I'm sure Michael and Sarah would love that."

As soon as she said their names, the two of them came through the swinging door and dragged themselves to the table. Michael sat with his head hanging to one side, but Sarah didn't fight her early-morning struggle. She dropped her head onto her crossed arms as she rested them on the table. Their nightclothes were adorable. Their mother had sewn them at the beginning of the summer. Charlotte would have to think about what they'd need to wear when school started in a few weeks.

The door opened again, and Nathan appeared. "Good morning to all of you." He almost sang the words. Like some rooster crowing in a yard filled with hens who'd been up laying eggs. It was a sound no one wanted to hear this early.

"Shh." Charlotte shushed him. "They just woke up."

"That explains their nightclothes." He picked up a mug from the shelf near the stove and poured himself a cup of steaming coffee. He looked at her then. "Which do not belong in this kitchen."

She wiped her hands on a nearby towel and walked around the table in his direction. A lesser man would have expressed concern at her direct approach, but he seemed undeterred. "I'd like to see you for a moment," she said. She pushed open the door and let it swish on its hinges behind her.

He walked into the dining room carrying his coffee and his Bible. He set both items on a table and pulled out a chair. "Would you like to sit?"

"No." She folded her arms across her chest and counted to ten in her mind.

"I've upset you? And so early in the day." He remained standing, but picked up his coffee and took a deep drink.

"You are here to handle things that relate to the hotel." She pointed at the door. "Not to tell me how to raise those kids. And not to tell them what to do or not do."

"What they do in the hotel kitchen is my business."

"No. It is not."

He put his cup back on the table and approached her.

"Charlotte, the kids live here. I understand. But you've got to look at things through the eyes of a guest." He pointed at the collection of tiny music boxes on the mantel of the fireplace. "I'm guessing your mother collected these."

"Yes. They're lovely."

"I'm sure to someone like your mother they are lovely. But I promise you that Mr. Thornhill hasn't noticed them."

"Then what difference does it make if we keep them?"

He leaned his head to one side and studied her until she became a bit uncomfortable. "Do you want your guests to be impressed by the hotel and the service, or are you satisfied that a large portion of your guests are unimpressed by your decor."

She opened her mouth and closed it again. There was no argument for that. "You're right."

"Thank you. I don't want to change the hotel because it's not nice the way it is. It *is* nice." He held his hands out palms up. "I want to change things so it will be memorable. I want our guests to go home and tell their friends and family about how great their stay was at Green's Grand Hotel. I want us to live up to the name."

"Okay, but what does that have to do with Michael and Sarah in their nightclothes?"

"I realize that you're all grieving. It's difficult to set that aside and make practical decisions when you're in such a state. And I'm sorry if the things I'm suggesting seem harsh or cold. That's not my intent. But consider this. Do you want your guests and their children to come into the dining room in their nightclothes?"

She backed up. "Of course not."

"Then don't set the precedent. If the kids want to wear their nightclothes, let them wear them. In your residence. I know they're eating in the hotel kitchen, but they had to walk through the lobby and dining room to get there."

He was right. Again.

"Set the example for your hotel. Your name is on the sign on the front of the building. If you want a clean, pleasant, relaxing environment, you have to set the example."

"You've really thought about all of this, haven't you?"

"It's all I've thought about for the last five years. Ways to make a hotel the best it can be. Ways to have an excellent staff and superior service for our guests."

"Can we do it?" She lifted her shoulders in query. "Can we make my parents' dreams come true?"

"If you work with me, we can."

She put out her hand to his. "I can do that. As long as we make the decisions in private and you consult me about everything."

He wrapped his hand around hers, and she wondered if it had been a mistake to offer it. His grip was firm without being painful. The warmth of it was distracting.

He smiled a smile that lit his eyes and sent an unexplainable flicker of hope to her. "Let's get to work."

The sound of glass breaking came from the kitchen. She knew it would be something the kids had done, but the look on Nathan's face warned her that it didn't need to happen again.

Lord, help me. I'm going to need it.

"I'll handle that." Charlotte pointed toward the kitchen.

"I'll be at the registration desk." He left the empty dining room. Breakfast wouldn't be served for another half hour. That would give her time to get the kids through the lobby unseen by any of the guests.

She took a deep breath and let her head fall back as she blew it out. She'd spent the last two hours in the kitchen. It was early in the day, but she was already tired.

Nathan was right. She couldn't keep up the pace she'd moved at for the last week. Had it been a week already? Only six days. How would she ever manage?

"Charlotte!" Sarah's voice rang out, and Charlotte squared her shoulders. It didn't matter what it cost her, she would not let her parents or siblings down. If that meant she was tired for the rest of her life, so be it. She'd be tired with a successful business and happy siblings who were well cared for.

There was no other choice. Failure wouldn't just affect her. It would ruin the lives of those two little ones, too.

Chapter Four

Charlotte walked into Gran Colina Church hand in hand with Michael and Sarah. Getting them dressed after the stress of breakfast had made them late. Michael had insisted the broken glass was Sarah's fault, and Sarah had cried until just before they'd left the hotel to walk to church.

Stares greeted them. Looks of pity from her friends saddened her. If only this were a normal Sunday. A day where she and her siblings would join their parents on their favorite bench and sing songs.

Today was different. Like every day for the last week, everything in their lives was done in a new way. And shadowed with grief. The singing that filled the room did nothing to alleviate the sharp pain in Charlotte's heart.

When they reached their bench, Michael refused to step out of the aisle. Charlotte nudged him, but his feet were rooted to the floor.

She leaned close to his ear. "Step into the row, Michael."

He stared at the empty bench. "No." His eyes grew

wide, and he yelled. "No." He jerked free of her hand and bolted down the aisle and out the door.

The commotion drew more unwanted attention to her family. The reverend's wife, Mildred Gillis, approached and bent down to speak to Sarah. "Would you like to sit with me today? I have a peppermint in my reticule."

Sarah clutched her doll and nodded. Charlotte whispered her thanks to Mrs. Gillis and went in search of Michael.

He hadn't gone far. She found him sitting on the bottom step of the barbershop. His Sunday-best pants would be soiled for it, and the shine of his shoes disappeared as he kicked up the dust at his feet.

Charlotte walked over and sat beside him.

He didn't stop kicking, and she didn't correct him. They sat in silence for several minutes.

Michael blurted out his pain. "I don't want to go to church."

"It's tough, isn't it?" Care for his pain was her utmost concern. She had to allow him to vent his emotions or he'd continue to bottle them up inside. She wished he'd express himself with something other than anger, but she understood. Sometimes, she even agreed.

"It ain't right to sit where Pa and Momma sat without them there." His feet stilled, and he turned to look at her. "I won't do it. You can't make me."

Movement behind her caught her attention, but she ignored it. "We don't have to sit where Pa and Momma sat, but we will go to church."

"I don't want to be there. It makes me miss them more." His little face hardened with resolve.

"What do you think Pa and Momma would want you to do?"

"They'd want me to go to church like always. With them."

Charlotte put an arm around his shoulders. "I'm sure that's true. But since they can't, I'd like us to honor their wishes and be in church every Sunday. It's the place they loved to go the best. I know right now we all miss them something fierce, but I think we'll come to be comforted by being there. It'll take time, but I feel it in my heart." She nudged him closer. "What do you say? Let's go sit with Sarah and Mrs. Gillis."

He shrugged off her arm but stood. "If we gotta."

When she turned to walk beside him toward the church, she caught sight of Nathan. He was standing near the corner of the barbershop. She nodded but didn't speak as they walked by him.

He lifted the brim of his Sunday hat and fell into step behind them.

After the service, Charlotte felt overwhelmed by the neighbors and friends who crowded around them to offer their continued condolences and help. Michael grew more tense with each passing moment, and Sarah was on the verge of tears. Charlotte wanted to get them home as soon as possible without being unkind to the people who were saddened by their loss.

Nathan inserted himself into the circle of church-goers. "If you'll excuse us, we have guests at the hotel and can't be away any longer."

Several people nodded and backed away. Nathan put a hand under Charlotte's elbow and guided them out of the church. The stifling August heat hit her in the face, but she was more aware of Nathan's unexpected touch than the weather. Michael broke free of her grasp and ran in the direction of the hotel.

Nathan squeezed her elbow. "Let him go. I'm sure he's going straight to his room."

Her shoulders slumped. "You're right." She turned to Sarah. "Do you want to run ahead home, too? Or would you like to walk with me?"

"I think I wanna go to Mrs. Gillis's house. She told me she made a pie for after lunch."

Charlotte stopped and stooped down to look into Sarah's face. "We've got pie at the hotel."

"But Mrs. Gillis says she wants to show me a doll she's making." Sarah held up her doll. "She said it's like my doll, only she gave her blue stitches for her eyes. Mine has green. Momma said it was to match my eyes."

Charlotte touched her gloved finger to the tip of Sarah's nose. "And just like Momma's." She gave her a big hug. "Let me speak to Mrs. Gillis, and I'll decide if today is the best day for you to go."

She straightened, and Nathan offered to wait with Sarah while she spoke to the preacher's wife.

"No." Sarah clung to her leg. "I don't want to stay with him." Her lower lip slid out, and she sniffed.

Charlotte looked at Sarah and then at Nathan. "Honey, Nathan is a good man."

"I don't wanna! Can't I go with you to talk to Mrs. Gillis?" She tugged on Charlotte's hand. "Please?" The plea was quickly escalating into a wail.

Charlotte tried not to be curt with Sarah. "I'm not sure it's the best day to visit with Mrs. Gillis. You seem too upset. Let's go home. You can visit another time."

Sarah sent Nathan her most ornery frown. Charlotte had seen it many times in the child's five years, though she had no idea why her sister should be upset with Nathan.

He took a step back and pulled his pocket watch from his vest. A touch on the latch opened it. "I need to hurry back to the hotel. It's almost noon."

"It's Sunday. A stroll home from church is one of the most pleasant parts of the day." Charlotte wondered at his abruptness. Perhaps he wasn't fond of children. Or was he so obsessed with his work that the needs of a little girl were viewed as an interruption instead of a need?

"Mrs. Atkins will be ready to serve lunch to the mayors soon. I want to ensure that everything is at its best. The hotel can't operate without someone at the helm."

"I've left a note on the desk that we'll return after services. It's the way Pa always did it."

"I agreed to attend church today. It's important that the people in town know you have help. In the future, we will either take turns on Sundays, or I will stay behind." His forthright tone didn't suit her. It rang with a twinge of arrogance.

"If you have an idea for a change you'd like to make at the hotel, you may bring it to my attention in private, so that we may discuss it before I decide if it is a change I am willing to make." She took a deep breath. "Between Michael and Sarah—and you—I can see that I'll be making a lot of decisions. But, rest assured, I will be the one to make them."

Nathan opened his mouth and closed it again. He slid his watch back into his vest pocket. "If it is not a problem for you, Miss Green, I'd like to go back to the hotel now." The firm set of his jaw might intimidate someone else, but Charlotte refused to turn over her responsibilities to him. He would have to adjust to that fact.

"Okay. We'll be along shortly."

Nathan picked up his pace and left her to walk with Sarah, who wanted to talk about her doll. Without warning the child burst into tears.

Charlotte picked her up and wiped a tear away with her glove. "What is it, sweetie?"

"I miss Momma. Mrs. Gillis said I shouldn't cry too much. I should remember that Momma is in heaven with Jesus." She gulped back a sob. "But I'm so sad, Charlotte. I really missed them in church."

Charlotte drew Sarah's head against her shoulder. "It was hard on all of us. You cry if you want to, Sarah. I'm sure Mrs. Gillis meant to make you feel better, but it's okay to be sad when you miss Momma and Pa."

Sarah cried all the harder, and Charlotte smoothed her hair. Her own tears were silent but heavy with the same grief her little sister couldn't contain.

When they stepped into the lobby of the hotel, Nathan was busy at the desk. Sarah's sobs had turned to whimpers, and Charlotte had dried her eyes. He pointed for her to go to the residence. The look on his face told her that Michael was inside. The sharpness of Nathan's nod let her know he wasn't happy with her.

Nathan heard Sarah cry out, and he closed the door to the residence. The children were having a difficult day. The weight of it on Charlotte prevented her from helping him at the desk. It could also keep her from seeing the magnitude of the work they had to do.

He was here to alleviate the load, even if she didn't see how much she needed him.

"Mr. Thornhill, we're pleased that you'll be extending your stay with us beyond the time of the meeting for mayors. Let me know if there's anything I can do for you."

The older man's thick brow wrinkled. "Is there anything I can do for those children? The Green family treated me with such kindness after my wife passed. And in all the years since. I'd like to repay the favor. It's so hard to listen to the little ones crying."

"Why don't you ask Charlotte the next time you see her. She's with her siblings at the moment, but your gesture is one I'm certain will be a comfort to her."

Mr. Thornhill cast a glance at the closed door of Charlotte's residence and shook his head. "I'll do that." He walked away from the desk, and Nathan knew the man's concern for the grieving family was genuine. The Greens had built something here in Gran Colina that was unlike the Turner Hotel in Dallas. These people cared for one another. It was refreshing, but he hoped the sentiments they shared wouldn't prevent Charlotte from seeing the need to implement the changes her father had initiated.

The children's upset trickling into the lobby was just the type of event he intended to keep out of the hotel. Guests on business or pleasure travel didn't need to know the inner workings of the proprietor's private life. Grief was normal but had no place in the hotel lobby. Not the sight of it or its sound.

There must be some way to get Charlotte to see his reasoning.

The door opened, and she joined him at the desk.

"Poor thing. She wrapped up in Momma's shawl and cried herself to sleep. Michael is on his bed with Pa's hat pulled over his face. I know he's not sleeping, but he won't talk to me. Neither of them wanted anything to eat."

Nathan looked around the lobby. "I'm sorry you are all having such a hard time. It's to be expected in a situation like yours."

"One minute I think they're coming to accept our loss, and then something happens that triggers their grief anew."

He hated what this family was suffering. He wanted her to know that—needed her to believe it. "They're young. I'm sure that makes it especially difficult."

"But?" She seemed to sense he wanted to say more.

"I was just going to say that I think you did the right thing by taking them into your residence. One's home should be a place of refuge and comfort. It affords them the privacy to cry themselves to sleep or deal with their sorrow in whatever way eases them."

"I don't know what else to do." She stood with her arms wrapped around her middle as if it was the only way she could hold herself together. Her face was pale, and dark circles contrasted against the blue of her eyes. He felt compassion for her, but there was nothing he could do to help.

Except run the hotel.

"I know one thing you can do."

"What?" She barely lifted her head.

"You can eat."

Charlotte shook her head. "I can't."

"You need to. It's been a week. I don't imagine you've eaten well since you got the news."

"I just can't." Her voice wavered.

"You have to, Charlotte. Michael and Sarah need you. You won't be able to care for them if you fall ill. You need nourishment."

She dragged in a slow breath. "But I'm not hungry."

"You've gone past hunger. It's understandable, but it's not healthy." He checked the time. "The lunch crowd has eaten. Go ask Mrs. Atkins for something substantial and have a quiet lunch in the restaurant. I can keep an eye on things here."

"I need to stay close to the children."

"If they need anything, I'll come for you." Why did he offer to do that? He wasn't here to take care of children. Or even keep an eye out for them.

"You aren't the most patient man with children."

Had he come across as unkind to her siblings? "I'm not impatient with children. I'm a focused man. You are putting yourself at risk of collapsing if you don't care for yourself. I'll listen for any sound from them. With the littlest one asleep, it shouldn't be a problem at all."

She twisted her mouth to one side and narrowed her eyes. "One peep and you'll call for me." It wasn't a question.

"One peep." He waved his hands to get her to move along.

Charlotte walked half of the distance to the restaurant doorway and turned back at him. "One sound."

"Go eat, or I'll be forced to get a frog to hurry you along."

She scowled at him and left the lobby. He had no intention of ever tormenting her with boyish pranks again, but it was all he could think of in the moment.

A half hour later she emerged from the restaurant and headed toward him. A few of the mayors lounged in the lobby in small groups that would erupt in laughter or raised voices trying to be heard as they all seemed to talk at once.

She made her way through the groups, stopping to speak to some of the guests along the way. At the desk she opened the registration book. "Do most of the mayors seem to be satisfied with their accommodations?" She perused the entries and didn't look at him.

"There have been small requests for more towels or extra pillows. Normal expectations. Overall, I think they are pleased with the hotel and service."

"That's good. I wasn't sure how they'd react when they found out my parents are no longer here. Some people seem to think a young woman can't handle a business. I need groups like this to continue to book here. Pa used to say they were the bread and butter of our establishment."

"He was right. Turner Hotels have guests who come every year for events. They expanded their properties to include large meeting rooms. They work with people in the area to establish entertainment for the guests during their stay."

"That could be interesting. I wonder if there is anything we could offer in Gran Colina."

"As the town grows more opportunities will open up."

"The most we've been able to do is offer the restaurant for meetings between meals. It's not ideal, though it is a large room, so it's functional. It also means that most of the attendees eat here. That's added income." Charlotte lifted a finger. "I should talk to Mayor Livingston.

He and Sheriff Braden talked about the possibility of a town hall being built in the center of town." A flicker of excitement darted through her eyes for a moment.

He nodded. "Now you're thinking like a proprietor. You need to keep pondering ideas. Ways to bring people to Gran Colina and your hotel. We can talk about them and decide which ones would bring the most profits."

The concern returned to her gaze. "Wouldn't it stand to reason that offering more things would bring more people? Then the profits would be greater."

"Yes, but if the things you plan cost too much, the income of the hotel could fall short of covering those new expenses. Raising the cost of staying here could turn people away. We should implement any changes gradually and record their success and failure."

"This is perplexing. Is this the kind of thing you handled in Dallas? The planning and such?"

"Among other things. I knew about everything that happened at the Turner Hotel in Dallas. And coordinated every event at one time or another." He was glad of the opportunity to share his expertise with her. "I was determined to learn everything I could about the hotel trade."

"If you were so good at your job there, why did you want to leave?"

He would never tell her, or anyone, of the regret he'd endured after pursuing Viola Turner. The woman had given him every indication that she'd viewed him as a proper suitor. She'd teased him and even flirted in the most demure way. He'd thought her intriguing until her ultimate rejection of him after she'd garnered the attention of a wealthy guest. Shame had filled him when he'd realized her coquettish behavior toward him had been meant to attract another man. That was a story he'd keep hidden. A valuable reminder to him that women of means could be treacherous.

"I wanted to attain things that were denied me by the Turners." That much was true. "My career is important to me. I was hindered in Dallas." Foiled by the Turner family, who saw him as presumptuous for thinking himself worthy of their precious granddaughter.

"You know I won't surrender the hotel. Not to Mr. Freeman, to you, or anyone else."

He appreciated Charlotte's direct approach. "I know. No one can accuse you of being unclear."

"I won't change my mind."

Nathan chuckled. "You're not one to dillydally or waver. I remember well that once you've made up your mind about something, you stand firm."

"As long as we're clear." She blushed. It reminded him of long-ago days when they'd played tag in the schoolyard. She'd kept up with the fastest boys and often won. Those lightly freckled cheeks had warmed with jubilant satisfaction every time.

He smiled at her and nodded. "We are." Possibility lurked in those tender memories. Possibilities missed and best forgotten. He picked up his notebook from the registration desk. "Let's follow your thoughts about expanding the services at the hotel. I think the timing is perfect for initiating new things. We have a few weeks to work out the details." He opened the notebook to a fresh page. "Tell me more about the mayor and this town hall plan."

"It's something that came up during the recent

elections. Mr. Freeman ran against Mayor Livingston. He promised a new town hall as a way to promote the growth of Gran Colina."

"Yet he lost the election? Do you think the people in the community were opposed to his ideas? That would hinder growth. Not just of a town hall, but of the local economy. Towns that resist change often lose business to nearby towns that embrace the future."

"The election was complicated, but all the candidates agreed on the need to build the town hall."

"Good." Nathan jotted a note to speak to the mayor about the time frame before the new town hall would be a reality. "I'll go see Mayor Livingston tomorrow morning."

Charlotte narrowed her eyes at him. "Why would you go? This is my hotel, so it's my place to talk to him."

"He is a businessman, Charlotte. Running a town is business. He'll most likely talk to me due to my experience."

She laughed. "You have been gone too long, Nathan Taylor. Mayor Livingston is like an uncle to me. Do you remember Rena Livingston?"

"The little girl with long braids who sat by you in school?" He had a vague picture of her in his mind.

"She's my closest friend. Her father is very dear to me. I'm sure he'll speak freely with me on any matter I broach."

Nathan made another note on the page. "That's great news. It will make our plans easier."

"Our plans?" She grabbed the corner of his notebook and read the open page. "Hmm. I see where you're going with this." She turned the book back to him.

"You may accompany me when I see him tomorrow. We'll leave directly after the guests of the mayors' meeting check out. Their last event is at eight in the morning. Most of them will leave by ten thirty. I'll have Mrs. Atkins watch the desk while we're out."

"Mrs. Atkins will be needed in the kitchen. We'll have to get someone else."

Charlotte thought for a moment. "I'll ask the mayor to meet with us here. And I'll find someone to watch the children for me. We can meet in my parlor, but leave the door open so we can assist anyone who needs us."

It was a good sign that she was planning around the guests. When she'd left the hotel desk unmanned for church that morning, he'd worried that her approach to the business was too relaxed. Her excitement over possible improvements was encouraging. Perhaps Green's Grand Hotel could grow into something that would compete with the likes of any hotel that chose to open in Gran Colina in the future. He needed the hotel to expand enough to require his long-term employment or he'd have to move. Again.

Returning to Gran Colina had brought him a comfort he hadn't realized he'd missed. Singing in church this morning, on the bench his family had occupied during his childhood, had stirred happy memories. Yes, he wanted Green's Grand Hotel to succeed. Not just for Charlotte's sake, but for his own future, too.

Inserting himself into his position required no slack on his part. If Mr. Freeman got the impression he wasn't fulfilling his obligations, he might try to move Nathan out of his new position. That would never do.

* * *

Charlotte brushed raindrops from her shoulders and stepped into the lobby. Nathan was at the desk. He'd become a fixture in the few days since his arrival.

He looked up as she approached. "Did you find someone?" His voice was tight.

"Mrs. Gillis will be here in a few minutes and walk them over to her home while we meet with the mayor." She went through the door to the residence and let Mrs. Atkin's daughter, Bertha, know she'd returned. "You can go back to help your mother. I'm sorry to have kept you from the preparations for the lunch meal. Thank you for watching Michael and Sarah."

"You're welcome." Bertha moved toward the door but avoided eye contact with Charlotte.

"Was there a problem?" She didn't hear a sound coming from the bedrooms.

"They are both in their rooms. Sarah is playing with her dolls." Bertha looked beyond Charlotte to the door of Michael's room.

"What about Michael? Did he give you any trouble?"

"I'm sorry, Charlotte. I tried to stop him." Bertha shrugged her shoulders. "He was just too quick."

"What happened?"

"Nathan caught him when he tried to run out of the lobby. He put him in his room and told him he had to stay there until you got back."

She let her head drop back and closed her eyes. Michael's antics had to stop. "Thank you, Bertha. I'll take care of everything."

Bertha left the residence, and Charlotte opened Michael's door. He sat on his bed with his back to the door and didn't turn when she entered.

Charlotte walked around the bed and sat beside him. They were both silent for a long time. He was probably waiting on her response, but Charlotte was praying for God's direction. She was unprepared to be a mother to these sad children, but without warning it had happened. She'd prayed more in the last week than she had in the last year.

"So…" She started the conversation. "Bertha tells me you didn't want to stay inside this morning."

"I don't have to. Pa always let me go where I wanted to go." Michael kicked his heels against the side of the bed.

"That's not how I remember things."

"You were always in the kitchen or off visiting with your friends. You don't know all the things Pa taught me. Nobody knows how we were except me and Pa."

"I'm glad you have memories of things you and he shared. Hold on to them tight." She longed to hear her father's voice now, to know what he'd say to Michael.

"What do you think Pa would say to you today?"

Michael shrugged his shoulders.

"You can tell me." She waited.

After a long pause he wrinkled up his face. "Pa would say he didn't want to die in that train wreck. He'd say he wanted to be here." He pointed toward the lobby. "That it's his place to run our hotel and not that man's."

Charlotte dropped her arm around his shoulders and hoped he wouldn't withdraw. "I think you're exactly right."

He turned to look up at her. "You do?"

"I do." She nodded. "Pa wouldn't have left if God had given him the choice."

"Why did God take him then?"

"I don't know. I'm not sure we can know." She gave him a gentle hug. "Like Momma and Pa showed us, we have to trust that God knows best. Even when we don't like the way things happen."

"I want to run the hotel, Charlotte. It's got our name on the sign. Not his." He jerked his head toward the lobby again.

"Nathan isn't here to take the hotel from us. He's here to teach us how to make it better."

"I don't like him being here."

"I know. It's hard for me, too." She cupped his cheek. "I make you a promise, Michael. This hotel will be ours. The Greens will own Green's Grand Hotel. As long as I can do everything like I'm supposed to, you and me and Sarah will have this hotel. It's what Pa wanted for us. It's why he and Momma went to Dallas."

"Really?"

"Yes. They met Nathan there. Together they planned for a lot of changes that we're going to make happen soon. I'll need your help though."

He perked up for the first time in days. "What do you need me to do?"

"I've got to learn a lot about how to run the hotel. You can help me learn it faster if you're a good boy."

"I am a good boy." Defiance returned to his eyes.

"You are, but I need you to be even better. The more time I have to worry about you and what you're doing, the longer it will take me to learn all Nathan is teaching me. And the more we'll risk losing the hotel."

"I promise I won't do anything to make us lose the hotel." He hopped off the bed and turned to face her.

"Good. And I promise to study hard and do everything the way I think Pa and Momma would want." She stood and took his hand. "Let's go see if Nathan is ready for our appointment."

"You're leaving again?" For all his tough exterior, Michael had a tender heart.

"We have a meeting with Mayor Livingston about some business. He's coming here." They walked into the parlor, and she saw Nathan at the door. Bertha must have left it ajar. He raised his fist to knock but lowered it when he caught sight of her.

"What about me and Sarah?" Michael didn't notice Nathan.

"Mrs. Gillis is coming. The two of you are going to her house. She kept the pie that Sarah told us about for today. You'll be sharing lunch with her and Reverend Gillis."

Her brother nodded. "I can help take care of Sarah, too. Sometimes she cries, but I can make her stop."

"Oh, Michael, it's okay for her to cry sometimes. We're all sad."

"But her crying makes us more sad."

Charlotte couldn't resist wrapping him in a big hug. "She'll be okay. We just need to give her time to cry it out. Sometimes I cry, too." He squirmed out of her embrace, but she caught his hands and looked into his face. "It's okay if you cry sometimes, too."

"Men don't cry." He pulled his hands from hers. "Men have to take care of the womenfolk. Pa taught me that, too."

"That's true. Men do take care of things. But remember that caring for people doesn't mean you get to boss them around. It means you help them through difficult times, or you protect them from things that could harm them."

He hung his head a bit, then looked back at her. "I'll do my best."

"Me, too. I'll try to be as brave as you are." She patted him on the head and straightened to her full height.

"You do pretty good for a girl."

Charlotte had no doubt Michael would do everything in his power to control his emotions and help Sarah and her. If only he were twenty instead of six. She accepted her responsibilities, but, oh, how she'd love to be able to lean on someone for help and comfort.

Chapter Five

Nathan buttoned his suit coat. "The mayor should be here any minute. Are you ready?"

"I am." Charlotte stood next to him at the registration desk. She gathered the papers she'd shared with him and made a note in the registration book. "That was the last guest scheduled to check out today. Mr. Thornhill is the only one who will stay longer, but that's not uncommon for him. The maids are cleaning the rooms. The ones on the left at the top of the stairs will be cleaned first. Anyone who checks in should be put there."

"It's good that you have a system like that in place." At least he wouldn't be building the business from the ground up. "Your folks did an excellent job with the hotel. It will be a simple matter of adding the things we discussed in Dallas. And any new things you and I decide."

The front door opened, and Mrs. Gillis entered the lobby. "Good morning, Nathan. It's so nice to have you back in town. I know Charlotte must be so grateful to have your help."

Nathan almost laughed. Mrs. Gillis was a boisterous soul who never missed an opportunity to try to encourage others. Even if she missed the mark, no one could fault her kindness.

"Thank you, Mrs. Gillis. It's good to be home again." He meant it. More than he'd known he could. "I especially enjoyed the service yesterday. It's been too long since I've been able to go to church."

Michael and Sarah came out of the residence. "We're ready, Mrs. Gillis. And we won't be no trouble. I promised Charlotte." Michael held his younger sister by the hand.

Sarah stood with her doll tucked under her other arm. "Charlotte said we can have pie."

Mrs. Gillis gathered the two with open arms much as a hen collected her chicks. "After a nice lunch of fried chicken and potato salad, we'll all have pie. Reverend Gillis can hardly wait."

Charlotte waved as the little group left the hotel. "I'm going to lay a tray of coffee in the parlor."

She'd been busy all morning. Every time Nathan had looked for her, she had moved on to another task. It pleased him after the heaviness she'd been under. Today marked one week since the accident, so he knew her grief wouldn't end soon, but it did appear that she was doing better.

When Mayor Livingston arrived, Nathan led him into Charlotte's parlor.

"Charlotte, my dear, how are you?" The mayor wrapped her in a fatherly hug. "You and the little ones have been in my prayers every day."

She thanked him and offered to pour the coffee. Nathan noticed her sniff a couple of times while they settled into their chairs, but she showed no sign of tears.

Maybe keeping the meeting on the business of the hotel would help her. He accepted his coffee from her and turned to their guest. "Thank you for coming, Mayor Livingston."

The mayor nodded as he stirred sugar into his cup. "Charlotte knows she can count on me for any help she needs."

"Thank you. It means the world to me." She set the coffeepot on the tray and sat on the edge of her chair. "I was telling Nathan about the town hall you mentioned. A lot of people have been talking about it since the last election. We're making plans to improve the hotel, and we think a town hall could be a big boost to all the businesses here in Gran Colina."

Nathan forged ahead as he intended to go in Gran Colina. He'd be honest and open, but forthright and determined at the same time. "Charlotte told me this is something you are in favor of. Is it planned or just being discussed?"

Mayor Livingston put his cup on the table. "It came up during the election. It's an idea that's caught on. Honestly, it's going to take a lot of work and commitment from the townsfolk, but all we've done so far has been received well."

The mayor was pleasant, but he seemed a bit vague. "What has been done?" Nathan knew how politicians could be.

"We've held meetings with some of the town leaders and business owners." The mayor turned to Charlotte. "Your father was at all of the meetings. Did he mention it to you?"

She shook her head. "He didn't usually talk to me of the business. I wish he had. If I knew more about it, Nathan—Mr. Taylor—wouldn't need to be here."

Her words cut him in ways he knew she didn't intend. "I think what Miss Green is saying, is that I am here to help implement her father's plans for the future of Green's Grand Hotel."

The look she sent his way was apologetic. "My parents' trip to Dallas was in regard to the future of the hotel. Mr. Taylor met with them during the course of their trip. He has personal knowledge of their plans. I'm trying to fulfill their wishes to improve the hotel so it will be financially sound, not just for me to raise the children, but so it will be viable to provide for all of us when they reach adulthood."

The mayor nodded. "That's wise. You've been left with quite a burden for a woman of your age."

"I'm a bit older than your Rena. Twenty on my next birthday. We're both of an age where responsibility is expected of us. It was delayed for me because I haven't married like she did. I'll admit that I was somewhat spoiled by Pa and Momma. But now that I am responsible to head our home, I'm determined to shoulder the burden well." She dropped her head. "By God's grace."

The meeting with the mayor ended a few minutes later with him expressing his hope for a town hall that would serve all their needs but no promises on a time for construction. Nathan feared his work in Gran Colina would prove difficult, at best. The future success of the hotel was tied to the growth of the town. Any delay in that growth could alter the goals he'd shared with Charlotte. He'd use all of his skill to prevent that from happening.

He came back to the parlor after seeing Mr. Livingston to the door. Charlotte was putting the coffee cups on a tray.

"Join me for lunch, and we'll talk about our next steps."

She straightened her slumped shoulders at the sound of his voice, but she kept her face turned away from him. "I'll have something here. I promised Mrs. Gillis I'd pick up the children."

"After their lunch, which was to include pie if I heard them correctly."

Charlotte lifted the tray. "I can't." She sniffed and headed for the doorway to her small kitchen.

As much as Nathan didn't think himself equipped to comfort her, he knew the signs of grief. Without thinking of the consequences of getting involved on a personal level, or about how she would receive his efforts, he moved quickly to take the tray from her. He set it on the round kitchen table and was surprised when he turned and saw her slip into one of the wooden chairs.

She rubbed her palm across the tabletop. "We ate here every morning." Pain filled her words and made him think of his mother. "Momma loved to ask about our day at supper. She wanted to know what Michael and Sarah had learned in school or what I was interested in at the time. It's so quiet now."

He sat across from her. "I'm so sorry. I know it's hard on you and the children."

She jerked her head up and looked at him. "Hard?" A tortured laugh escaped her. "Hard is being sick or losing your favorite pet. Hard is not knowing if anyone will ever want to marry you. This isn't hard. It's unbearable. I don't know how to cope. How can I raise those two precious little ones? They need their parents." She dropped her head onto her arms and sobbed.

Nathan came around the table and knelt beside her chair. He put a hand on her shoulder. "God will help you." She was a lovely young woman. How could she wonder if anyone would want to marry her? He marveled why she hadn't accepted anyone yet. There was no possibility that no one had asked. The grief must be clouding her thinking.

Charlotte lifted her head. "What will God do?" She shrugged. "I don't have the money I need to pay the bank, or the training to make this place successful." She flung one hand out in the direction of the other chairs. "And I have no idea how to comfort the children who sit here with me, aching to hear our mother's laugh or see our father drop a kiss on her forehead." She gulped back another sob and stilled.

He hadn't meant to be so close to her. Sorrow permeated the blue of her eyes. "I know the ache. It takes away your breath and squeezes your chest until you don't think you can breathe in again. And when you finally gasp for enough air to survive, more pain flows into your soul. It's a hot pain that can't be soothed or touched. A pain you long to escape, but you know if you do you might start to forget. And you'd rather feel the pain than escape the memories of the love that's gone. Not even the promise of heaven can ease it when it's fresh. Your mind knows the promises of God and the hope of the future, but your shattered heart is in too many pieces to accept it. Not when the pain is so heavy and new." He moved the hand that rested on her shoulder and brushed away the tears that wet her cheek.

She gasped. "That's exactly how I feel." She met

his gaze. Not a superficial connecting of two people glancing at one another, but a locking of eyes and minds—a deep understanding that someone else sees the scars of your heart.

Charlotte couldn't look away. Nathan was the last person she would expect to understand her grief, but here he was—closer than any young man had ever been to her—showing her compassion.

How had she forgotten the clear blue of his eyes? They mirrored hers, in color and pain. His hand on her cheek was warm and comforting. She leaned into it and tried to breathe in. His touch bore witness to the harsh loneliness she'd endured for the last week. She wanted to lose herself in the closeness he presented. Did she dare?

The bang of the kitchen door swinging open jolted them apart. Nathan backed up to the wall by the stove.

"Charlotte, I was on my way to see you when I saw Papa on the street. He said you were having a bad day." Rena Braden, the mayor's daughter, held baby Cordelia in her arms. She stopped a couple of steps into the room. "Oh, Nathan, I didn't expect to see you here." She looked from Nathan to Charlotte. "Is this a bad time? I can return later if you're busy." Rena's face crinkled into an expression somewhere between embarrassment and humor. The baby whimpered, and her complete attention left Charlotte and Nathan.

"I was just going." Nathan made his way to the kitchen door. "Charlotte, I'll be at the desk going over the information we've gathered so far." His stilted manner let Charlotte know the situation was as awkward for him as it was for her. "It's nice to see you again, Rena." He stopped to smile at the now-quiet baby. "Congratulations on your little one."

Rena nodded. "Thank you. You'll have to stop by the sheriff's office and meet my husband, Scott."

"Maybe in a few days, after I've settled in, I can do that." The kitchen door closed behind him as Nathan left the room.

Rena pivoted toward Charlotte. "What did I just see?"

Heat crept into Charlotte's face. "Nothing."

"Nothing? Nathan was in your private kitchen. And the two of you were looking very…friendly." Rena sat in the chair Nathan had vacated. "If that was nothing, I've never seen anything." Her laugh was friendly. "You tell me all about it."

"Like you told me all about you and Scott?" As soon as the words left her mouth, Charlotte knew they were unkind. "I'm sorry, Rena. Please forgive me. I didn't mean that." Rena had married the town sheriff without so much as a word to Charlotte about their courtship. Charlotte still wasn't clear on how they had ended up married, but her lifelong friend was full of happiness. The baby in her arms wasn't the only reason for that joy.

Rena leaned back in the chair. "Why do you think I'm here?"

Charlotte tried to smile at her friend. "Because you're a dear friend."

"I know what it's like to feel alone, Charlotte. I've been through some hard times in the last year." She loosened the baby's wrappings and lifted her to rest against her shoulder. "I've seen how God can take difficult days and turn them into a happy life." She patted Cordelia's back to soothe her.

Charlotte reached a hand across the table. "Thank you."

"I'm sorry I wasn't in church yesterday. Scott told me about Nathan being in town. I'd wanted to welcome him back to Gran Colina, but Cordelia was fussy. She seems to be fine today. I didn't really want to have her around too many people yet." Rena smiled at her baby. "But I had to see you. I'm sorry I couldn't be at the funeral or come before now. How are you all doing since the accident?"

"Michael had a difficult time yesterday." Charlotte looked around the room. "Sarah is clinging to me, and Michael struggles with anger."

"Where are they?"

"I had Mrs. Gillis take them so Nathan and I could meet with your father. We're working on ways to improve the hotel."

Charlotte spent the next few minutes sharing the details with Rena. "So you see, it was all something Pa had planned. Only he never told me about it."

Rena nodded. "It's a blessing that Nathan was willing to come back to Gran Colina and help you."

"I don't think he'd have done that if he'd known Mr. Freeman didn't own the hotel outright. You're probably right, though. Having him here is awkward, but it's better than trying to tackle it all on my own. I don't know what I'd have done if the things Pa ordered were delivered in a few weeks with no warning. At least this way, I have knowledge of his plans."

"The Good Lord does send us help in the most amazing ways sometimes." Rena grinned at her.

"What are you saying, Rena?"

"I'm saying that God knows you needed someone, and He sent Nathan." The grin grew. "I will admit that it's a bit humorous that He chose Nathan. A boy you secretly admired until he teased you."

"He's not a boy now." Charlotte stood and pulled the kettle forward on the stove. "Would you like a cup of tea?"

"So you noticed?"

Charlotte wouldn't pretend she didn't understand Rena's question. "I noticed. And I remember that Momma warned me away from people like him. She told me God would bring the man for me when He knew I was ready." She held her hands out, palms up. "I'm not ready for anything now. I'm so upside down with a broken heart and more work than I'll ever get done." She took cups from the hooks on the cabinet near the stove.

"I don't think God wants you to do it all alone."

"I have too much responsibility on me. I can't think about a man. Not even one who intrigued me when I was a girl." Charlotte looked straight at Rena. "My days of being a carefree girl are over."

When Rena left, Charlotte took a few minutes to compose herself. She washed her face and headed back to the lobby.

Nathan came out of the restaurant and stopped in front of her. "There you are. We still need to do the detailed inventory we talked about." He checked his notebook before continuing. "And we need to go to the bank and arrange the accounts so you and I can write checks. There's fabric to be purchased for the lobby drapes, too."

"The bank accounts?" She must have misheard him. She saw no reason to add him to the bank accounts.

Mr. Thornhill entered the lobby. "Ah, Miss Green, I've been hoping to see you. I'd asked Mr. Taylor to see if there is anything I can do for you or your siblings."

Charlotte looked at Nathan.

"I do apologize, Mr. Thornhill. I haven't had time to relay your message to Miss Green. We've been very busy today."

"You are too kind, Mr. Thornhill. I don't know that there's anything that can be done for us at the moment. We're all adjusting to our new circumstances as best we can." She hooked her hand in Mr. Thornhill's sleeve and steered him toward a settee near the front of the lobby.

Nathan went to the registration desk to greet a new guest who'd entered behind Mr. Thornhill.

"Miss Green, your family has been the very soul of kindness to me. I know my missus would have wanted me to do something for you and the children."

They sat on the settee. "She was a dear one, your wife." The smile on his face let her know she'd distracted him for a moment from her troubles. "I do miss her visits."

The next ten minutes passed in a flurry of memories and a few tears on his part. "You just know that if you can think of anything I'll be glad to help."

Mr. Thornhill left her, and she went in search of Nathan. She'd seen him leave the desk. The lunch crowd trickled in. She'd need to leave within the hour to collect the children.

Mr. Eaton, the guest Nathan had checked in on Friday, stopped her as she made her way to the restaurant.

"Miss Green, I'd like to extend my stay. I'm not sure how long I'll be in town."

"We're happy to have you with us. Let me just make a note in the registration book." Charlotte returned to the desk and handled his request. "Is there anything else I can do for you today?"

"Can you give me directions to the land office?"

"Certainly." Charlotte gave the directions. "Will you be moving to Gran Colina, Mr. Eaton?"

"Um, no—" He cleared his throat. "I'm in Gran Colina on business for my employer."

She would have inquired further, but one of the maids had a question about a torn curtain in the room she was cleaning. Mr. Eaton slipped away while she dealt with the maid.

An hour had passed before Charlotte realized it was gone.

Nathan descended the stairs and joined her at the registration desk. He carried his ever-present notebook. "We need to talk about the inventory. I've done an assessment on my own, but there are details we need to discuss together before the new furnishings arrive."

"Yes, of course. I just need to go get the children from Mrs. Gillis."

The front door was flung open with a force that banged it into the wall and bounced it back again. Michael ran through the lobby and into the residence. That door slammed as Mrs. Gillis and Sarah came through the front entrance. Sarah was crying, and Mrs. Gillis looked as if she might join the child with sympathetic tears at any moment.

The preacher's wife held Sarah's hand. "I'm sorry,

Charlotte. I tried to see they had a pleasant outing, but Michael is in such a state."

Sarah flung herself at Charlotte and wrapped her arms around Charlotte's legs. "Michael is mean, Charlotte. He won't stop saying mean things to me."

Mrs. Gillis shook her head. "I didn't know what to do except bring them home to you."

"Thank you." Charlotte rubbed her hand across Sarah's back to soothe her. "I'm sorry they were so much trouble."

"They're children in pain. It's been a tough blow to them. They'll settle down." Mrs. Gillis was kindness itself, but Charlotte knew the children had upset her.

Nathan stood at the desk watching the scene before him. The disapproval on his face did nothing to help the situation.

"I'll take care of them. Thank you again, Mrs. Gillis." Charlotte reached to lift Sarah into her arms, and Michael opened the door to the residence.

"I'm hungry!" He stomped his foot on the floorboards and glared at his little sister. "Sarah ate the biggest piece of pie. She's such a baby."

"I am not!" Sarah wailed. "You're mean!"

"Children, you will be quiet." Charlotte's words did nothing to stem the flow of their tantrums.

"I won't be quiet. I'm hungry." Michael put his hands on his hips and dared Charlotte to reproach him again.

"I want Momma." Sarah's sniffles turned to sobs.

Nathan took a step toward her. "You need to get them into your parlor." He nodded toward the few guests in the lobby. "They are upsetting people."

Charlotte swallowed the anger that threatened to

spew out of her at him. She kept her voice low, but it resonated with the protectiveness she felt for her siblings. "The children are the ones who are upset. If the guests cannot make allowances for young children at a time like this, they can check out."

"That is just the kind of attitude that will make me sell this hotel." Thomas Freeman's voice came from behind her. The banker had picked the worst possible moment to come to the hotel.

"Mr. Freeman, I assure you that I have everything under control." Nathan's words surprised her more than Mr. Freeman's sudden appearance. "I've just asked Charlotte to take the children into their parlor. They've had a trying morning and are understandably upset." He waved a hand behind his back so Mr. Freeman wouldn't see it.

Charlotte obeyed his gesture and ushered the little ones into their parlor. She peeked into the lobby as Nathan dealt with the banker before closing the door and turning her attention to Michael and Sarah.

She knew Mr. Freeman wasn't making idle threats when he spoke of selling the hotel.

Lord, help me with Michael and Sarah. There must be some way for me to comfort them and provide for them at the same time. Give me wisdom.

Sarah whimpered against Charlotte's shoulder. "Hush, little one. Michael loves you. Let's go find him." She went into her brother's room and found him facedown across the bed. His shoulders shook with the power of his weeping.

She sat on the side of the bed with Sarah still in her arms and tried to soothe both children. Today was their day for weeping. Charlotte had known it would come. She'd expected it before now.

Lord, I know it's too much to ask for joy to come in the morning, but could You please give us a measure of peace to get through today?

One week after her parents' deaths and Charlotte knew the world would never be the same. She prayed for strength and wisdom. She'd have to show Mr. Freeman he was wrong about her. And she'd have to start now.

Chapter Six

Nathan shook his head. "Mr. Freeman, this has not been the way of things since you brought me to Green's Grand Hotel. The children are having a moment of sadness over their recent loss, but Charlotte—Miss Green—is in agreement with me that the hotel must be separate from every aspect of their personal lives."

"I'm a banker, Mr. Taylor. I don't hold with children putting my investments at risk." Mr. Freeman held his fancy hat in one hand and curled the brim in his tightened fist. "Seeing this display puts in mind the notion that Miss Green is nothing more than a child herself. Though why her parents spoiled her so is beyond me. She should be married with her own family at her age." He frowned. "You must make certain this does not happen again." He looked over his shoulder at the guests who'd gone about their business as soon as Charlotte had taken the children out of the room. "The people who provide the funds to pay the obligations of the hotel must not be disturbed. On any account."

Charlotte came out of her parlor and stood beside Nathan at the desk. The tenseness in her posture let him know she was here at great effort. "Mr. Freeman, I apologize for the outburst of my siblings. They are settled in their rooms and will not be in the lobby again until they have recovered from their emotions."

"Miss Green, I am not willing to stand by and see the hotel's success fade under your inexperience." He turned to Nathan. "If you cannot take control of this situation immediately, I will call Turner Hotels and sell the property to them."

"You can't do that." Charlotte gripped the edge of the registration desk.

"I can, and I will." He looked at them both. "You have six weeks to show me progress and a plan that I can trust, or the hotel will be sold." His mouth was set in a firm frown. "Good day to you." He turned on his heel and left them.

Charlotte held on to the desk as if to keep from falling. The muscle in her jaw flinched, and Nathan knew the banker had crossed a line that she would defend until she won.

Without taking her eyes off the closed front door, Charlotte drew a deep breath. "I will not lose this hotel." She turned to Nathan. "Give me half an hour to find someone to sit with the children until the school term begins next month. Then you and I will go over the plans you've been yammering about for the last few days. With God's help, we'll make them work." She went into the restaurant and left him standing there.

Nathan had to smile. Mr. Freeman thought he'd won the battle, but Nathan sensed he'd only stirred up the fight in Charlotte. A fight Nathan had seen before when they were young. A resolve he expected would help her keep her hotel. For the present. And the future.

True to her word, Charlotte came to the desk thirty minutes later with a notebook of her own. He didn't realize she'd returned from her errand to find someone to look after the children.

"I'm ready." She opened to the first blank page and held her pencil at the ready. "Where do we start?"

"Well, let me see." He opened his notebook and tried to take in the change in her in such a short time. She'd pulled her hair back into a neat, though stark, bun, unlike the loose bun she usually wore. Gone were the curling tendrils that brushed her neck. The watch pinned onto the shoulder of her dress added to the seriousness of her demeanor. He preferred the softer look, but this Charlotte would probably get a lot more work done. It would be easier for him to stay focused anyway.

He hadn't realized what a distraction she was until this moment. That would never do. If he was going to establish himself in the hotel business, he must keep his eye on the prize. The pretty, young owner of a hotel on the brink of being owned by the bank was not the prize. Keeping the hotel afloat and growing was.

Pretty, young owner? Yes. Pretty. Charlotte was pretty. He admitted it.

Nathan took a deep breath in an effort to clear his mind and immerse himself in work, or he'd be in big trouble. Mr. Freeman hadn't made an idle threat. He had six weeks to put Green's Grand Hotel on the right path or he'd be out of work with no prospects.

For the next hour he shared his ideas and listened to Charlotte's responses. As they finished the discussion about redecorating the lobby, Sarah cracked the door of the residence and asked to see Charlotte.

"What is it, dear?"

"Miss Libbie says I need to take a nap." The little girl's eyes were puffy from her crying spurt earlier on.

Charlotte smiled at her young sister. "Then you will do as Miss Libbie says."

"Must I?"

"You must. She'll be your teacher in the new term. It's best you begin to respect her authority now."

Libbie Henderson appeared behind Sarah in the open doorway. "Come along, Sarah. I'll read you a story." Libbie held out her hand, and Sarah took it.

"Hello, Libbie." Nathan greeted Libbie. "I haven't seen you since my return to Gran Colina."

"Hello, Nathan. I've been away for a few days and only just returned. It was my last opportunity to visit with my grandmother before the term begins in a few weeks. Welcome back. I hope you're settling in nicely."

Sarah tugged on Libbie's hand. "I want you to read me a story now." She yawned. "But not poetry. When Momma read it, the words sounded like she was singing. I think it might make me sad."

Charlotte kissed Sarah on the top of her head. "I'll be home soon after your nap."

The door closed, and Charlotte dabbed at her eyes with a handkerchief she'd pulled from a pocket in her skirt.

"Would you like to take a break?" They needed to keep working, but he didn't want to be insensitive to her grief.

"No. We must take advantage of the time we have with Libbie here. Mrs. Atkins suggested her. I should have thought of it earlier." She looked down at her notes from the last hour. "Only I know it's important to use care in how I spend money. More so than ever before."

"I agree, but I think having Libbie here to help with the children while we get things sorted out is an investment in the future of the hotel." He closed his notebook. "But let's at least have something to drink and a piece of pie. I imagine Mrs. Atkins could do with a rest after the busy lunch crowd we had today. Let's ask her to sit at the desk. It's a quiet time of day. You and I can work at a table in the restaurant."

She nodded. "Okay, but only for an hour. Mrs. Atkins will need time to finish the supper preparations."

The rest of the afternoon passed in a flurry of note taking and inspecting the rooms that would need to be done over. Charlotte wore a brave face when she agreed to the changes he suggested for room eight.

"Your father was very specific with the furnishings he chose. I think you'll be pleased." Nathan caught a breath of the scent of Charlotte's hair as she walked past him on the way to her parlor. The sweetness of it had assailed him all afternoon.

"We could ask at the mercantile and see if the Busbys order from the same company. Perhaps you could show me the choices. It may help me to pick out fabric for the draperies if I can see the style of things."

"That's a good idea." He watched her disappear into her rooms and sent Mrs. Atkins back to the kitchen. He'd love a walk on the busy sidewalk to clear his head, but there wasn't a moment to spare. He and Charlotte had covered a lot of territory this afternoon. He needed to put his notes into some sort of order so they could begin the work of implementing everything.

He was deep in thought when a gentleman not much

older than him approached the desk. He looked familiar, but Nathan couldn't remember his name.

"Mr. Taylor, I'm Alfred Murray." The man spoke in a slow, deliberate pace.

Recognition dawned on him. "Yes, Mr. Murray. You were here the other day to speak to Miss Green."

"Yes. I've come to see if she's available now." The man's words were rife with tension.

"Is anything the matter, Mr. Murray?"

He shook his head. Too fast. "No. Nothing is the matter."

"Miss Green has had a busy day with the hotel and her siblings. Would you consider coming at a later time?" Nathan didn't know what the man wanted, but he didn't need Charlotte to be upset or distracted by anyone or anything. This man looked like he was bringing trouble—even if he didn't intend it.

"I really want to speak to her as soon as possible." Mr. Murray pulled at the sleeve of his jacket. "I've already waited a few days. Do you think she might be able to spare a moment?"

Nathan pondered the request while he observed Alfred Murray. His hair was thick with the look of some sort of oil. The marks of the comb he'd used had left a pattern in the slick style. It was late afternoon, but he was freshly shaved. These things weren't what Nathan would notice about a man except that he was so perfectly turned out. Mr. Murray wasn't dropping by to check on Charlotte. He was here to come calling on the owner of the hotel.

"If you'll take a seat there by the window, I'll see if I can find her."

Mr. Murray positioned himself on the settee across

the lobby, and Nathan tapped on the parlor door behind the desk. He kept one hand on the handle to keep whoever answered from flinging the door wide.

Sarah tugged the door ajar and looked up at him through the narrow opening. "We're busy."

He almost laughed, but she was so serious that he didn't want to upset her. He bent down to be on her level. "I need to ask Charlotte something. Can I come inside for just a minute?"

"No. Every time you talk to her she comes home sad. Me and Michael won't let you make her sad anymore. We talked about it." Sarah's calm reserve was noble.

"I'm sorry she's sad, but I think there are a lot of reasons for that. I'm not trying to do anything that would make her sad."

"You don't have to try. You just do it. Like when Michael makes me cry. He says he doesn't mean it, but he does it all the time." She leaned closer. "And he told me you shouldn't be at our hotel. He says he's the man now that Pa is gone, and he should be running the hotel. He says we don't need you here."

All this information from a little girl who'd avoided him from the moment he arrived.

"I'm here to help Charlotte. And you and Michael." He stood up tall. "And I need to speak to Charlotte, so be a good girl and let her know I'm here."

She shook her head. Blond curls swung around her shoulders. "Michael won't like it." She closed the door with a click.

Nathan laughed. Sarah had done to him what he was doing to Mr. Murray. They were both trying to protect Charlotte.

He knocked again. This time with enough force for Charlotte to hear.

From the other side of the door he heard Michael speak. "Go away. Charlotte is making us dinner."

Nathan considered letting Mr. Murray try his best to get past the two protectors. But only for a moment. Mr. Murray was the second person to call on Charlotte in the last few days. If Charlotte accepted the attention of one of the men who came, she might marry and turn over the management of the hotel to her new husband. Not even Thomas Freeman and all the money in his bank could make Charlotte keep Nathan on as manager in that event. He could find himself without a job or income.

But it wasn't only for his sake that Nathan wanted to protect Charlotte. These men had known her for a long time. If they'd truly been interested in her as a wife, why would they have waited until now to share their intentions?

No. Charlotte might not realize it, but Nathan had every expectation that many of the gentleman callers would be motivated by her new financial holdings. They would be unaware that her inheritance was encumbered by a substantial loan from the bank.

Michael and Sarah might choose to protect her from him, but he'd protect her—and her hotel—from suitors who might want more than a wife.

Nathan knocked again. And again.

The door finally opened, and Charlotte stood there wiping her hands on a dish towel. "What is it? The children were frightened by your knocking."

"I doubt that." He looked around her to where they

stood with guilty faces. "They were trying to protect you from me."

Charlotte turned. "Is that so?"

Sarah whimpered into the handkerchief doll she held up to hide her face.

Michael bowed out his chest and pushed his shoulders back. "We don't need him here, Charlotte. Pa wanted me to run the hotel after he died. He told me so."

Charlotte leveled a look on the child that only a maternal figure could master. "And when he told you this was he speaking of sometime in the future when he was too old to do the work? Perhaps when you grow up and have a family of your own?"

Michael kicked at the rug beneath his feet. "It don't matter. He's dead, and I'm the one he wanted to run the hotel." He poked his finger in Nathan's direction. "Not him."

"Michael, you will respect your elders. Apologize."

"I'm sorry for being rude." The boy gave Nathan a stern look. "But I'm not sorry for saying the hotel is ours. Pa told me all the time that it's my job."

Nathan wanted to applaud the child's bravery in a difficult situation, but Mr. Murray had made his way back to the registration desk. The man's nervous cough drew Charlotte's attention.

"Miss Charlotte, I'd like to have a word with you." Mr. Murray looked around Nathan at the children. Then he gave his full attention to Charlotte. "It's a personal matter, if I could speak to you privately."

Charlotte's face stiffened. A shadow crossed her eyes. Mr. Murray was too far away to notice, Nathan was sure. But why was Nathan noticing?

"I was coming to tell you that you had a caller, Charlotte." He stepped back from the door. "I'll be in the lobby."

He walked to the front of the room and adjusted the embroidered pillows on the settee. It wasn't necessary, but he didn't think he could stand within earshot of Mr. Murray and not be drawn to listen. It would be unfair to the man who'd asked for privacy.

Before Nathan could walk back across the lobby to the desk, Mr. Murray was on his way through the front door. The man's gaze never left his shoes. Nathan wondered how he didn't bump into the furniture on the way out.

Charlotte stood at the door watching Mr. Murray leave.

"Are you okay?" Nathan didn't want to pry, but her focus had to be on the business. She was vulnerable. If she gave her heart to one of these callers, and later found that the man had an ulterior motive, it would devastate her. A broken heart caused by a disingenuous romance would be more than she needed on top of the grief and responsibility brought on by the death of her parents.

"I am." She huffed out an unladylike sigh. "Mr. Murray is a nice man, but why did he approach me now? He could have spoken to Pa or Momma at any time in the past. Honestly, I've never considered him in any way as someone for my husband. I appreciate that he is a good and kind man, but that doesn't make him the right person for me."

"Charlotte, these men are coming because you own this hotel. You should prepare yourself for the attention that a woman of means receives from prospective suitors."

"The hotel isn't secure. Not at the moment. They'd just be asking for a load of debt and work."

Nathan took a step closer to her as Mrs. Atkins entered the lobby. He lowered his voice. "No one knows of the debt, save the banker. He won't tell because it would put his investment at risk for people to think the business could fail."

Acknowledgment of the truth filled her eyes.

Mrs. Atkins approached them. "Miss Charlotte, I need to go to the mercantile. I'm out of some of the spices I need to finish the supper for tonight. Would you be able to mind the stove for me? I had to send Bertha home early to cook for her pa."

The door to the residence opened wider, and Michael and Sarah came out. "I'm hungry." The words were spontaneous but rang out in unison.

Nathan assured Mrs. Atkins that she could run her errand.

"But—" Charlotte started to protest.

"Take the children with you to the kitchen. I'd like you to consider the possibility of you and your family eating from the restaurant for the foreseeable future. You don't really have time to prepare meals on top of all the work you'll be doing for the next many weeks."

Her shoulders slumped. "Our mother always cooked. She said we were a family and family should sit around the family table every evening and share the news of the day. It's a special time for us."

Sarah chimed in with her opinion. "I want to eat in the restaurant. Mrs. Atkins is a good cook. I like her biscuits."

"Me, too." Michael headed for the restaurant.

"Go ahead." Nathan put a hand on her arm. "It's one less thing for you to worry over."

Her gaze settled on his hand. "You may be right. We'll eat there tonight, but I'll have to decide if it's something I want to do on a regular basis."

The warmth of her arm through the sleeve of her dress distracted him. He dropped his hand. It was imperative that he keep his distance. "You can bring the food back to your table if you choose. Then you could have a good meal and still share in your family traditions."

"That's a good idea." Sarah tugged on Charlotte's skirt. "Let's go see what's cooking. I'm real hungry."

Nathan rubbed his hands together as they left the lobby. He needed to keep his distance in more ways than one. He needed to guard against an emotional attachment to Charlotte and the children, but he also needed to keep space between them in a physical sense. If his light touch on her arm had the power to capture all of his attention that would not be good for either of them.

On Wednesday afternoon Charlotte helped Mr. Thornhill make a reservation for his next stay in Gran Colina. "Thank you for your loyalty to our establishment, Mr. Thornhill. It's guests like you who keep us in business."

"You are most welcome. I do wish you could think of some way for me to help you and the children."

"Just keep coming to visit." She smiled and finished her notes in the registration book. "Does your schedule still have you leaving us tomorrow?"

"I'm afraid so. There are things I must attend to at home." He nodded at Nathan when he joined them at the desk. "I've been added to the board of directors for a group of farmers. It works like the Grange. We're planning a meeting in October, and I've received a telegram today that there is a problem with the location we've chosen. The town is a good area for our members, but there was a fire in the hotel there a few days ago. They won't be up and running again before our meeting."

Nathan turned one ear closer to the conversation. "So you have a group that needs a meeting place and a hotel?"

"Yes. That's right." Mr. Thornhill put a hand on the desk. "I wish I'd known earlier. I'd have tried to book them here."

She couldn't believe what she was hearing. "You are the person who makes that decision?"

"Yes."

"Is our hotel large enough to accommodate your members?" Was God sending Mr. Thornhill as an answer to one of her many prayers?

"Wait, Charlotte. There is a lot more to hosting a group than having enough rooms."

She didn't appreciate Nathan's response. "I'm aware of that. The group of mayors have been coming for years."

Mr. Thornhill smiled. "I'd love to have you host the gathering. It would bring a good bit of business to the hotel and restaurant. I don't know why I didn't think of it before."

"We'll need the dates and the number of guests before we can offer to accept the reservations." Nathan pulled the registration book toward him. "We need to make certain that other, prior reservations won't conflict."

The three of them worked out the dates, and Nathan turned to Mr. Thornhill. "Please give Miss Green and I the afternoon to ponder this. There are a lot of things we'll need to consider."

Charlotte pushed forward. "We can do it. I know we can." They needed events like this. Nathan had said as much himself.

He tapped on the registration book. "Let's not bore Mr. Thornhill with our discussions. I think we have enough information from him."

"I want to stop in at the train station and buy my ticket this afternoon. I'll come by the desk after supper and see what's been decided." Mr. Thornhill left with a smile on his face.

If Charlotte had her way, he'd be whistling a happy tune when he returned for their answer.

"Why did you send him away? We could have confirmed everything right then and there."

"There's more to hosting a meeting than having open rooms on the right days."

"I know that." His presumption of her ignorance perturbed her. "The mayors just left very pleased with their days here."

Nathan leaned his hip against the registration desk and folded his arms. "Who arranged that meeting?"

"My father." She stiffened to match his posture.

"And who handled all the food arrangements?"

"Momma did." She didn't like the uneasiness in the pit of her stomach. "With Mrs. Atkins."

"How many more farmers are in this new group as

opposed to the number of mayors?" In all this time he hadn't budged from his leaning position.

"You sure do seem confident leaning there, like you know all the answers to the questions before you ask them. Confident to the point of arrogance. I might be wrong, but you don't need to show me in such a condescending manner." She frowned at him.

"That pretty little pout might have worked on your father, but it won't work on me."

"What?" Pretty? The way his eyes grew wide as he stepped away from the desk let her know he hadn't meant to say that aloud.

He cleared his throat and straightened the notes he'd made into an orderly stack. "I mean you can't pout and expect me to give in to your way of thinking."

"I wasn't pouting."

"Really? So what do you call it when you push out your lower lip when you know you're about to be found out? You looked just like Sarah when you did it." He mimicked her frown, and it made them both laugh.

"Okay. I see it now."

He smiled the most genuine smile she'd seen since he'd returned to Gran Colina. "Good. Does that mean you'll listen to what I have to say about Mr. Thornhill and his group?"

"I will." She almost felt coy when she answered. "As long as you don't stay upset with me."

Nathan was facing the desk again, but he cut his eyes toward her and stilled his work. "Not upset. Never upset." He rubbed his hand across the shadow of beard on his chin. "Not if you let me join you for supper and we talk about what having a group this size would require."

"Since I'm not cooking, I think I could arrange for dinner on such short notice. Let's eat in the residence though. The restaurant is noisy. And we can leave the door open to hear in case anyone comes to the desk for assistance."

An hour later the children had eaten their fill and gone to play in the parlor. Charlotte poured Nathan another cup of coffee and sat down opposite him.

"Thank you for clearing away the dishes while I settled the kids."

He spread his notes out on the clean surface. "I thought this would be the best place for us to work."

She stirred cream into her coffee as he started to point out what would be needed to host the group of farmers.

"There's the matter of extra help since the hotel would be completely booked with that many farmers. And Mrs. Atkins would need another assistant for those days. Is Bertha still in school?"

"No. She finished her studies in the spring. She works with Mrs. Atkins here and helps out at their home."

"Okay, then we'll only need one additional assistant. The shopping for the week will be heavier than usual. Do you think you will have mastered that in the weeks before the meeting?"

Charlotte sipped her coffee. "Before this week, I'd have said so with no hesitation. If you hadn't been here last week, we'd have run out of food." She twisted her cup in the saucer. "You'll have to teach me."

Nathan nodded. "That's settled then. There's also the rooms. With all of them rented, we'd need more help with the laundry and cleaning the rooms."

"There are some girls in town who are friends with the maids. I'm sure one or two of them would appreciate a small job."

"So, the food and cleaning would be handled. I can take care of the lobby and make the bank deposits. You can oversee the cleaning staff and kitchen. Would you allow someone to help you with the baking? Just for the week."

"You're talking fast, but I'm listening just as fast." She leaned forward with her elbows on the table and tried to read his notes though they were upside down. "I will handle the banking."

Nathan rested against the back of his chair. "I mentioned this the other day to no avail. Charlotte, you can't handle all the business alone. Thomas Freeman has been here every day to check on our progress. He's asked why you haven't had me added to the accounts for the hotel."

"The accounts for the hotel are mine. Pa handled all the money. I think he'd want me to do the same."

"What do you know about the bills? The account at the mercantile, the butcher's bill and the various things that must be purchased to keep the hotel going. Have you any idea how much money is taken in and how much must be set aside for slow seasons? There are expenses that are paid monthly and others that need to be paid on delivery."

"I can learn that."

"It's more complicated than shopping for the restaurant." His face softened as he spoke. "I don't want to overwhelm you, but running an establishment like Green's Grand Hotel could take months—or even a year—to learn."

"I don't have a year to learn it, Nathan." She looked again at the notes he'd made. "According to Mr. Thornhill, this meeting will commence on the first Monday in October. That's just over seven weeks. When do the new furnishings arrive?"

"Five to seven weeks."

She smiled in triumph. "Then we'll have everything ready before they come. This meeting will be our big debut of our new and improved hotel."

"Charlotte, that doesn't allow a moment for error. What if something is delayed? The furnishings could be caught up by the train schedule. We could be forced to work at a slower pace on the individual rooms. Any number of things could go wrong. You or I could be ill."

"I'm never sick." She picked up her coffee. "And God knows how desperate I am to make this work. Thomas Freeman will be powerless to take the hotel from me."

"I would love for it to be that easy."

"It can be. You can make it happen." She knew he could. Somewhere inside, a faith in his abilities had taken root. "The very fact that you are here is proof of it. Thomas Freeman wouldn't have brought you if he thought you weren't able to succeed."

"It's a lot of work, Charlotte. I'll do everything I can, but it's taken me five years to learn what I know. You're going to have to trust me on some things."

The bell on the desk rang, and she knew it would be Mr. Thornhill. She sprang to her feet. "I'm going to tell him we can do it."

Nathan didn't look convinced. "I'd be more comfortable if we had more time."

"We don't. So we'll have to do it. We'll go to the bank tomorrow. It's just the sort of news I need to keep Mr. Freeman from coming around to trouble me."

"I would imagine he'll come no matter what you tell him." Nathan stood as the bell rang again. "Let's go tell your friend that we'll do our best."

Mr. Thornhill was pleased with their acceptance. "Are you sure it's not too much to arrange. I know it's more people than the mayors' group."

Nathan asked, "You've given us adequate time to prepare. We'll be ready."

"That's good to know." He smiled. "It'll be a nice boost to your business here. And don't worry about the farmers. They're a good sort and don't need as much tending as a bunch of grumpy mayors." He laughed at his own joke.

"We'll do our best. I'm so grateful to you for your trust in our establishment." Charlotte blinked away tears at the thought of how proud her father would be that she was able to make this happen so soon after taking the reins of the hotel.

"I've no doubt in you. You're from good stock, Charlotte Green. If anyone can do it, you can."

As soon as he left to telegram the other board members of his decision, a lump of worry filled her throat. What if Nathan's concerns were true? What if something went wrong? What if she failed?

Nathan hit the bell on the desk and snatched her out of her thoughts.

"Don't you do it."

"Do what?" She crinkled her forehead in an effort to concentrate on his words.

"Don't back up now that the deed is done. The plan is in motion, so we need to prepare."

She nodded and smoothed her skirt with her palms. "You're right." She blew out a slow breath.

"I think the best thing we can do is start to take our lunches together. It's the best time for us to work without interruption. Libbie will have the children, and you'll still have your suppers with them as a family."

She'd asked him for a lot this afternoon, and he'd risen to the occasion. To refuse him on this request would be rude payment for his effort.

Somewhere inside, a warning voice told her that spending time with Nathan Taylor every day could be the biggest change in her life. The one with the most impact on Charlotte Green. More than anything Nathan the hotelier could ever do or say to change Charlotte the hotel owner.

Chapter Seven

Nathan and Charlotte climbed the steps to the porch of the hotel on Friday morning. He held the door open for her to precede him into the lobby. "That went well, I think."

She had been silent on their walk from the bank. "If you mean the business of signing the papers went smoothly, it's no surprise since Mr. Freeman had them prepared and waiting for your signature."

He tried to ignore the tension in her tone. "It has to be difficult for you. Every day you've had to do something you never imagined before."

"Thank you for saying that. It means a lot that you understand how strange all of this is to me." She gave him a forced smile. "I'm going to talk to Mrs. Atkins about the grocery order. It has to be placed today."

"May I join you?"

"Of course. Just let me check in with Libbie first. Michael and Sarah were not in good humor when I left earlier."

When Charlotte came back into the lobby Michael

was on her heels. "I don't want to stay home today. I want to go outside and play with my friends."

"Michael, you will do as you're told." Charlotte didn't give him a hint that she'd relent.

"It's not fair. You used to take us on walks by the river and to see Mrs. Braden's animals." His anger escalated with every sentence.

Nathan didn't think Charlotte deserved any more back talk from the boy. "Michael, Charlotte has answered you. Arguing with her is not helpful, nor should you continue to do so in the hotel lobby."

Charlotte spun around and pinned Nathan with her stare. "I will handle this, Mr. Taylor." Her tone was low and even—and full of grit. No one listening would have criticized her manner, but Nathan knew just how serious she was. The suddenness of her reaction warned that he may have overstepped a boundary with Michael. One she would guard with all the maternal instincts he'd witnessed in her as each day passed.

She turned back to Michael, and Nathan returned to the desk as the front door of the hotel opened. Dennis, the errand boy from the train station, lugged in several valises and a box.

Michael yelled out. "Those are Pa's things! And Momma's!" He bolted around Charlotte and almost tackled Dennis.

"Whoa, there, Michael." Dennis set the bags down. "I've got to give these things to your sister."

Charlotte walked at a steady pace across the lobby. A stoic dread surrounded her posture. "Michael, return to the parlor." She brooked no argument from the child at this point, and he knew when he'd been conquered. The slouch of his shoulders deepened as he walked closer to the parlor door. He pulled it closed behind him without looking back.

Dennis handed the small box to Charlotte. "The stationmaster wanted me to make sure I put this in your hands. The valises are the ones your parents carried on their trip." He pointed at the box. "These things were with your parents at the time of the accident. It took a while for the railroad company to go through all the personal things and sort them to return to their rightful owners." He removed his hat. "Please know how sorry everyone at the station is for your loss."

"Thank you, Dennis. I appreciate you bringing their things home."

Nathan had walked over to stand beside Charlotte. "I'll take care of everything from here." He tipped the young man discreetly and picked up the valises. "Where would you like me to put these, Charlotte?"

"I don't know." She stared at the top of the box. "I don't know why it didn't occur to me that their things would eventually be returned. I'd asked about them the first day but had forgotten them in the stress and busyness of the days that followed."

"If you'd like, I can put everything in your parents' room. You could choose the best time for you to go through them later." He waited, but she didn't answer. "Charlotte."

She jerked her head up. "I'm sorry. I was just so taken off guard." She lifted her face to look at him. "Just when I think I'm dealing with it all, something comes out of the blue and sends me reeling back into the abyss of grief." A tear slid down her cheek. He wanted to drop his burden and pull her close. To hold her head against his shoulder and comfort her. That would never do.

"I'm so sorry. Please let me put these things somewhere for you. You don't have to deal with them until you're ready."

"You're right. I can wait." She led him through the parlor and down a short hallway. The door she approached stood closed. She froze to the spot. "We should put everything in there—only I haven't been in their room since I chose the clothes for their funerals."

"Let me do it. You put the box on the floor, and I'll put everything inside. You can wait until you're ready."

Charlotte set the box down and retraced her steps to the parlor. She dropped onto the settee with her back to him. He moved everything into the room as quietly as possible. One look around the space showed why it was difficult for Charlotte to enter the room. A picture of her father stood on the corner of her mother's dressing table. Her father's Bible was on the table by the bed. Cheerful yellow curtains hung at the window. The room had been a sanctuary for her parents. The feminine touches that were evident in the lobby were on full show in this room. A framed picture of a yellow rose was on the wall above a chair near the opposite side of the bed. Small figures of children lined a shelf on another wall. Everything spoke of Nancy Green's love for her family and her home. Even the rag rug at the foot of the bed made the room feel cozy.

Charlotte would need courage to face the emptiness of a room so full of memories of her parents. He closed the door and joined her in the parlor.

"Do you want me to check on Michael? I heard noises coming from the next room."

"No. He does best if he's left alone to calm himself when he's upset." Her tone was distant. The arrival of her parents' belongings must have brought fresh grief.

"Is there anything I can do for you?"

"We'll be fine. Libbie took Sarah for a walk. They'll be back soon. If you don't mind, I'm going to wait a few minutes and speak with Michael. I'll be back to work soon. We can finish the inventory and perhaps go to the mercantile after lunch."

"Okay, but if you think of anything, all you have to do is ask." She nodded, but he didn't think she really heard him. He decided it was best to leave her alone to deal with this unexpected wave of sorrow. He headed toward the lobby.

"And, Nathan," Charlotte called after him. "I will be having meals with the children. You may join us for lunch on their good days. I feel it's best for me to spend that time with them. I know we have a lot of work to discuss, and I think it's best if we try to meet together as much as possible. At the same time, I have to do what's best for the children."

"What about the hotel? We are just beginning to make progress."

"We can finish the inventory and go to the mercantile today. Then I'll take a few days to ponder things and decide how we'll proceed."

"So you're only going to hear my ideas and then put me in my place? I'm sorry if it sounds harsh to you, but this kind of business requires drive and planning. You need to do both."

"I'm sorry, Nathan, but I don't have the luxury of letting anyone, including you, think they can get the upper hand over my business. Or my family." She perused the lobby. "This is my life. I'm responsible for myself and those two little ones. I won't abdicate that to anyone."

He was so handsome standing in the parlor doorway. And he'd been helpful. She'd almost broken down when Dennis had returned with her parents' belongings. If Nathan hadn't been there, she'd no doubt be up to her elbows in the box and valises at this very moment, letting the memories carry her on an emotional journey. It would never have occurred to her to wait and open them when she felt stronger.

But as much as he'd done—as much as she wanted to rely on someone—she wouldn't let her attraction to him pull her into a deeper relationship. She was his boss. Plain and simple. As hard as it was to face the fact, she knew she was drawn to Nathan. Her mother had been right. She wasn't ready for marriage. She had too much to learn about life.

Momma had even warned her about Nathan when Charlotte was still in school. She hadn't liked to see Charlotte upset after Nathan's teasing.

Charlotte had to protect Michael and Sarah. If that meant she had to protect herself from any emotional entanglements, too, then so be it.

"You've been very good about showing me things that will help the hotel, but in the end, the hotel is mine. Mine and my siblings. You're here to do a job. That job is to teach me how to run the place."

"I see. And am I to have a place here after you've learned to buy the groceries and handle the accounts? Or am I to be out on my ear as soon as you think you can manage without me?"

"That's not fair, Nathan. You know I would never have taken you on if Thomas Freeman hadn't insisted."

He grunted. "And you should know that I'd never have left my job in Dallas if I'd thought I'd have no future here."

She hung her head and twisted her fingers together in her lap. "No, I guess not."

Michael came to the end of the hall. "I can hear you fighting."

Charlotte held out a hand to Michael, and he went to stand by her. "We're not fighting."

"Yes, you are. You don't want him here, and I don't want him here. Why don't you just make him leave?" The child never looked at Nathan.

"I'll be at the desk. I know you want to handle this alone." Nathan pulled on the door.

"Wait." She called him back. "I won't be unfair to you. I promise."

"I hope you're able to decide what's fair. It's not an emotional decision. It's a business one." Nathan walked into the lobby and closed the door behind him.

"I told you we don't need him here. I don't think he likes me and Sarah." Michael's constant anger had prevailed since their parents had died. As much as she hoped he wasn't right about Nathan, she longed to see another emotion surface in her young brother.

"I wouldn't say Nathan doesn't like you."

"You don't have to say it. He doesn't like anything we do. He wants us out of our own hotel. He won't let me sit behind the desk like Pa used to, and he wants us to be quiet. This is our hotel." Michael stomped his foot. "He's not the boss."

Charlotte dredged up her mother's methods of dealing with Michael's strong will. "Michael, you are not an adult. You do not get to make adult decisions. You may tell me anything, and I will listen to you. I never want you to think you can't talk to me. But I will not allow you to be disrespectful." She put a finger under his chin and angled his face toward hers. "Do you understand me?"

"Yes." He scuffed his shoe against the carpet.

"As for the hotel, it belongs to me and you and Sarah. We are the Greens of Green's Grand Hotel. You're right about that."

"And he's not the boss." He poked the air between him and the door to the lobby.

"No, he isn't. But neither are you." Charlotte put an arm around his shoulder. "I am."

"But I'm the man of the house. Pa always said I'd be the man of the house if he wasn't here."

"You are. But just because I'm not a man doesn't mean I'm not the boss. I'm the oldest. So I'm the boss." She touched her finger to the middle of his chest. "And when you're an adult, you can be the boss with me. You and Sarah, too."

"I wanna help now."

"You can."

"How? You don't think I'm big enough to do the stuff Pa did."

"No. You'll have to be older to do those things. You can help me by being a good boy. If you're good in school, you'll learn things you need to know for when you are one of the bosses at the hotel. If you're good at home, you'll help me learn all the things Nathan is here to teach me about being the boss. Then the hotel will be big and successful when you're all grown up."

"Can I have a glass of milk?"

"You just had milk with your breakfast. Why do you want another glass so soon?"

He puffed out his little chest and stretched to his highest height. "Milk makes you grow. I need to grow fast, so I need some more milk."

Charlotte laughed and hugged him. "Yes, you can have some milk. I'll even let you go to the hotel kitchen to get it if you promise to behave."

"I'll be good." He took off for the door and tugged it open. "I promise."

Lord, please help me. People in every direction are pulling at me for answers and their very way of life. I can't do this without Your help.

What would she do? Learn all she could from Nathan and send him away? At the moment, it was the only thing she knew to do.

Nathan jotted down the last items on his list. "That takes care of the inventory."

Charlotte brushed dust from her sleeves. "Good. I'm not sure when I was last in the attic, but I don't remember it being so dusty."

Nathan watched as she ran a hand over her hair. "You were probably a child. Attics are an adventure to children. Dust is never a deterrent—it's part of the mystique."

"I do remember coming up here in search of one of Ma's old dresses. Not Michael and Sarah's mother, but my mother." Her eyes glazed over. He got the sense that her mind took her on a trip to a place in her memory where no one left on earth had been. "I wanted to wear it to Pa's wedding to Nancy, my second mother."

She looked at him then. "She was so good to me. I never felt like she didn't truly love me. Her wisdom and guidance protected me in ways that make me forever grateful."

"Did you find the dress?"

"I did, and she altered it for me to wear to the wedding. She had a new dress. Pa got Mrs. Opal Pennington to make it up from fabric he bought for her. She was beautiful. It was like a lovely dream. An autumn day in the cool of the morning. The harvest was over, so the townsfolk gathered and celebrated with them in the hotel restaurant after the ceremony in the church."

Nathan remembered a picture his mother had had of her and his father on their wedding day. It was one of her prized possessions. Now his father kept it on the table by his bed. "It's wonderful that you have such fond memories."

"It is. I know I should be grateful for that. I am." She shrugged. "But I am so very sad at the same time."

"Let's get you out of the attic. You can take your happy memories from here with you." He held the door open for her and caught her light floral scent as she passed him to stand on the landing. The fragrance mingled with a hint of dust must be like her memories. Sweetness covered with the age of life.

"What's next on the schedule?" She descended the stairway onto the landing on the second floor.

"We still need to go to the mercantile and see if they have the catalog your father ordered from."

Charlotte opened the watch she wore pinned to her dress. "Although it won't be time for supper for a couple of hours, I'm not sure we can be away from the hotel any more today. The trip to the bank was early, but we have guests scheduled to arrive this afternoon. And I'm hoping for more to come from the train."

"Let's leave that for next week then. We've accomplished a lot in one week. There is plenty for us to plan from the notes we've made. All that will need to be done at the mercantile is to choose fabric for the draperies. Everything else is coming with the order your parents placed in Dallas."

"Okay. I'll just go make sure everything I ordered for the restaurant this morning has been delivered."

She headed across the lobby while he made his way to the desk. Without discussing it, they'd fallen into a natural habit of him manning the desk and working on the notes they'd made and her checking on the staff and supplies.

"Mr. Taylor, I'd like a moment of your time." Mr. Eaton had walked up without his notice. He was too taken with the Charlotte. She was getting to him, and that would never do.

"Certainly, Mr. Eaton."

"I'd like to extend my stay again. By another week, at least."

Nathan checked to see that they had availability. "That will be fine. I'll adjust your information here." He made the note for Charlotte to see. "I assume you're having a productive time in Gran Colina. Miss Green told me you're in town for your employer."

"Yes. Things are going well. Thank you." He lifted a hand and left the lobby. His quick gait made Nathan wonder what had prompted his hurry. Was it the work he was here to do, or had he wanted to avoid any conversation about his job?

Charlotte joined him. "Is that Mr. Eaton leaving?"

"No. He said he'll be staying for a minimum of another week."

She leaned against the desk. "I wonder what kind of work he does. I haven't had an opportunity to ask."

"I was about to ask, but he left in a hurry."

A frown creased her brow. "Do you think he doesn't want us to know?"

"It's possible. Though I can't think what difference it would make to you or me."

"You're probably right. He asked for directions to the land office the other day, but he said he's not moving to Gran Colina."

Nathan squared his shoulders as the front door opened, and the guests from the train entered. "We'll most likely know soon enough. Gran Colina may be growing, but there's still enough small-town charm here for someone to notice Mr. Eaton and share his purpose with others."

They helped their arriving visitors before Charlotte had to relieve Libbie. She carried their family supper on a tray as he made his way toward the restaurant for his evening meal.

"Why don't you join me and the children for supper? I've enough here, I'm sure."

He stopped to look over his shoulder at the empty lobby. "If we can leave the door ajar so I can hear the bell."

"That's fine. Whenever you're ready, we'll be in the kitchen."

Ten minutes later, he knocked on the kitchen door and pushed it open. "May I come in?"

Charlotte sat at the table with Michael and Sarah.

Sarah scooted closer to Charlotte. "We didn't think you would come."

"I'm sorry." Nathan smiled at the sweet girl. Her shy demeanor and the way she clung to Charlotte was endearing her to him. "I had to help someone at the desk."

"We are just about to offer thanks." Charlotte motioned for him to have a seat and held out her hands to the children.

Nathan took the offered chair and reached a hand to each child. Sarah snuggled even closer to Charlotte but slid her tiny hand into his. Michael bowed his head and kept his hand in this lap.

Charlotte gave thanks for their food and the blessings of guests to fill the rooms of the hotel. When she lifted her gaze, she saw Michael glare at Nathan.

"Michael, you will apologize to Nathan or leave the table." Her voice was steady and even. She was mastering her maternal instincts.

The chair legs scraped across the wood floor, and Michael stood. "I ain't hungry no way." He stomped toward the door.

"You are not excused from the room, Michael. You may apologize to Nathan, or you may stand in the corner while we eat. Then you will eat and wash all the dishes afterward."

"But—"

"No. You may not sass me. Not on this or anything else." Charlotte kept calm through the entire exchange, and Nathan marveled that she wasn't already a wife and mother. She'd taken the children in hand in a loving and maternal manner.

Michael studied his shoes for a moment, then jerked

his head up and looked at Nathan. "I'm sorry." He plodded back to his seat and slumped into it.

Charlotte put stew on their plates and added a biscuit. "If you finish your meal, there is pie." She smiled across the table at Nathan. "That applies to you, too."

This was the real Charlotte. The girl who smiled and laughed.

"Yes, ma'am." He returned her smile and glanced at Michael to see how he was faring. The boy wasn't happy, but he was eating. That was something, and it spoke well of Charlotte's tactics.

Sarah ate her biscuit first. Charlotte had to coax her to eat her stew. "You know you love pie. I made buttermilk pie today."

Sarah perked up. "Buttermilk? That's my favorite."

Charlotte tapped the tip of Sarah's nose. "That's why I made it."

Michael talked around a mouthful of food. "I like sweet potato pie." He loaded his spoon with another generous bite of stew.

"I'll make that for you as a special treat soon."

They finished the meal, and the children put their plates on the cabinet for Charlotte to wash. She added her plate to the stack of dirty dishes.

"I want to go on the front porch and rock my doll." Sarah straightened the folds of the doll's dress.

Charlotte thought for a moment. "If Michael goes with you."

"Do I gotta?"

"No. You can stay here and help with the dishes if you'd like."

Nathan tried not to laugh at Charlotte. Her eyes gleamed with amusement.

"Come on, Sarah. I'll bring my horses and play, too." Michael grabbed two wooden horses and went through the parlor with his young sister.

Nathan could stand it no longer. He dropped his head back and laughed. "You have tormented that poor boy with your logic tonight. He can't win a minute of reprieve."

"It's awful, isn't it?" Charlotte giggled. "He needs to remember his manners, but I don't want him to feel as though I'm being unfair to him. I've found he responds well when given a choice of two things he doesn't want to do."

"You are a smart one, Charlotte Green." He picked up a towel. "You wash, and I'll dry."

She took a step back. "What? The great hotelier is going to serve as kitchen help?"

"I've done my share of dishes. And cooking, for that matter. Don't think I don't know my way around the household chores. Life without a mother or wife can make a man resourceful." He leaned close to her. "You'd be surprised."

She drew in a quick, low breath. "Oh. I hadn't thought of that."

Nathan stared into her blue eyes. He hadn't meant to be so close. Hadn't intended to tease her. But the look in her eyes wasn't teasing. They'd both turned serious in an instant. His eyes roamed the contours of her face. The worry lines that were new to her young face deepened on her forehead. He didn't want her to be uncomfortable, but he didn't trust his feet to hold him if he tried to back away.

He reached out and tried to smooth the worry from her forehead. "Don't fret, Charlotte. I'm here to help you." Without forethought he added, "Not just with the hotel. I'll help with anything you need." As his finger traced across her temple and down her cheek, he leaned closer.

"Sarah dropped her doll and it fell into the street. Now she's crying." Michael's voice startled them both, and Nathan backed up until he bumped into a chair at the table.

Charlotte tucked a loose tress of brown hair behind her ear. "Tell her to bring it to me. I'll wash it after I've done the dishes."

Michael cast a wary eye over Nathan. "Were you trying to kiss Charlotte?"

He felt his face flush hot. "No. I was—" What should he say? He had thought of kissing her. He'd wanted to. If the boy hadn't interrupted them, he might have. Then where would he be? On the street with no job in all likelihood. "I was telling your sister that I'd help her with the dishes." He held up the towel he'd tossed over one shoulder. "I'm going to dry."

Charlotte turned her back on them and slid the first dishes into the soapy water.

Michael didn't seem convinced. "You don't need to stand that close to dry the dishes." He twisted toward the door and back to look at Nathan. "I'm watching you." He pointed his little finger at Nathan and went to fetch Sarah. If Nathan hadn't been so embarrassed he'd have laughed again.

This time there was no humor in the moment. He'd almost kissed Charlotte. Something he'd thought about as a gangly boy, but not something he should entertain now that Charlotte was his boss.

He took the glass she handed him and wiped it dry.

They worked in silence, carefully avoiding eye contact, until the children came back into the kitchen. Charlotte washed each dish and placed it on a towel on the cabinet. He assumed it was her way of eliminating the risk of an accidental touch. She wasn't just wise about how to handle the children—she was proving to be more mature in how to handle her relationship with Nathan than he was. And his past failure with Viola Turner should have taught him better.

Where had she learned to be so cautious? And was she cautious of all men? Or just him?

Sarah came to stand between them and held her doll up for Charlotte's inspection. "She's awfully dirty, Charlotte."

"It's okay, sweetie. I can get her clean. You just put her over on this other side of the cabinet."

Sarah motioned for Charlotte to stoop over and whispered, "Michael said Nathan was trying to kiss you."

Nathan watched Charlotte's cheeks fill with color.

"No, he wasn't. Michael is mistaken." Charlotte put another plate on the towel. "He's helping with the dishes because he ate supper with us."

Sarah peeked up at Nathan. "Charlotte is pretty. Pa always said she was pretty and that some boy would want to kiss her but she wasn't to let him do it." She tugged on Charlotte's skirt. "Don't let him do it."

Charlotte leaned close to Sarah again and whispered, "I won't."

Well, if Nathan needed to know what Charlotte thought of the idea of being kissed by him, he knew now. He wanted to relieve her of the uncomfortable situation they found themselves in, and he wanted to put her mind at ease for the future.

"Your father was right, Sarah. Someone is going to want to kiss Charlotte." Charlotte's face turned another shade of pink. He seemed to be making matters worse instead of better. "I promise not to kiss her. She should only be kissed by someone when she wants to be kissed." He lowered his voice to mimic the whispers the sisters had shared. "She doesn't want to kiss me, so you don't have to worry." He turned to Michael. "You don't, either. You're a good brother to look after your sisters. Your pa would be proud."

He folded the towel and draped it over the back of the chair he'd occupied during supper. "If it's okay with all of you, I've got some more work to do before bed. May I be excused?"

"Thank you for your help. We can finish here." Charlotte seemed to breathe easier, and the color in her cheeks was fading. "Children, tell Nathan good night and go get ready for bed. I'll be in to check on you both as soon as I've finished here."

Michael watched Nathan as he went through the parlor and closed the door.

Lord, this family doesn't need me to complicate their lives. You sent me here for a job. I didn't realize that helping them would be a part of the job. I need Your strength. Charlotte is beautiful, and I wasn't prepared for how spending time with her would waken my heart. It's not right. I won't hurt them. And I'd be grateful if You'd keep me from hurting myself.

Chapter Eight

Charlotte put a hand on Michael's knee to still his fidgeting during the church service on Sunday morning. Norman Lewis glanced over his shoulder at her and nodded a subtle greeting. Why would the owner of the feed and seed be greeting her? She acknowledged his nod and turned away to see how Sarah was doing. Reverend Gillis finished his sermon, and they stood for the closing prayer.

In the aisle, with a child holding on to each hand, Charlotte was surprised when Mr. Lewis pushed in close to them. "Miss Charlotte, I want to personally extend my condolences on your loss." He was tall and leaned over to say the words.

She was uncomfortable looking up at him so near behind her. "Thank you." The children pulled her forward as they continued to the church doorway.

"Hurry, Charlotte. Mrs. Atkins told me she's making dumplings for lunch, and I'm hungry." Sarah tugged on her hand.

"I don't want dumplings." Michael persisted in his

anger at everything. Charlotte would need to have another talk with him about it.

At the door, Reverend Gillis smiled at them. It wasn't a smile of pity, but concern. "How are you, Miss Green?"

"We're doing the best we can."

The preacher offered his hand for Michael. "How about you, Mr. Green? Are you able to help your sisters now that you're the man of the house?"

Charlotte wanted to hug the preacher for knowing the exact words to boost Michael's spirits.

"I do all Charlotte will let me." Michael put a hand beside his mouth as if he were sharing a secret. "She thinks I'm just a kid, but I'm not."

"I understand, Mr. Green. I have a big sister, too." The preacher winked at Michael.

Sarah chimed in. "I'm a kid. I don't want to be a grown-up. Charlotte is a grown-up, and she's sad all the time. I'm sad sometimes, but I can play with my doll and feel better."

Reverend Gillis patted Sarah on the shoulder. "You're a wise young lady."

Charlotte appreciated the encouragement the preacher offered, but Mr. Lewis was so close behind her that the feeling of unease she'd experienced when he'd turned to greet her in the service grew.

"We best be on our way." She led the little ones down the steps and turned toward the street.

"Miss Green, I'd like a word with you." Mr. Lewis had followed her down the steps without stopping to speak to Reverend Gillis.

She lifted her arms to show that she still held Michael and Sarah by the hand. "I'm busy with the children. Could we wait for another time?"

"The children can step aside. It won't hurt them to wait while we talk." Norman Lewis was her father's age. He'd been widowed for several years and had no children. Perhaps that explained his impatience. People who lived alone seldom had to take the needs of others into consideration. He must be accustomed to having his way with things.

"I really must get them home."

"I insist. It will only take a moment." He looked at the children. "You two go stand by that tree over there. I need to speak to your sister."

Her temper was bubbling to the surface at his high-handed treatment of, not just the children, but her as well. The desire to handle whatever he wanted without delay caused her to shoo the children out of earshot. She turned to him and clasped her hands together to keep from balling them into fists in her frustration.

"What is it that you'd like to say, Mr. Lewis?" The words were measured, but her attempt to keep the tension out of her tone failed.

"I see the struggle you're having with the children. I'm sure the hotel is more than you can handle on your own. I want to offer myself to you as a way to give you the security you need since you've lost your parents."

"We are managing just fine, Mr. Lewis."

Sarah called out, "Stop!" She swatted at Michael when he tried to snatch her doll.

Charlotte snapped her fingers and signaled Michael to move away from Sarah.

Mr. Lewis frowned. "You obviously need time to teach those two how to behave in public. I suggest that you allow me to call on you for a respectable amount of time. While we are courting, I can take over the management of the hotel. You'll be free to tend to the children. Then we can marry, perhaps in six or eight weeks. I can provide for you in a manner that frankly will be better than you've any chance of with another man in Gran Colina."

Her mouth dropped open. "Excuse me?"

"I believe I've made myself plain, Miss Green. I'm a man of business, and you are a young woman—too young to deal with what's been thrust upon you by God. I am willing to take you on and absolve you of your burden."

That was more than she could stand silently for. "You mean absolve me of the responsibility of my hotel." She took a step closer to him. "I do not need to be rescued, Mr. Lewis. Not by you or anyone else." Her temper was at full wrath. "I will not give away everything my parents worked so hard to give to me and my siblings." Fists at her side, she took another step, and he backed up. "I am not the next wife of whoever decides they want me. You, and every other man in Gran Colina or the whole of Texas, can stand back and watch me make the most of Green's Grand Hotel. Not just for now, but from now on. The hotel will provide for me and the rest of the Green family— just as my father intended—for as long as the Greens choose to run it."

She motioned for Michael and Sarah to come to her. "I trust I've made myself clear."

"You are a silly girl, Charlotte Green. I hope you come to your senses soon, or no man will want you. You're past the age of marrying for most young men.

A man like myself won't beg to take on the load of another man's family."

"I am in complete possession of my wits, sir, and will take care of my family without being made to feel I'm a charity case."

Mr. Lewis shook his head. "A man trying to do a Christian duty and make life easier for someone too young to handle it isn't something to be scoffed at. I'll take your ignorance into account if you come to me with a change of heart." He frowned at the children who stood by her side. "I'd recommend you take those two in hand. Good day." He spun on his heel and walked away.

Charlotte almost couldn't breathe. How dare he speak to her like that?

Rena must have noticed something amiss. She handed her baby to her husband and came to see about Charlotte. "What's wrong? You're so pale." Rena took her hand.

"Pale? I'm surprised my face isn't bright red." Charlotte pointed at the retreating back of Norman Lewis. "I cannot believe what I've just been told."

Rena told the children to go visit with Mrs. Gillis. They skipped away, unaware of the depth of Charlotte's anger.

"What did he say to you, Charlotte? I've never known Mr. Lewis to be unkind. Arrogant, yes, but that should come as no surprise."

"He told me I need to take the children in hand and let him court me and take over the hotel." Her voice rose with each word. "As if I'm unable to function because I'm a mere woman." She clinched her fists. "And a young one at that."

Rena started to laugh.

"This isn't funny."

"Oh, Charlotte." Rena pulled her into a brief hug. "I'm sorry for laughing, but I wish you would."

"How? I've been insulted to the highest degree."

"You have, but think about it. Mr. Lewis made a preposterous gesture. No woman would accept such an offer."

"It's still not funny."

Rena grinned at her. "How many men have approached you in the last two weeks?"

"He is the third. How did you know?"

"You are an unattached young woman with respectable means. Every eligible man in Gran Colina is going to come calling. Hopefully, one at a time, but they'll all come."

All but one. Charlotte wondered about Nathan and the respectable distance he kept from her at all times. Well, not that moment in the kitchen when she'd thought he might kiss her.

"Not one of them would be approved by Momma."

Rena nodded. "And that's what you can tell them. Tell them you know your parents wouldn't want you to make such an important decision when you have so much new responsibility."

She took a slow breath. Would she resist Nathan if he approached her? It had never occurred to her to ask such a thing. He was the boy who had teased her in school. But no more. Now he was the man who helped her with the hotel. He understood her need to keep it and work it.

"It's still not funny." They walked toward the spot where Mrs. Gillis stood with Michael and Sarah.

"It is." Rena held up her hand with her finger and thumb indicating a small distance. "A little bit. To think someone that old would be of interest to you. Maybe that's why he chose to berate you. He might think you're the kind to be intimidated into a situation."

"That is a funny thought." Charlotte laughed. "Anyone who speaks to Nathan Taylor will learn that I'm not intimidated, nor will I stand to be pushed around."

"Good." Rena gave her another hug. "You go take care of your siblings, and I'm going to feed my husband a big lunch. As soon as Cordelia goes to sleep."

Michael and Sarah walked with Charlotte back to the hotel. Attending church hadn't been as difficult today. Her heart ached at the void left by the loss of her parents. Why then did her mind keep straying to the man at the registration desk of her hotel? He worked for hours on end to help her improve her hotel with no promise of any benefit to himself except a temporary position.

Gilbert Jefferson and Norman Lewis wanted her hotel. Their motivation was clear. Charlotte thought Alfred Murray's motivation for coming to call was the most sincere of anyone. He'd offered her companionship and security. She had refused him kindly, but the pain it caused him wasn't lost on her. He was not a greedy or selfish man, but he held no appeal for her.

Won't I feel drawn to the man You put on this earth for me to spend my life with, Lord? It's too much to consider. Help me maintain my resolve to rebuff all this unwanted attention.

The face of a handsome man in a business suit

floated to the forefront of her mind's eye. A serious expression with the bluest eyes refused to fade.

Would attention from Nathan be unwanted?

Nathan closed his Bible and tucked it onto a shelf in the back of the registration desk. He didn't like missing church, but someone had to stay at the hotel. Attending the service last week had been a welcome treat, but it was more important for Charlotte and the children to be around people who loved them. Grief was always eased in the presence of love.

The lobby door opened, and Charlotte entered with her siblings. Her deliberate stride and heightened color warned him to tread with care this afternoon.

"Did you enjoy the service?"

She sent Michael and Sarah to change out of their Sunday clothes and stopped at the desk. "The service was very nice. The songs were sweet, and the sermon was encouraging."

He leaned his head to one side and studied her face. "I gather there is more to the morning that you aren't telling me."

"There is more to the morning, more to the week, more to life than what I've shared. I just can't imagine what men are thinking." She flapped her reticule onto the desk and peeled her lace gloves off one finger at the time. "Why would a man think it acceptable to approach me and offer marriage in exchange for this hotel?" She tossed her gloves beside the reticule. "I'll tell you what he thinks. He thinks I'm a silly school-girl who can't find her way through life without the help of a big, strong man. That's what he thinks." She balled her hands into fists and shook them together in front of her. "He actually said I was silly."

Nathan chuckled. "So, the heart of the girl I knew in school is still inside this young woman who has pulled her hair back like a grandmother and worn the same two black dresses since I returned to Gran Colina. I was fearful I'd never see her again." He pointed at her watch. "You've tried too hard to be someone you're not, Charlotte."

She stopped still. Her hands dropped to her sides, and her shoulders relaxed. The flames that had darted from her eyes during her outburst became burning embers that showed life in her soul instead of anger.

And she giggled. A lighthearted tinkling sound like rain on a windowpane. It was delightful. Her smile became full, and the giggle turned into laughter.

Charlotte fingered the watch on her dress. "A grandmother? A grandmother who is always late." She took a step closer, and he could see the faintest freckles on her cheeks.

"Those clothes are too big for you." He touched the sleeve of her dress.

She smiled and looked at the sleeve. "It's Momma's dress. I didn't have anything black. She only had these two dresses. Wearing them made me feel I was showing how sad I am that she's gone." Her blues eyes moved to his. "I know it doesn't make a difference. Momma hated to wear these dresses."

"The sadness in your heart is in your eyes, Charlotte." His gaze captured her eyes. "Right there with the love you have for your parents. You can be Charlotte and still honor the memory of your folks."

"You're right." She pulled her lips in and stared at

him. "Would you like to join us for lunch? I know it's Sunday, and we shouldn't make it a working meal, but I think we could share a table for the sake of good company."

He lifted one brow. "You think I'm good company?"

"Don't make me reconsider and withdraw my invitation." She scooped up her reticule and gloves. "Give me a half hour to change and get the food from the restaurant."

"Why don't we eat in the restaurant? There isn't a large crowd of guests today. You could use a break from having to wash the dishes." He pointed over his shoulder to her door. "You go change and get the children. I'll let Mrs. Atkins know to save us a table."

"Okay. I'll be ready in a quarter of an hour."

She went into her parlor and closed the door. What would she think if she knew he was staring after her wondering what life would have been like if his parents had never left Gran Colina? She'd caught his eye when he was a young lad. If life hadn't treated them both with such harshness, maybe he'd be willing to risk exploring what it would be like to court Charlotte Green.

But life *had* been harsh. Viola Turner had toyed with him until he'd thought he had a future with the granddaughter of Turner Hotels. Then she'd rebuffed him, saying she'd never marry beneath her station in life. She had scoffed that an employee of the hotel would never be a suitable mate to anyone in the family of the owners. He'd been foolish to allow himself to think she'd returned his growing affections. Affections that died in the face of her cruel rejection.

Nathan knew he couldn't court anyone until he

secured his future. Charlotte's anger at the men who approached her hoping to gain her business reinforced his failed attempt to win Viola's heart. A woman in her position would be suspicious of any man's interest in her. Rightly so.

As long as Charlotte was determined to make Nathan leave as soon as she learned the hotel business, he would keep his heart tucked away from anyone. No woman wanted to risk giving her heart to a man without the means to support her. And if he lost this job, he'd be without means.

He'd never seek any woman's affection in those circumstances. Not even one who would work alongside him. It was too much to ask.

Fifteen minutes later, Charlotte and the kids came into the restaurant. Nathan stood and held a chair for Sarah. She giggled and climbed into the chair. He told Michael to pull out the chair for Charlotte.

Nathan took the seat next to Sarah and across from Charlotte. Charlotte had changed into a blue dress. It wasn't ornate, but it fit properly and suited her much better than the black she'd worn earlier. Her hair hung around her shoulders in lovely waves of dark brown. He liked that the watch peeked out from behind her tresses. She was growing into a responsible woman and learning that she didn't have to lose herself in the process.

"Your dress is very pretty." He wanted to comment on her hair but decided that might give her the impression that he was flattering her. He didn't want to mislead her in any way, so he kept that admiration to himself.

Her eyes widened ever so slightly, and she looked away. "Thank you."

Had his comment made her uncomfortable? He needed to keep the conversation on polite terms. "Mrs. Atkins said the dumplings are good today."

"I don't want dumplings." Michael didn't seem to miss an opportunity to be negative.

Charlotte gave him a look that all women must be taught when they are girls. "You do not have to eat dumplings, but you will remember to be kind." Nathan decided that the look worked as intended, because Michael sat silent in his chair.

"I want dumplings. I like them best of all the food." Sarah tucked her doll close beside her into the chair. "Except pie. And cookies. I like pie and cookies better."

"I do, too." Nathan winked at Sarah, and she gave him a shy grin in return.

Mrs. Atkins arrived to take their orders and promised to return in a few minutes.

"Were you busy while we were at church?" Charlotte unfolded her napkin and draped it across her lap.

"Not overly. Two of our guests left. I had time to read the Bible for a bit."

She studied him. "Are you certain we couldn't leave a sign like Pa did so you could join us at church on Sundays?"

Nathan would like to give her this concession, but his years in Dallas proved it would be impossible. "I'm sorry. As much as I'd like to attend, there are responsibilities here that must be met. As the hotel grows, the responsibilities will increase."

"I suppose we could hire more help when that happens. Perhaps we could alternate the Sunday duties to keep anyone from having to miss services on a regular basis."

"An excellent idea."

Mrs. Atkins brought their food, and Charlotte prayed a blessing before they began to eat.

"Would you share the subject of the sermon with me?" Nathan knew she'd had a rough morning and hoped that retelling the preacher's words would distract her from the unpleasant encounter she'd described to him.

Lunch passed with general conversation over good food after Charlotte gave a brief summary of the sermon. Nathan enjoyed the time with this young family more than he'd expected he would. Michael and Sarah ran into their parlor, and he thanked Charlotte as they entered the lobby.

"I appreciate your invitation to lunch. It was nice. When my mother passed and my father immersed himself in his work, I lost that sense of family."

"You're welcome." She looked through the open door to her parlor and watched Sarah on the settee with her doll. "What we're feeling must be like you felt back then. I'd hoped it would be better in time, but I see you still suffer from your loss." She turned back toward him. "I'll have to make certain they keep a sense of family. Thank you for sharing that with me."

"I'm sorry. I didn't mean to sound as if I hadn't moved beyond the loss. I have. Of course, I still miss my mother. You must miss yours, too. I know you were young when she passed and your father remarried, but that doesn't stop you from remembering her love. I was only saying it was nice to sit down to a meal and not feel alone." He hadn't realized how alone he'd felt in the last five years until he spoke the words aloud to Charlotte.

She nodded. "I think I understand. Even when the kids are right there with me, they're so young that I can't share with them the things that I have on my heart and mind."

"You can always share with me. I'm a good listener, and I know what you're going through." He didn't know if she'd accept his offer of a deeper friendship— or if he wanted her to—but the words just spilled out of him before he even considered them.

Michael called out to her. "Charlotte, can I go to play with Archie?"

"Well, I understand a lot of what you're going through." Nathan smiled at Charlotte. "Not the part about taking care of young children."

Michael raised his voice when she didn't answer. "Can I?"

Charlotte put her hand on his sleeve. "Thank you. That means more than I can say." She ducked into the residence as Michael yelled out for the third time.

Nathan admitted that he had no idea how difficult Charlotte's life was. When his mother had died, he'd been younger, but he'd only had to care for himself. And his father had handled the funeral and their finances. Nathan hadn't inherited a hotel, and he wasn't raising young children on his own.

He decided to be more compassionate toward Charlotte and the kids. It was his Christian duty.

If he gained something—perhaps a strong friendship with Charlotte—there could be no harm in that.

Could there?

Chapter Nine

Charlotte tried another tactic with Michael. She'd called him into the parlor after supper that evening, and he sat beside her on the settee. At six, he was big enough to understand that their parents were gone, but he didn't know how to control how that made him feel.

"Being angry won't make it easier for you. You want to be the man of the house, but do you ever recall Pa acting like you've been acting?" She hated to use guilt, but every approach she'd tried had failed. He'd rebuffed everything—from compassion and understanding to being threatened with discipline.

"I can't be happy anymore." He squinted his eyes together and frowned.

"Do you think Momma and Pa would want you to be happy or angry?"

He blew a heavy breath through his nostrils. "They aren't here."

"Their love didn't stop when they went to heaven. The love they gave you is still here." She eyed him closely. "I think they'd want you to share it with others. The way they shared it with you."

"But all the hurt used up all the love." Defeat filled his voice.

Charlotte put an arm around his small shoulders. "You can't have used up all that love. There was so much of it." She pulled him close to her side. "When we think about them the love grows. It's the way our heart remembers them."

"I miss them." For the first time since the funeral two weeks earlier, Michael snuggled next to her in a hug. He usually stiffened or, at best, endured her attempts to comfort him.

"I know you do. We all do." She dropped a kiss on the top of his head. "Tell me your favorite memory of Pa."

"That's easy." Michael launched into a tale of fishing with their father. Before long he was laughing and telling about the time he'd startled their mother with a frog he'd captured in the schoolyard.

Sarah heard the laughter and came from her room. "What are you doing?" She climbed onto the settee beside them.

"We're telling memories of Momma and Pa and growing their love so we don't lose it." Michael seemed excited at the idea that he could keep their love alive in his heart.

"I wanna tell one." Sarah told of the day Momma had given her the doll she held against her chest.

A half hour later, both children were smiling and succumbing to fatigue.

"Let's get you two to bed. I think you'll have happy dreams tonight."

Charlotte settled into the corner of the settee after they were tucked up for the night. She was exhausted after the emotional day. The ups and downs had taken their toll.

The joyful memories hadn't only helped the children. Her heart was lighter than it had been since they received the awful news. She considered the valises in her parents' room. Was she ready to see what they held?

The thought of her mother's favorite dresses and her father's newest suit threatened to steal the joy they'd discovered tonight. The valises could wait. For now, she'd close her eyes and enjoy the happy thoughts.

Monday morning she woke stiff in the corner of the settee.

"I'm thirsty." Sarah stood clutching her doll and pushing on Charlotte's arm.

Charlotte stirred from her slumber and stretched. "Okay, sweetie. Let me wake up a bit, and I'll get you a glass of water."

"I want milk."

Michael dragged his feet across the floor and slumped onto their father's favorite chair. "Sarah woke me up."

"Me, too." Charlotte smiled and hugged Sarah close. "You are a sweet girl to wake up to." She stood and regretted not going to her bed the night before. "I'll get changed and make us some breakfast while the two of you dress for the day."

She had them fed and under the watchful eye of Libbie Henderson in time to be at the registration desk before Nathan made an appearance in the lobby.

His brows lifted. "What is going on here?"

Charlotte knew he was teasing her and played along. "I'm getting the day started. Unlike some people who think they can just show up to do their work whenever they decide." She pulled a hoity face. "I'm guessing you haven't had breakfast. You best be quick about it, or I'll have all the work done before you're in your place." Try as she might to keep a straight face, she felt the corners of her mouth drawing upward.

"So, you're going to let me have the late shift today? I thought it was your preferred time to work." He smiled back at her. "You seem to be better this morning."

"I think I am. A bit." Sober thoughts threatened her, but she kept them at bay. "A little better each day."

"You look as though you rested."

"I did. It's the first night I've slept through."

"That's good." He pointed at the restaurant door. "I'll just have a quick bite and then help you deal with the people who are checking out today." Before he turned to go, he added, "Yellow is a nice color for you."

Charlotte watched him walk away. She'd wondered if it was too soon to wear the yellow dress. It was cheery and made her feel pretty. Her mother had made it last summer. She smoothed the skirt and decided she'd made a good choice for the hot summer day.

Nathan helped the last guests take their bags to the hotel porch and went back into the lobby. Charlotte was talking to the maids about their chores for the day, so he went in search of Mrs. Atkins. She was cleaning up the remainder of the breakfast dishes.

"Can you take a break when you've finished?" Nathan caught sight of stew simmering on the stove for lunch. The workings of a hotel kitchen had always fascinated him. The preparations for one meal began before the previous meal was finished. It was like well-orchestrated music that required precision timing and thoughtful planning.

"Certainly. Just give me a few minutes. Should I meet you in the restaurant? We can talk over a cup of coffee, if you'd like."

"That sounds great. Bring three cups, and I'll get Charlotte to join us."

The three of them pored over the menus for the week. Nathan complimented Mrs. Atkins on the way she prepared the meals based on what had worked in the past and new items that travelers mentioned to her when they visited.

"Thank you. I like to vary the offerings. It all seems a bit stale if we don't mix it up on occasion."

"Momma always loved trying your new recipes." Charlotte poured another cup of coffee for herself. "And I think the townsfolk dine here more often because of the variety."

Nathan made notes as they talked. His notes would serve him well as they made the changes he had in mind. "How do you decide which items to drop from the menu?"

Mrs. Atkins looked at Charlotte. "Your mother made those decisions."

Nathan wondered if there was a method to the decisions or if it was done at random. "I suggest that we make the determinations based on popularity of the dish, cost to prepare it, and the price we must charge the guest when we serve it. Plus seasonal availability of the ingredients."

Charlotte ran her finger along the edge of her saucer. "There are some items I'd like to remove." Her next words came out in a rush. "I'd like to drop the tea cakes and two of the pie flavors."

Nathan was surprised at her suggestion. "If you're having trouble keeping up with the demand for baked goods, we can hire someone to do it for you. I have been concerned from the beginning about your putting in such late hours on the nights when you bake."

Mrs. Atkins offered, "Perhaps Bertha could help."

"It isn't the amount of work." Charlotte picked at the edge of her napkin. "I don't have the heart to keep making all of Momma's recipes. She guarded them so closely. I can't hire someone and give them her secrets. I may want to add them back in time, but for now, I want to drop those options."

"You poor girl." Mrs. Atkins patted Charlotte's hand. "I should have thought of that. The way you and your sweet momma worked side by side in the kitchen. Please forgive me for not realizing what a toll it's taking on you. I can do the baking."

Charlotte thanked her. "I thought I could do it. At first it was comforting to be in Momma's place. I even wore her apron the first couple of times I baked. But I can't keep doing it. Not right now."

Nathan watched Charlotte bare her soul to Mrs. Atkins. The woman was probably closer to Charlotte than any other adult now that her parents were gone.

"Charlotte, Mrs. Atkins has offered a good solution. We could hire someone to do some of the things she is doing. She could take over the baking. At least a big part of it." He turned to Mrs. Atkins. "Would that be acceptable to you?"

She squeezed Charlotte's hand. "I'll do anything that will help to ease your burden."

"Okay, that's settled then." Nathan turned the page in his notebook.

"Excuse me." Charlotte gave him the same look she'd given Michael when she'd corrected him. "I haven't agreed to this arrangement."

Nathan sat back in his chair. He hoped she wasn't about to scold him like a child.

"I'd like to think about it for a day or so." She nodded. "It may be the very thing we need to do, but I'd like us to talk about it when we discuss other things we're planning, Nathan." She pushed her cup and saucer away from her. "Mrs. Atkins, we'll let you know as soon as we make a decision. And if we decide to take on extra kitchen help, I'd like for you to offer any suggestions you may have on their duties and who might be a good candidate for the position. We'll want to make certain we keep things running smoothly. The wrong personality might upset the well-run service you provide for the restaurant." She stood. "If you'll excuse me, I need to check in with Libbie about the children."

Nathan was impressed. Charlotte had grappled with whether or not she agreed with him, but she'd handled it in a professional manner that would have been acceptable in any business. Even something as well respected as the Turner Hotels.

Charlotte showed growth in her knowledge of business in the short time he'd been in Gran Colina. Her determination would be the root of her success.

He only hoped he wasn't working himself out of a job.

On Tuesday evening Nathan put away everything on the desk. He'd worked steadily for the last two days to clean out the desk and anything in the lobby that needed to go. More than once he and Charlotte had disagreed over an item. In the end, she'd taken the personal items to her living quarters, leaving only a portrait of her parents on the wall over the fireplace. She'd wanted to honor their legacy of establishing Green's Grand Hotel. It was in keeping with the business side of things, so Nathan saw no reason to resist her on the subject. All her mother's trinkets had been removed.

The door to the private residence opened, and Charlotte walked into the lobby. "I've got the children to bed. Do you need anything else before I retire for the night?"

"Would you make a pot of coffee? We could go over the details of the plans. Time is passing quickly, and we need to decide on the details before Mr. Thornhill arrives with his group of farmers."

She stretched her neck from one side to another. "It would probably be best to do it while things are quiet. You get your notes, and I'll put on the coffee."

They settled at a small table in her parlor and spread out their notes. They started with the things they agreed on and worked through much of the details in less than an hour.

"I think we can arrange the new furniture in most of the rooms to achieve a fresh look. It won't be necessary to paint, but every room needs to be cleaned from top to bottom." He drained the last of his coffee and set the mug on the table.

Charlotte wrote in her notebook. "I'll speak to the maids tomorrow morning. They can choose a room to do each day. That will keep the work from being too much at once."

"That's a fine idea." He leaned back in his chair and studied her in the light of the lamp. "You've taken to the business side of things. It seems you have a natural ability for organization once you get into the practice of the work."

She eyed him in that snappy way she had when they were in school together. "You seem surprised."

"Not surprised as much as pleased. You need to stay on top of things, or you'll fall behind and never catch up." It was true. He hadn't expected her to be prompt after the first few days of watching her be distracted. She had put that behind her. A monumental task for someone struggling with so much loss and responsibility.

"I'm not going to let Thomas Freeman take this hotel. I won't fail." She shrugged. "Even if it means I don't sleep or that I have to let you have your way on some of the things that you say need to be changed."

"I know you think the changes are all coming from me. I give you my word that I'm staying as true as I can to the things your father told me. It's almost impossible to remember every detail, but the fact that our conversations were so recent has helped."

Charlotte nodded. "If only he'd talked to me. I would have been more prepared."

"He never imagined he'd be gone so soon. His job wasn't dangerous like a sheriff or rancher. A businessman in town leads a relatively safe life."

"If he'd given me any clue... Momma and I worked together in the restaurant, so I know what I'm doing in there. The kitchen and the dining room are very well known to me. All except the ordering." She shifted in her chair. "I should have paid more attention to Pa's work."

"He would no doubt have shooed you out of his way. I imagine he had Michael in mind for that part of the hotel. And little Sarah would have grown up to help you and your mother."

Her eyes misted over again.

Nathan reached across the table and put his hand on hers. "I didn't mean to make you cry. I'm sorry."

"It's just such a sweet thought. Momma had already let Sarah stand on a stool beside her while she worked sometimes. Sarah was learning to roll out the dough for dumplings or cookies."

"I'm glad you have those memories. I treasure the little things like that about my mother. Sarah will, too. She's young, but she's old enough to have the image of her mother and that love in her heart forever."

"They both left us pleasant memories. Michael would sit by Pa and help tote valises up the stairs."

He hadn't realized this. "If you think it would help with his behavior, Michael can spend some time in the afternoons with me. I can let him do those things." As he made the suggestion he thought he might have just opened himself up to a load of trouble with a small boy.

Charlotte's face lit up. "Would you? That may be what brings him out of his anger. We had a long talk on Sunday evening. He's been better, but there are times he seems to be holding on to this temper with all his might. He doesn't want to be angry, but it's easier for him than being sad."

"Do you think he'll resent my authority? It wouldn't do for him to be rude in front of the guests."

"I can make it part of the agreement. He can only help if he's mature and represents the hotel as if Pa was standing beside him."

"That could work. We can try it if you like."

"I hope Sarah isn't jealous." Charlotte laughed. "That little girl thinks she should be included in everything. Since we've agreed to hire help for Mrs. Atkins, maybe Sarah can help me or Mrs. Atkins on occasion."

Nathan began to understand why she was so concerned about the children. "A wise choice. It's hard to imagine that they didn't just lose their parents—they lost their way of life. You're doing an excellent job with them. They are blessed to have you."

He hadn't meant to, but he'd embarrassed her. The clock on the mantel struck the hour.

"Oh, my. We've been working a long time." Charlotte stood and gathered their coffee cups.

Nathan rose from his chair and reached for the sugar bowl. Charlotte grabbed it just before him, and his hand closed around her warm fingers. He looked up and released her as she pulled away. "I'm sorry. Let me help you." He picked up the sugar and followed her into the kitchen.

She put the cups down and took the sugar from him. He was careful not to touch her hand or look into her eyes. She might see how the brief contact had affected him. The longer he spent his days and evenings with Charlotte, the more he knew the young man he'd been had chosen wisely when he cast his affections in her direction.

If only he'd known how to deal with his youthful feelings, maybe he would have drawn her into friendship—

and something deeper in time. Instead, he'd teased her and driven her away.

He searched for a way to take her mind off the awkward moment. "Did you open the valises yet?"

The discomfort in her face turned to sorrow. She moved away from him. "No. I tried not to think of them."

They went back into the parlor, and he looked through the door that stood open to the lobby. "I'll gather my notes and be going."

Charlotte stood near the door. "I think we made a lot of progress tonight."

"We did. I don't think you have to worry about the banker coming to take your property. We're on track to make a substantial increase in the income of the hotel with the new furnishings. And a successful stay for Mr. Thornhill's group will make it even better." He headed toward the door.

Charlotte put her hand on his arm. "I'm glad you were able to come to Gran Colina. I'm sorry I resisted you at first. It was childish."

"You had only our history as children on which to base your opinion of me." He smiled at her. "I'm glad we've both grown out of that stage of our lives."

"If you hadn't shown up, I wouldn't have known about the furnishings or where the money went. I'd have lost the hotel before the order ever arrived. Even if I'd held on until then, I wouldn't have been prepared for the changes that needed to be made. By coming, you brought my father's vision back home. For that, I'm eternally grateful."

"I have offered a prayer of thanks for that very reason. It would have been an added tragedy for the three of you to lose the hotel when your parents' purpose for being away was to make it better for you." He wanted to offer her comfort, but his arms were full of the work they'd done. "I wish we had your father's papers. They were so detailed. He even drew out his vision for the rooms and changes. If we had that, we could know we were doing everything exactly as he'd planned."

Charlotte's future had become very important to him. Admitting that fact to himself wasn't as hard as he'd thought it would be. He refused to ponder why. He wasn't ready to deal with the answer.

Chapter Ten

Charlotte dropped her hand from Nathan's arm and went as quickly as she could to her parents' room.

"What is it?" Nathan's voice followed her.

"Just a minute." She called the words over her shoulder and looked at her parents' belongings that Dennis had brought. She opened the box first. He'd said it contained the items her parents had with them. Her mother's reticule and her father's watch were inside. She opened the valises next. She rummaged through the first two without stopping to treasure the scent of her mother on the dresses and nightgown. The third one held her father's things. She turned it upside down, and the clothes tumbled onto the bed. "It has to be here."

Nathan asked again. "What is it, Charlotte? Are you okay?"

She turned to look at him. He still stood near the lobby door, but she could see him through the open door of her parents' room. "Yes." Her tone was clipped, but she wouldn't give up her search. She dropped the valise onto the bed and picked up each article of clothing to shake and toss aside. "I'm looking for Pa's notes.

He wouldn't have left them in Dallas. They must be here."

Nothing. She'd looked through everything in his case.

"It's not here." She sank onto the side of the bed. "He must have been carrying it in his hands when the train wrecked. It was probably lost amid the wreckage."

Nathan pointed at her mother's valises. "What about those?"

"Those are Momma's."

"Perhaps he had her put them there."

"I looked."

He indicated the piles of clothes on the bed. "You seem to have searched your father's valise more thoroughly. Give it another look."

She gave a deep sigh. "I don't know what good it will do, but—" She dumped the contents of the first valise and went through each item carefully. "Nothing."

The second case was heavier but not as large. She turned it upside down and shook it. "I don't see anything here, either." She rummaged through the clothes anyway.

"What about inside the case? Perhaps it lodged in the bottom when you turned it over." Nathan's voice held hope.

She didn't know if the hope was for her sake or the hotel's. The result would be the same if he was right.

Charlotte looked in the bottom of both of her mother's valises and found nothing. When she picked up her father's valise she heard a thump and turned to Nathan. "Could it be?" She stuck her hand into the bottom of the valise and pulled out her father's leather journal.

Excitement filled her. "It's here!"

She raced into the parlor and threw her arms around Nathan's neck. He stumbled backward from the force of her approach, and his papers fluttered to the floor in disarray. He wrapped his arms around her waist and steadied her. The gentle strength of his embrace invited her to relax against him. The need for relief from the constant weight of her burdens begged her to stay in his arms.

But she couldn't. Nathan worked for her. He had helped her, but could she trust that he wasn't like the other men who wanted her hotel? He'd made it clear from the beginning that he wanted to take it over. Was this desire of his to follow through with her father's vision a way to make that happen? She couldn't be certain.

Charlotte would accept his help and expertise, but she wouldn't depend on him for her happiness or peace.

She jerked away from him and felt the heat climb into her face. "I'm sorry." She put a hand at the base of her throat. "I was overcome by the discovery."

He bent to retrieve the papers that surrounded them and laughed. "It's quite all right. I haven't had a young woman fling herself into my arms before. I could think of more unpleasant experiences."

He was teasing her. She knew she should accept it as such, but the thrill she'd felt when he'd held her close had surprised her. It hurt to think he would dismiss it in jest. Her head spun with the emotions that warred inside of her. Reality stopped the whirlwind.

They were working together to save her future. Silly emotions could jeopardize their success. She'd never forgive herself if that happened.

She pushed her hair back over her shoulder and opened the journal. "Thank you for telling me about this." She turned the pages quickly and saw drawings and long lists. "Now we can do everything like Pa wanted."

Nathan stood beside her and looked over her shoulder. "I don't know why I didn't think of it before. He made so many notes in our meetings."

Charlotte went back to the table where they'd spent the evening. "I won't be able to sleep until I've read this."

Nathan put the notes they'd made on the table and sat across from her. "Do you mind if I stay?"

She flipped to the end of the journal and back to the front. The pages thrilled her. "No. I don't mind. Just let me absorb the overview. I imagine there will be things you'll have to interpret for me." Nathan's chuckle drew her attention away from the journal. "What are you laughing about?"

"The idea that you won't understand the notes."

"It's a lot to take in. You worked closely with my parents on this. There are bound to be things I'm unfamiliar with."

"Maybe unfamiliar, but not out of the scope of your understanding." She stared at him, and he continued. "You've learned so much, Charlotte." He leaned back in his chair. "I'll sit here while you read. You'll see. It's no longer foreign to you."

"Okay." She nodded and turned back to the journal. The pages were filled with details. Everything that had been ordered and where it was to be placed in the hotel was listed. She skimmed the pages knowing she'd have to read it all again at her leisure, but she couldn't resist looking at every page.

Nathan sat quietly while she read. A full half hour must have passed. She finished and looked up at him. "Everything you've told me is confirmed here, including plans for room eight." She rubbed her hand over the leather cover. "There is even a page of things Momma wanted to move into the residence."

One eyebrow on his handsome face shot up. "Really?"

She swatted at the air between them. "You must have made a convincing argument for her to agree to remove her mementos." Had Momma approved of the man Nathan had become? Her agreement with him on the things about the hotel meant she'd accepted his wisdom to a certain degree and followed it.

His brow lowered, and a smile replaced the teasing expression. "They were earnest in their efforts to implement changes that would make Green's Grand Hotel into the kind of business that would endure."

"Thank you for taking the time to help them when they were in Dallas. I have a feeling that Michael and Sarah and I are more indebted to you than I ever imagined. More so than the money I owe Mr. Freeman at the bank."

His eyes narrowed. "This experience has not been without benefit to me." He swept one arm out in the direction of the lobby. "I've been afforded the opportunity to make a real difference here. I don't take that lightly." Then he leaned close and put his hand over hers on the journal. "You could have sent me away the first day."

"I think I did." She didn't move her hand. The urge to turn it over and wrap her fingers around his was strong.

"I'm not the kind to run from a challenge." A gentle pressure of his hand on hers warmed her heart. Then he released her hand and stood. "We can spend the morning making certain we're on track with your father's vision." He picked up his notes. "Get some rest. You're going to need it. I think our days are going to be full for the next many weeks."

He smiled and wished her a pleasant evening before closing the door behind him.

The evening that had started out as such a challenge had ended with vision and direction. And great relief. Knowing she would be able to fulfill the dreams of her parents made her work at the hotel more rewarding.

Having a partner like Nathan to help her in the process was exciting.

She carried the journal with her to her room. Sleep might be a long time off. She could study the pages while she waited for it.

Much later, when she put out the lantern, Charlotte wondered when she'd begun to think of Nathan as a partner instead of a burden to be borne while she learned the hotel business.

His face was the last thing she saw in her mind's eye before sleep overtook her. He was smiling at her. A smile filled with hope and promise.

Was it merely a dream? Something between consciousness and slumber. Or was it something she longed for in her heart?

* * *

On Thursday morning, Nathan closed Charles Green's journal and corrected the final discrepancies in his notes to conform to the man's vision. He and Charlotte had gone over the notes with great scrutiny. Nathan was encouraged by her eagerness to move forward with every aspect of the changes.

Charlotte came out of the restaurant wearing a green dress with a high collar that ruffled around her neck. She still wore the watch from her mother, but her hair hung down her back in waves. She had pulled the front of it away from her face with two combs. He tried not to stare, but he wanted to remember every detail of how she looked. If she forced him to leave after she'd mastered her newfound duties, he'd only have the memories to comfort the hollowness he knew would take the place of his heart.

It would be in his best interest to resist such thoughts and fight for his place at the hotel. He should warn her that it could all change in a heartbeat and leave her in worse shape than when he'd arrived. He could tell her all the things that could go wrong.

If he worked for Turner Hotels and had been sent here to take over the property that was exactly what he would tell her. But he was here for his own future. Back to a place where he'd been happy in the past. He dared to hope that he might have a new beginning in Gran Colina. And maybe that new beginning would include the beautiful young woman who stood across the desk from him and said something he didn't hear. He noticed the way her lips moved, but her words didn't reach his ears. He blinked and shook his head.

"I'm sorry, Charlotte. What did you say? My mind drifted to other things."

"Other things?" She grinned. "Let me guess. You were thinking about one of those lovely young ladies who checked in yesterday. They told me they are only in town for a few days. It seems they have an aunt in Gran Colina who wanted to see them. They stopped off here on their way to California. You'll not be pleased to see them go if you get all dreamy eyed thinking of them."

"What?" He didn't remember the guests she referred to. "What ladies?"

"I see. So you weren't standing here thinking of an attractive young lady and how she might fit into your life? The life you've filled with business to the exclusion of all other relationships?" There was teasing in her tone but truth in her eyes. She taunted him, but she believed the words she spoke.

"And if I was?" Two could play her game. "Would you be jealous?" As he said it, he hoped it was true. He didn't want to hope it, but he did.

She turned her head in a coy manner and fanned herself with one hand. "Oh, Mr. Taylor, you have found out the deepest secret of my heart." Her tone became an elongated drawl that rang with the exaggerated sweetness of generations past.

"Have I?" He leaned on the desk. Her eyes grew wide, and he could feel her breath on his face. He lowered his voice to mimic a male counterpart to her pattern of speech. "What else do you have buried in the recesses of your soul? Have you carried a torch for me from the time of our youth?"

The door of her parlor swung open, and Michael

stepped into the lobby. Nathan backed away from the desk, and Charlotte schooled her features into the serious expression she'd adopted in recent weeks. She must think it fitting for the owner of the hotel.

Michael looked from Charlotte to Nathan and back. "Charlotte, your cheeks are blotchy. Are you too hot? You know it ain't good to get too hot. You'll get sick. Want me to get you some water?"

Nathan turned a chuckle into a cough. "I'm going to see if Mrs. Atkins is pleased with her new helper. Mrs. Baxter seems to be just the sort of person we needed in the kitchen." He left Charlotte to deal with her brother. He didn't want to make her uncomfortable in front of others. He'd only teased her in response to her provocation.

If he felt like whistling as he crossed the lobby, he wouldn't admit it. But he would allow that he'd enjoyed the brief banter with Charlotte. If things were different—if she wasn't the owner of the hotel, and he wasn't an employee at her mercy—he'd be tempted to smile back at her or try to recreate another moment that would be as invigorating as the last few minutes had been. But he knew he wouldn't serve either of them well if he allowed their relationship to move beyond a business association. He needed his job, and Charlotte was in a vulnerable state. Even if she'd begun to feel better in the last few days and was adapting well, it would be unkind to take advantage of her. Time would have to heal her pain.

And after that? No one knew. But, if the steady stream of men he'd seen seeking her attention since his arrival in Gran Colina was any indication, Nathan was sure she'd have plenty of suitors who could offer her more than he could. At least, until he secured his financial future.

When he spoke to Mrs. Atkins, he discovered that she'd talked with Charlotte just before he came to the kitchen. Charlotte was proving herself in every way.

He opened the restaurant door enough to peer into the lobby to see if Michael was still there. Charlotte was at the desk with Mr. Eaton. He approached as the man settled his bill in full.

"So you're leaving us, Mr. Eaton?" Nathan hadn't discovered the nature of the man's business in town, but he was prompt in his payment and had been a pleasant guest who hadn't required extra attention. "I thought you would be in Gran Colina through tomorrow."

Mr. Eaton thanked Charlotte for his receipt. "I've finished my business earlier than expected." He picked up the valise at his feet. "Thank you for recommending this place to me. My stay here was more rewarding for having been a guest here."

"Please come again."

"I'm sure I will."

"We'd be grateful for any recommendation you could give for us to other travelers."

"You can rely upon it." Mr. Eaton took his hat from the desk, and Nathan watched him walk away.

"What do you think he was doing in town?" Charlotte seemed as curious about the man as Nathan was.

"I would love to know. He was very quiet and to himself. I can't imagine what business he had here."

"Well, no matter. I'm grateful that he stayed as long as he did."

Nathan picked up his notebook. "And that I invited him?" He grinned without looking up.

"Yes." He could hear the smile in her voice.

"Let's get Mrs. Atkins to watch the desk for a few minutes and go over to the mercantile. We need to pick the fabric for curtains. Time is getting away from us."

Ethel Busby greeted Nathan and Charlotte as they entered Busby's Mercantile. He remembered her and her husband, Cyrus. "Hello, Charlotte. It's so nice to see you." She moved forward and patted Charlotte's arm. "You and the little ones have been in my prayers."

"Thank you, Mrs. Busby." Charlotte's reply was genuine and came naturally. He didn't hear the thickness of emotion in her voice that had been so prevalent when he'd first returned to town.

Nathan cupped her elbow in his hand. His intention to comfort Charlotte reverberated and eased his concern for her.

She stepped away from him and opened her father's journal. She showed the owner of the mercantile the information about the order Mr. Green had placed in Dallas. "Mrs. Busby, do you carry the catalog my father ordered these furnishings from?"

"No, we don't have much call for large orders like that."

"Of course. I don't know why that didn't occur to me. If he'd thought you could order these items, he'd have waited until he returned to Gran Colina." The realization that he'd never returned flashed across her eyes.

Nathan stepped up to keep Charlotte's silence from becoming awkward. "We'd like to purchase fabric for new drapes in the hotel lobby. Can you show us something that would be suitable? We're looking for the latest options. We'd like it to be something classic, so it doesn't go out of fashion any time soon. The goal is to update the furnishings and decor. Gran Colina is growing, and Charlotte—Miss Green—would like to provide the best possible accommodations to her guests."

Mrs. Busby headed for the long tables near the windows in the front corner of the store. "What a lovely idea." She stopped in the middle of the store, and Nathan and Charlotte almost bumped into her. "Maybe Mr. Busby and I should spiff up our place, too. Why, all of Gran Colina could use a fresh coat of paint." She waved at her husband when he came out of the storeroom. "Cyrus, we need to order paint. Remind me to pull that brochure the salesman gave us the last time he came through town. We need all the latest colors." She held her hands wide and smiled. "Thank you for such a wonderful idea."

"You're welcome." Nathan and Charlotte shared surprised expressions after Mrs. Busby started off again at a rapid pace.

"I have some wonderful new bolts." She unrolled a length of fabric from the first one. "This is a lovely shade." She held it up to the window. "Just look how the sun shines through and fires up the colors of the birds in the pattern."

Nathan didn't think it was in keeping with the vision he'd shared with Charlotte's parents. "Perhaps something not quite so bold."

Charlotte fingered the fabric. "It's very pretty."

Mrs. Busby ignored him. "You have such wonderful taste, Charlotte." She looked at Nathan over the rims of her glasses. "This is the sort of decision a woman should make. Men are not given to decorating and such."

Charlotte cast a glance at him and looked as if she might burst out laughing. She cleared her throat. "Mrs. Busby, we're looking for something that will blend with the other pieces that my father ordered." She touched the fabric again. "This pattern, while perfect in its color and quality, is too ornate for the pieces that are coming."

"I see." Mrs. Busby rolled the fabric back around the bolt. "Why don't you tell me what color you have in mind? Perhaps that's the best place to start."

"I was thinking of something gold. A medium shade that will make the room glow as the sunshine comes through the windows." Charlotte seemed to be enjoying herself.

Her enthusiasm pleased Nathan. "That sounds perfect to me." He refused to let Mrs. Busby's scolding stare push him away. "The hotels in Dallas put on quite a show with their stunning lobbies."

"What do you think of this one?" Charlotte pointed at a bolt on the far end of the table.

Mrs. Busby unwound a length of the fabric and held it up to the window. She looked over her shoulder, anticipating Charlotte's reaction.

"I think that's the one." Charlotte turned to Nathan. Her face beamed.

"I agree." He was happy to encourage her. "The result will be elegant."

She rewarded him with a smile. "We'll take this, Mrs. Busby."

Back at the hotel, she had him hold the fabric up to the window. She inspected it from every corner of the room. "I couldn't be more pleased." She took the fabric from him and added it to the stack of bolts. "It's wonderful that Mrs. Busby had enough of it in stock to do all the windows in this room."

"I'm sorry you'll have to wait for the dining room fabric to arrive." He carried part of the stack of fabric to the storeroom in the corner of the lobby. "You'll have to go see Opal Pennington about making them up for you."

"I'll do that now."

After she'd left the room, Nathan put the rest of the fabric away. He pivoted to examine the lobby and assess the changes they'd made.

"We're going to make it." He nodded in satisfaction. "We're going to finish in time for the farmers' meeting. Green's Grand Hotel is entering a new era. An era that should carry the Green family safely into the coming generations."

Nathan wasn't in the habit of talking to himself, but he was as pleased as if the hotel belonged to him. In many ways, he was responsible for the transition. It would be wonderful to see it through to completion.

Lord, if You could make a way for me be a part of this hotel for the long term, I'd be grateful.

It was a selfish prayer, but Nathan decided it was time to ask for something for himself. The Bible said people didn't have things because they didn't ask God for them. Well, he was asking.

Chapter Eleven

August was nearing an end, and everything was on schedule for the arrival of the new furnishings in mid to late September. Charlotte sat curled up in the corner of the settee in the parlor and drank a cup of tea. The spot had become her place to think since the death of her parents. She found herself there every night and morning. This morning found her peaceful and rested. It was a welcome state.

She admired the row of music boxes on the mantel. Her mother had loved having them in the restaurant, but Charlotte and the kids enjoyed choosing one to listen to every evening after supper. It was like having a bit of their mother's joy in the room with them.

Sarah came into the room, clutching her doll with her head hung low. She climbed onto the settee to snuggle into the crook of Charlotte's arm.

"I'm too tired today, Charlotte." She pulled the doll close.

"It's going to be a beautiful day, sweetie. We'll go to church, and maybe we can take a long walk on the way home."

"I'm too tired to walk." Sarah yawned and cuddled closer.

"I'm sorry. I was hoping you'd be able to have pancakes for breakfast." Charlotte twirled one of Sarah's curls around her finger. "Mrs. Baxter is cooking this morning."

Sarah bolted from the settee and ran toward her room. "I'll be right back. I gotta put on my clothes first."

The two kids were ready to eat within minutes. Charlotte led them into the kitchen. "Good morning, Mrs. Baxter. I hope you're enjoying your work here."

"It's a good job. Mrs. Atkins and I get on well. And seeing my daughter, Nora, during the day is an added blessing. I've missed her at home since she started her duties here as a maid."

"I'm glad it's working out so well. You're a great help to us." The children took their seats at the table. "Do you think we could have a couple of plates of pancakes for these hungry ones?"

Mrs. Baxter turned from the stove with a smile. "I'm sure we can manage something."

Charlotte settled the children with a cup of milk and left them in Mrs. Baxter's charge.

She encountered Nathan in the lobby. "Hello."

"Good morning to you." A broad smile accompanied his cheery greeting. He paused and took a step back. "I'm sorry." His whisper made her laugh.

"It's okay to be yourself, Nathan. I've actually been up for a couple of hours." She looked over the registration book. "I fell asleep as soon as my head hit the pillow last night. I woke refreshed and ready for the day."

"That's good to hear." He gathered his notebook. "Will you man the desk while I eat then?"

"I will. And Mrs. Baxter is ready to cover for us while we attend services this morning."

He nodded. "Excellent. Shall we walk together?"

"Okay." Charlotte wondered what it would be like to be invited to walk to Sunday service alongside someone who preferred her company. Nathan's growing friendship made his offer sound natural and unencumbered. If only that were true for her. The longer they were together the more she wanted to forget her mother's warning about a boy who would torment her. She ached for one more talk with her mother. One where she'd share that Nathan wasn't a boy anymore. One where her mother would give her permission to allow Nathan to court her. Only that conversation could never happen. And Nathan gave her no indication he'd ever want to court her—or any other woman. "We'll be ready."

If he thought her response took too long or lacked enthusiasm, he didn't show it. Charlotte watched him disappear into the dining room.

After weeks of working together, she now welcomed Nathan's constant presence and knowledge. Maybe more than she should. But it was no use dreaming of things that weren't going to be. Nathan's expertise was her only hope of saving Green's Grand Hotel from any plans Mr. Freeman might have for it. Nathan had come to teach her to run the hotel, and she'd finally convinced him that she wanted nothing more than that from him.

Too late her heart tugged at her to consider more than the help he was with her business. The same way she'd refused to budge from her original opinion of him as a schoolboy, she knew that he would no longer accept even a slight indication from her for more than a working friendship. At one time he might have been interested in her, but she'd shied away from him any time he'd made overtures that could be considered more than friendship. She wondered what would have happened if Michael hadn't come into the kitchen on the night Nathan almost kissed her.

She'd never know.

While she sorted through the list of guests who would leave the hotel that morning, Junior Conrad walked through the front door. "Miss Charlotte. Just the person I'm here to see." He approached the registration desk as if she'd invited him for a visit. He opened his hand and rang the bell. "Could I get some service here, ma'am?" He laughed at his joke, while she slid the bell to one side, hoping he'd take the hint to let it rest.

"What can I do for you, Junior?"

He was taller than when they'd finished school together, but he had the same playful attitude. "I've come calling. I thought I'd walk you and the children to church this morning." He pulled on the cuffs of his dress shirt at the end of his jacket sleeves. "My pa says you need a suitor. I've come for you."

It took all the restraint Charlotte possessed not to laugh in his face. "Excuse me?"

"Good morning, Junior." Nathan came up behind the man and clapped him on the shoulder. "I haven't seen you since I've been back in Gran Colina. What are you doing with yourself these days?" He walked around the desk and stood by Charlotte.

"Today, I'm taking Charlotte and the little ones to church." Junior's lips turned up in a confident smirk. "She's needing a man in her life, and I've come to her aid." He reached across the desk and rang the bell again. "It was as easy as ringing that bell. Pa said she needed me, and here I am."

Charlotte tucked the bell on the shelf under the desk. "I am sorry you've gone to so much trouble, Junior." She slid her hand into the crook of Nathan's elbow. "I've already accepted Nathan's invitation to walk me to church this morning." She squeezed Nathan's elbow and hoped he would interpret it as her need for his rescue from this forward man.

Junior leaned his elbow on the desk and propped his chin in his hand. "Charlotte, you know Nathan can't offer you the things I can." He stood up and tugged the bottom of his vest. He puffed out his chest much like Michael would do if he won a game of tag or carried a large valise up the stairs alone. It was endearing on her brother, but annoying when Junior did it. "Why, my pa is the land agent for this entire county. Poor Nathan here doesn't have any claim to anything that would be worthy of a woman of your means now that your folks have gone and left you this fine hotel." He spread his hands out to indicate the lobby. "Even if it does need some sprucing up."

Charlotte tugged on her hand, but Nathan put his other hand over it and held her fast. He stepped a bit closer to her and said, "Junior, you make a fine case for yourself. You are like no other suitor Charlotte could hope to have call on her." He turned and looked straight into her eyes. With the right side of his face out of Junior's line of vision he winked at her and pressed his elbow into his side. She couldn't help but smile at him. He was rescuing her. The wink was his way of asking permission, because they both knew she could refuse Junior on her own. "I must insist that she go with me, though, having given my word that I'd escort her and the children today." Nathan looked back at Junior. "You know how important a man's word is."

"Well, you could release him from his obligation, Miss Charlotte." Junior pulled the bow on his tie with both hands. "On account of getting a better offer and all."

Charlotte gave a sincere effort at letting Junior down easy. "Thank you, Junior, but I'm indebted to Nathan. He's done so much for my family since coming to manage the hotel. I don't know how I'd have made it without him." Junior really was a nice young man. If only he had some ambition—any ambition— some young lady would be glad to have him come calling. Especially with his father's substantial holdings. At least, anyone who believed his father's protestations would think their family to be financially blessed. It seemed they were so well off that Junior never had to work at all.

"Well, I must say I didn't think you'd refuse me, Charlotte. I know you've turned men down left and right. If you don't choose someone soon, you may end up with the likes of Nathan. Then won't you be wishing you could do it all over again? Nathan may be keeping you company now, but he won't be courting you. We all know he's here because he thought this business belonged to the bank." Junior turned his back on her and walked out the hotel.

Charlotte pressed her free hand against her abdomen and held her breath. Nathan's shoulders shook, and she shushed him. She waited until Junior's shadow crossed the last window of the lobby and gasped at the gall it took for Junior to say those things to them.

"I was ready to pounce on him for saying such things."

Nathan laughed and patted the hand he still held. "He can't be helped. You'd have felt bad later if you'd told him how rude he was."

"True, but he had no right to speak to either of us in such a manner."

"No, he didn't. But I've learned a lot working behind a registration desk. You can be right. You can even argue and win, but not every fight is worth the effort. Especially when your energy is short. It must be saved for battles that will reward you with their spoils."

Nathan's wisdom calmed her irritation, and his nearness closed around her. She was grateful that the lobby was empty. In that instant it dawned on her that they would face the consequences of their actions as soon as they arrived at Gran Colina Church together. She pulled her hand free and covered her mouth. "What have we done?"

Nathan looked puzzled. "Avoided an unnecessary argument and sent a man away without giving him what he wanted."

"No. Don't you see? Before, when you asked if we could walk to church together, it would have looked like the friends and coworkers that we are. Junior is probably telling his father about our conversation right this minute. Before we arrive, word will have spread to anyone who will listen."

Nathan shook his head. "Charlotte, you missed the most important thing Junior said."

She tried to remember anything their schoolmate had said that was of importance. Most of his words were worthy of immediate dismissal. "What?"

"He said no one will believe that you would allow me to court you."

Junior's words came back to her with clarity. Everyone in town knew Nathan had returned to town for the hotel. Not for her. She took a step back. Try as she might to forget, the truth of those words would always be there. Nathan had come to town for her hotel. Everything he'd done since he'd arrived had put the hotel in a better position to secure his future with Mr. Freeman.

Charlotte clasped her hands together in front of her. "If it's all the same to you, I'll walk to church with the children. I don't want anyone to gather a wrong impression about the two of us."

"I see." His mouth settled into a firm line. "And by *anyone*, do you mean to include me?"

"Of course not. You and I know the truth. Neither of us is ready to court anyone. You have your career, and I have this hotel and my siblings. That's more than a body could be expected to handle at one time."

Nathan entered the door of the church and took a moment to observe the people who'd assembled for the service. Mrs. Gillis was making her way up the aisle to the piano. It didn't take long for him to spot Junior Conrad next to his father in an animated discussion. Junior pointed at Charlotte and then at Nathan. Davis

Conrad turned around and met Nathan's gaze with an air of dismissal and a shake of his head.

Charlotte gave every appearance of ignoring Junior, but the stiffness of her shoulders and the tilt of her head proved to Nathan that she was aware she was the topic of their conversation.

Sarah turned on the bench and climbed onto her knees. She gripped the back of the wooden bench with her doll in one hand. "Mr. Nathan, come sit by me." Her curls bounced in response to her exuberant greeting.

Several people turned to watch him. He would have refused Sarah, but there were so many onlookers. He didn't want to risk her displeasure. The little girl was still given to tears if something made her unhappy. Nathan had no good choice save to accept her invitation.

He came to stand at the end of the bench and endured the clandestine glare Charlotte sent him from beneath the brim of her Sunday hat. The straw creation was tied into place with a wide, green ribbon under her delicate chin. Even in a state of aggravation she was beautiful. He smiled an apology and sat beside Sarah.

"I'm glad you came today. Mrs. Gillis said it's important for everybody to go to church." Sarah leaned in and whispered, "She said it can heal your heart, but I don't think Charlotte's heart is healed yet."

Nathan looked over Sarah's head at Charlotte. She stared ahead, but the twitch of her cheek proved she was aware of his gaze. "She is better, Sarah. Sometimes Charlotte is trying to make decisions, and it makes it seem like she's hurting. She's just trying to get things right. Don't you worry about your sister. She's very strong. Inside and out."

Mrs. Gillis began to play the opening hymn, and everyone stood to sing along. Nathan was hard-pressed to concentrate on the sermon. He was too aware of Charlotte's discomfort and the furtive glances they received from every direction throughout the service.

Charlotte drew his attention with a small cough. Nathan hated that she was enduring the service that should have brought her comfort. He looked at his watch. Reverend Gillis would preach for at least another twenty minutes.

Nathan leaned over to Sarah. "I'm going to leave now. You make sure your sister takes a nice long walk on the way home today. Okay?"

"Oh, goodie. I want to walk by the river. I'll tell her you said we need to." Sarah's pleasure contrasted with Charlotte's mood. Perhaps the girl's joy would spread to her sister.

Nathan winked at Sarah and left the church.

By midafternoon Nathan's back was tired. He shifted on his feet and pulled another journal toward him.

The figures on the page swam in front of his eyes, and he remembered he'd skipped lunch. Several tasks in rapid succession had greeted him when he'd returned from church. By the time he had handled them all, the restaurant had closed for the afternoon. He marked his place in the journal and went to the kitchen in search of something to eat.

He opened the door and found Charlotte and the children at the kitchen table. He backed up. "I'm sorry. I didn't realize you were here. I'll come back later."

Michael's mouth was full, but he managed a few words. "You gotta try this pie. Mrs. Baxter is a good baker." He scooped up another big bite on his fork, but Charlotte lowered his hand with a touch on his wrist.

"Have some milk first."

Michael dropped the fork to his plate with a clatter and drained his milk cup. A wipe of his sleeve removed the white ring from his lip.

"Slow down, Michael." Charlotte put a plate with two large cookies in front of Sarah.

Nathan took another step back as Charlotte cut a piece of pie and slid it onto a plate. She set it on the table in front of the empty seat beside her. "You may as well join us for pie. Everyone in town now assumes we are a pair, so dessert in the privacy of this kitchen can't do us any harm." She took two cookies for herself and broke off a small piece of the first one.

"A pair of what?" Sarah picked up a cookie.

Nathan caught Charlotte's gaze. "A pair of friends, Sarah. Your sister and I are friends." Charlotte smiled at his innocent explanation.

He slid a chair out and smiled at Michael. "I'm not sure I'll like the pie as much as you do."

"It's better'n Charlotte's."

"Is that so?" Charlotte laughed. "You may find yourself waiting until Mrs. Baxter cooks it again to have another slice."

The four of them ate dessert and laughed at Sarah's recounting of their walk by the river. It seemed Michael had been dangerously close to falling and knocking Charlotte into the water. A nearby branch had saved her.

Michael pointed at the hem of her dress. "She only got a little bit wet, and I caught the cricket."

"What did you do with the cricket?" Nathan enjoyed their boisterous telling of their outing.

"I put it in my pocket." Michael reached into his pocket and retrieved the insect. "See." He opened his hand a bit for Nathan to admire his catch, but the cricket leaped for his freedom and disappeared behind the pie safe. "Oh, no! I wanted to show him to Archie."

Charlotte narrowed her eyes at Michael. "I'm quite sure you'll hear him chirping later. You can find him then. And no more bugs inside." She wagged her finger at him, but they all laughed knowing she was as amused as Michael had been.

The kids soon lost interest in the kitchen and headed for their rooms to change out of their Sunday clothes.

"I didn't see you come home." Nathan stacked the plates and took them to the basin.

Charlotte followed with the cups. "We came in the back door. I didn't want the children to disrupt anyone in the lobby."

Nathan wiped his hands on the towel that hung on a peg near the basin. "You don't have to avoid me, Charlotte."

She put the cups in the basin. "What makes you think I was avoiding you?" She picked up the towel he'd used but didn't look at him.

"The fact that you've never come in the back door before. Not in the entire time I've been here." He leaned against the cabinet and folded his arms across his chest.

"Michael and Sarah were laughing and playing when we got here. It was nice to see them enjoying themselves. I didn't have the heart to ask them to settle down. They've had almost no fun in the last few weeks."

"I understand that, but you still could have entered through the front. Children of our guests come in laughing and happy all the time."

"I know."

"But—"

"I don't know how to act around you sometimes." Her words were quiet.

"I'm your friend. You don't have to act around me. Just be yourself. I've never known a more genuine person than you."

Charlotte looked up then. "It's so hard with everyone in Gran Colina talking about me. If they aren't talking about Pa and Momma and feeling sorry for us, then they're talking about the hotel. I've heard the whispers about me being too young to know how to handle things." She flung the towel onto the cabinet. "I don't need the added worry of everyone questioning my every move." She threw her arms out wide. "Do you know that three different ladies approached me after the sermon to tell me who they thought I should be courting?"

"I see. So that's the root of your attitude."

"My attitude?"

"Yes. That somber and worried grumpiness that isn't you." He reached out and flicked a bit of her hair over her shoulder. "You're much too sweet of a person to be so serious. You should laugh when they make their suggestions and tell them you're waiting on God to bring the right man to you. That you'll know him when you see him."

"You think I'm grumpy?"

"You are grumpy." He leaned his head to one side. "It's going to give you wrinkles, too. You better stop it or you'll have lines between your eyes, and people won't see your freckles because they'll be buried in the crevices of your wrinkles. You'll look like a grandmother before you ever marry. You're much too pretty to look like a grandmother. Yet." He laughed.

She leaned away from him and stilled. "You think I'm taking them too seriously?"

He sobered to match her mood. "I do. You'll never be happy if you listen to everything people say to you. Or about you. All you need to do is pray. God will direct you. In subtle ways that will comfort you. Not by berating you with the town's busybodies." He pushed away from the cabinet. "Now, go check on those two before they get into something. I'll manage the desk for the rest of the day. And we need to get out of this kitchen before Mrs. Baxter arrives to cook supper and finds this mess we made."

Nathan held the door open and followed Charlotte into the restaurant. At the doorway to the lobby she turned back to him.

"Thank you."

"For what?"

"For not hurting Sarah's feelings in church. You knew it would wound her if you refused to sit with her."

He raised his brows. "I didn't think you were pleased about that."

"At the time, I was uncomfortable, but it was because Junior and his father were gossiping like two jealous cranks at a wake."

Nathan chuckled. "Those two are used to pushing

their will on others. I remember how Junior was always there to take credit for some project or another, but I don't seem to be able to recall him ever doing any of the actual work."

She smiled. A pretty smile that crinkled her eyes and rounded her cheeks in a way that showed her freckles at their best. "He's still the same. You know, he doesn't even have a job. I'm not sure why his father lets him meander through life without a purpose. My pa wouldn't put up with any of us being idle."

"Your pa was a good man."

They went into the lobby, and Charlotte opened the door to her parlor. "Let me know if you need me. We're going to be here for the rest of the day."

"I will." He opened the journal he'd looked at earlier. "Will you send Michael to see me? We've got quite a few people checking out in the morning before the train runs. I want to ask him to help me tomorrow."

"I will." The joy in her eyes was all the thanks he'd ever want for having helped her and her family.

He tried to remember that the next morning when Michael tossed a valise down the steps and left a guest standing, mouth agape, on the landing.

Chapter Twelve

Charlotte opened the door of the parlor just in time for Michael to plow into her skirts. "Michael, what's the matter?"

Her brother untangled himself from her grasp and ran into his room. The door slammed.

She looked over her shoulder into the lobby. Nathan stood at the foot of the stairs apologizing to Mrs. Peabody. The lady and her daughters had stayed with them for three days and were leaving on the morning train.

Charlotte hurried to see what had happened.

Nathan picked up Mrs. Peabody's valise and dusted it off. The handle was broken. "I'm very sorry, ma'am. Please allow me to send someone to the mercantile to buy a new valise for you. I can have Miss Green transfer your belongings while you eat. Your breakfast will be complimentary, of course."

"I don't understand what got into the boy." Mrs. Peabody frowned. "I must insist that someone else retrieve the rest of our things from our rooms. The child's behavior was unacceptable."

"Yes, ma'am. I'll take care of it myself."

Charlotte extended her arm in the direction of the restaurant. "I'll show you into the restaurant and see that you're taken care of." She led the lady and her daughters to a table and left them in the care of Mrs. Atkins. She returned to the desk.

Nathan gave Nora Baxter, the maid, some money from the money box. "Make certain that the valise is of an equal or greater quality to this one." He showed her the broken valise. "And hurry, please."

Nora nodded and tucked the money into her skirt pocket before she left.

"What happened?" Charlotte had tried to assist Nathan but, now that everything was under control, she wanted an explanation.

"I don't know. Last night I told Michael what I needed him to do this morning. He seemed excited to be here. Then, as Mrs. Peabody was following him down the steps, she said something, and he threw down her valise and ran off. I simply cannot allow him to be in the lobby if he can't behave properly." He pointed at the broken handle. "We've just had to pay for three meals and a new valise. The profit we've made on their visit is greatly diminished because of that."

"It makes no sense that he'd do such a thing. Michael has never been one for throwing a tantrum."

Charlotte picked up the valise and set it on the registration desk. As soon as she did, the scent of roses drifted to her. Visions of her mother danced in her mind. The aroma was strong and brought raw memories of love and loss with it.

"Oh, Nathan. I know what upset Michael."

"What? There was nothing said to him. Mrs. Peabody assured me."

"It wasn't something she did or said. It was this." She pointed at the valise. "It smells like our mother. Mrs. Peabody must use rose water like our mother wore. If you lean close you can smell it. I'm sure Michael had to use both hands to carry it. When he lifted it near his face, all the memories of our mother must have overwhelmed him."

"Why do you think that would cause such an outburst?"

"He hasn't really grieved. You've seen how angry he's been. It's been easier for him to lash out at others than to feel his own pain. He has barely cried or shown any emotion except anger."

Sarah came out of the parlor. "Charlotte, come quick. Michael's crying. He won't let me in his room, and he's crying something awful. He makes me to go away when I open the door."

Charlotte turned to Nathan. He put a hand on her arm. "You go take care of him. I'll get Nora to handle Mrs. Peabody's things."

She covered his hand with her own. "Thank you." The comfort she drew from that small touch was something she'd think about later. For the moment she needed to concentrate on Michael.

"Sarah, I want you to go into the kitchen and play with your doll at the table. Don't get in Mrs. Atkins's way."

Nathan asked Sarah if she'd like to sit on the chair behind the registration desk. "You can help me put the keys on the board when our guests leave."

"Can I, Charlotte?" Sarah looked hopeful.

"You may." She smiled at her sister and closed the door to the parlor.

Charlotte heard Michael's cries when she entered the hallway. She tapped on the door. "Michael, I'd like to come in."

"Go away!" He yelled the words, but they were muffled as if he had his face buried in his pillow.

She opened the door enough to see him sprawled across the bed. Sobs racked his small frame. For all his anger and strength, he was a six-year-old boy without his parents. Charlotte had known this time would come.

She sat on the side of the bed and rubbed the back of his shirt, grateful when he didn't push her away.

A full ten minutes passed before he said another word. He rolled to one side and dried his eyes on the bedclothes.

"I want them to be here, Charlotte. I miss them so bad. It hurts in here." He pushed on his chest with both hands.

"Me, too." She opened her arms, and he flung himself at her.

"Why did they have to die? I miss how good Momma smelled. That lady smelled like Momma."

Charlotte hugged him close and rocked him back and forth the way she'd seen their mother do time and again. "I don't have an answer for why, Michael. Only God knows the answer to some questions."

While he cried until he had no more tears, Charlotte rocked him to sleep. She laid him back against the pillow and tiptoed out of the room.

The door closed with a quiet click, and she went to her room to splash her face with water. The bowl and pitcher had been her mother's. The mother who had given her birth. The sweet memories she had every time she used it flooded her mind. She knew Michael and Sarah would heal from the pain that tormented them now. Just as she'd healed when she'd lost her mother. But watching them grieve was as hard on her as grieving for their parents. She'd gladly bear their pain if it were possible.

A glance in the mirror showed her swollen eyes. The cool water had helped, but she'd have to face Nathan and her job anyway. It wasn't fair to leave him alone. She hoped to be able to speak to Mrs. Peabody and explain Michael's actions.

Sarah was standing on a chair behind the registration desk when Charlotte entered the lobby. She grinned as she slid a key into the highest row of slots on the wooden cabinet. "I'm a big girl, Charlotte. Mr. Nathan is making me work."

Nathan thanked the guest who was leaving. "We look forward to having you stay with us the next time you are in Gran Colina."

"Making you work?" Charlotte asked. She was so relieved that Michael had finally broken through the wall of anger to his pain that she would gladly tease Sarah and Nathan. "Isn't Mr. Nathan supposed to be working for you? You're one of the owners of this fine establishment."

Sarah giggled. "I'm too little to be a boss though. Mr. Nathan said so." She climbed from the chair. "I don't want to work anymore. Can I go play on the porch?"

Libbie opened the front door at that moment, so Charlotte sent her sister out to play under her watchful eye.

Nathan marked the registration book. "Is Michael better?"

She nodded. "He's asleep. He's cried his heart out. After all this time, I was worried. He's kept it all bottled up inside. The pressure of trying to hold himself aloof from it was overwhelming. I think he'll start to heal now."

"I'm glad." Nathan handed her the valise Nora had bought for Mrs. Peabody. "This should make up for the inconvenience. Nora transferred everything from the broken valise. I told her she did well to choose this one. She may be a good person to move up as we hire more staff in the future. She's a smart young lady with plenty of enthusiasm. What do you think?"

The ease of Nathan asking her opinion on matters to do with the business of running the hotel boosted Charlotte's confidence. "I agree. She's always punctual and does her best. She never argues when asked to work late or do things that are out of the ordinary for her."

Nathan took out his notepad. "I'll make a note of it."

Mrs. Peabody and her daughters came out of the restaurant. Nathan picked up the valise, but Charlotte took it from him. "Let me talk to her, please."

He nodded and turned his attention to the journal he had open on the desk.

"Mrs. Peabody, please accept my sincerest apologies for my young brother's behavior."

"It was most shocking."

Charlotte agreed. "You are quite right. Your disapproval is understandable, but I'd like to explain if I may."

"We're in a bit of a hurry to get to the train station."

Mrs. Peabody folded her hands together and held them at her waist. Her velvet reticule hung from one wrist. The bag must have cost a week's wages. The elaborate beadwork was unlike anything Charlotte had seen at the local mercantile. This lady was a person of means and would no doubt share her opinion of the service at Green's Grand Hotel with others in her circle of friends. Charlotte couldn't risk a bad reputation. Not for the sake of her family privacy and pride.

"It will only take a moment."

Mrs. Peabody huffed a short breath. "Do be quick then." Her posture reinforced her desire to leave as soon as possible.

"My brother is recovering from the loss of our parents a few weeks ago." A tiny shift in the woman's shoulders let Charlotte know she was doing the right thing. "Michael has been angry ever since their accident. I've been ever so worried that he hasn't cried like my sister and I have. He's kept his pain tucked away in his heart."

"So this anger is your excuse for his behavior?" The shoulders stiffened a bit.

"No, ma'am. Just the opposite. You see, Michael is so small that carrying your valise was a big job for him. No doubt, he had to tuck it up under his chin to take it down the stairs."

"If he's not able to do the work, he shouldn't be given the task. You might be better served to wait until he's older."

"But our pa taught us that we should learn to work at a young age. He said it builds character and strength."

A nod of approval was Mrs. Peabody's reaction.

"The point is, when Michael lifted your valise up

near his face, he caught the scent of your rose water. You see, our mother wore rose water. Holding your case and smelling the scent of our mother broke the dam of pain that he'd built up in his heart. While you ate your breakfast, he wept and wept. He's asleep now, and I daresay it's the best sleep he's had in the weeks since they passed."

Mrs. Peabody wiped a tear from her cheek and put her hand on Charlotte's arm. "Oh, the poor dear. I'm so sorry. If I'd known, I'd never have been sharp with the boy."

"Thank you for understanding."

"Please tell him not to worry about it. Not for a minute."

"I will." Charlotte smiled with relief. "I didn't want you to leave here thinking that I would tolerate such behavior in our hotel. We value your business and welcome you to stay any time you are in Gran Colina."

"You may count on it."

Charlotte lifted the valise, and Mrs. Peabody took it from her. "This is a lovely bag. And thank you for the wonderful breakfast."

As the door closed on the Peabody family, Nathan came to stand beside her. "You were marvelous, Charlotte. I tell you, there isn't a Turner in Dallas who could have smoothed over an issue with a guest any better than you did."

She looked at him. "But I wasn't trying to smooth anything over. I was making things right. She deserved to know the truth, and Michael deserved mercy given the circumstances."

"All of that is true. Not only did you handle it with

professionalism, your motive was pure. You have all the makings of a fine businesswoman."

Charlotte's face warmed with his unexpected praise. It took great effort to whisper her thanks. She hadn't wanted his help in the beginning, but to win his approval meant more than she could express.

Would she be ready to take the lead on managing the hotel quicker than Nathan imagined? She hoped so. The sooner she learned everything, the sooner she could pay the bank and secure the future of her family.

And the sooner Nathan would be free to get on with his life.

She remembered the list of salary requirements he'd presented when he'd first arrived. He'd made it clear that he'd stay for the long term. She'd agreed to his terms with conditions.

Would she still want him to leave after he'd taught her all he knew?

On the first Monday in September Nathan waved to Michael and Sarah. "Be good in school, and I'll let you help me this afternoon."

Sarah held tight to Charlotte's hand and beamed at Nathan. "Me, too?"

"You, too."

Michael swung his lunch pail in a slow rhythm. "I'll help with the hard work. Miss Henderson said she's gonna teach us math at school, so I can write in the journals like Pa did."

"Study hard, and you'll be ready before you know it."

"We best be going. You don't want to be late on the first day." Charlotte smiled at the children. She caught Nathan's eye. "I won't be long."

Nathan spoke with the maids about which rooms still needed to be cleaned. If things went as he hoped, the new furnishings would arrive at the end of the next week. The curtains would be ready by Friday. It seemed everything was on schedule for Mr. Thornhill's meeting.

There was one other thing that troubled him. He'd speak to Charlotte about it when she returned.

The maids went to turn out the next room on their schedule, and Nathan looked over the list of names of possible staff to help set up the new furnishings and take care of the extra work that would come their way when Mr. Thornhill's group arrived.

He was crossing off a young lad's name who hadn't impressed him when Mr. Freeman came into the lobby.

The banker stopped inside the door and looked around. "I don't see a lot of guests milling about. Is Miss Green having a problem keeping the guests happy? I heard about an incident with her brother last week."

"Good morning, Mr. Freeman." Nathan wouldn't dismiss proper business manners to appease the man who'd brought him here under false pretenses.

"I'm not interested in pleasantries, Mr. Taylor. I'm interested in my investment paying off at the bank." He lifted a hand toward the restaurant. "And unless that room is full of paying customers, I think we have a problem."

"No, sir. We do not have a problem. You just arrived at a time of day when the lobby is empty. Many of our guests are having breakfast, but some are packing for their departure. Remember that the hotel business is built on people coming and going. You can't judge by how full the lobby is. Any more than you'd want people to think there was a run on your bank when you have a line at the teller's booth."

Mr. Freeman bristled at the comment. "I'll need more proof than your word. The Turners could easily improve this situation without delay."

"Mr. Freeman, you asked me to come here because of my vast experience with Turner Hotels. I'm doing my job. And I'm doing it well."

Charlotte entered the lobby carrying a large bundle wrapped in brown paper. Nathan went to assist her.

Mr. Freeman headed for the door. "I won't wait a moment past the six-week mark. If you want to stay on here after that, you'll have to prove your worth to me."

Charlotte watched the banker leave and turned to Nathan. "What was that about?"

"He visits every week, and it's almost the same conversation. He wants to know how the hotel is doing. Today he thinks that no one in the lobby means we're failing."

"Everyone is in their room or at breakfast. Or out for the day." She let him take the bundle from her.

"I told him."

"Is he offering to keep you on if he takes the hotel from me? You know I won't let him take it." She untied the string that held the paper around her package.

"I know. He was rambling on about so many things. I was too busy to pay him much mind." He didn't want her to think about the possibility that he would stay on if Mr. Freeman succeeded in taking the hotel from her. It wasn't what he wanted to do, but he'd be a fool not to consider it. Even the thought made him feel disloyal to Charlotte. "I suggest you do the same." He lifted the paper from one side of the bundle.

"It's not your livelihood at stake." She was pulling the other side of the paper away from the package, and he caught her hand.

"Yes, it is, Charlotte. I don't know how to impress on you that my future is tied with yours here. If you fail, I fail. If you lose the hotel, I have no income or home." Unless he stayed on for Mr. Freeman or whoever bought the place.

She stood still. "I'm sorry. I know you came here for a permanent position. I wish things were different. I would try to keep you on. But with the banknote coming due, I don't know if there will be enough to take care of everything the kids will need for the next couple of years. Paying off that note is my main concern. I won't let Mr. Freeman have that kind of power over me for one moment longer than necessary to satisfy the note."

Charlotte lifted a curtain from the paper. "These are lovely." She shook it out and let it drape across the registration desk. "I saw Opal Pennington on my way back from the school. She told me she had these ready. They go in the dining room. She said she couldn't resist making these as soon as the fabric arrived. The lobby ones will be ready on Friday as promised." A touch of anticipation turned her blue eyes bright, and she pulled the top of the curtain under her chin. "Can we hang these today?"

He smiled at her excitement. "I think we might be able to do it tonight after the restaurant closes. I remember seeing a ladder in the attic."

"Wonderful! We'll finally start seeing the results of

all our planning. Well, all the planning Pa and Momma did with your help." She folded the curtain back into the bundle.

"You helped make this happen, Charlotte. For all the effort that went on before you learned of their plans, you've been the one to see it through."

"Thank you. It means a lot for you to say that. I've been so busy and sad that I wondered if anything I've done is working out well." She fingered the golden trim on the curtains. "Do you think we should wait and do everything at one time?"

"No. We'll have so much to do that we may fall behind." He helped her tie the string around the curtains. "And, Charlotte, it's all working well. That's what I just told Mr. Freeman. I know you wouldn't have believed it when I first arrived, but I do want you to succeed. I want you to make Green's Grand Hotel into everything your parents ever imagined. And more."

"I believe you." Her words were quiet and measured.

Chapter Thirteen

Charlotte tried to focus on the tasks at hand. "We need to choose the extra helpers we need for when the furnishings arrive and for Mr. Thornhill's meeting."

"Great. Let's put this bundle of curtains in the parlor and get started while it's not too busy."

An hour later, the final decisions were made for the renovations and the upcoming meeting. She stood and stretched her neck from side to side. "Time is moving quickly. At first it stood still, and now it's as if I can't hold it back."

Nathan closed his notebook. "I'll go out this afternoon and make sure everyone we've chosen knows when to come to work." He looked around the empty lobby. "Do you want to join me for an early lunch?"

"I'd like that."

They finished their light meal, and Mrs. Atkins removed their plates from the table.

Charlotte touched the fabric of the curtains they would be removing tonight. "These are very old. As much as I liked them when they were new, I'll admit I won't be sorry to see them go."

"I'm glad. Some things are easier to let go of than others." Nathan checked his watch. "I spoke to the maids this morning. There are only two rooms left to deep clean. They are doing one of them now. The other will be done tomorrow."

"I'll make a final round of all the rooms and gather the rest of the items we decided would be best removed."

Nathan straightened the tablecloth. "You aren't still upset about removing the sentimental trinkets?"

"As a matter of fact, we're enjoying having some of them in our residence." She smiled and pointed at the mantel. "The music boxes that were over the fireplace are among our favorite things. We listen to one every night. They remind us of the joy in our mother's heart and the happiness she and Pa shared."

He smiled. "You should have seen them at the Turner Hotel in Dallas. They danced after supper on their last night. Their love for each other was evident."

"Was she wearing her blue dress? It was Pa's favorite."

"I think so. They had a wonderful meal and spent the evening talking and dancing."

"They would dance in the parlor here. Michael and Sarah would dance, too."

Nathan frowned. "What about you? Don't you dance?"

"No. There was never anyone Momma approved." It was strange that she no longer resented her mother's protectiveness. She would miss having someone to guard her from life's pitfalls.

"Seeing the procession of intended suitors who've

called since I've been here, I can see why she was so careful." He chuckled, and it made her laugh.

"It has been quite an assortment of fellows. Some not so bad but others I could never accept—under any circumstances."

"Has there been anyone you'd like to consider?"

"Not yet. There has always been an idea of the kind of man who'd suit, but he just hasn't made himself available yet." She smiled at Nathan. She didn't think she'd be sorry if he'd never moved away and the two of them had courted. But if they had, he wouldn't be here helping her keep the business running. All he'd learned was benefiting them both. Sometimes when life didn't turn out like you'd hoped, it could be a good thing.

Just before time for the children to return from school, the young man who made deliveries for the train station appeared.

"Miss Green, there's a big shipment for your pa at the station. It was on the morning train. We only had time to unload it, but it's all on the platform. The stationmaster wants to know when you're coming to pick it up."

Charlotte looked at Nathan. "Could it be so early?"

"Dennis, is the shipment a lot of large crates? Something the size of furnishings and such for the hotel?"

"Yes, sir. It's all powerful heavy, too. I wore myself out toting things off the train with some of the others at the station."

Nathan looked at her. "It is."

"We'll have to make arrangements to bring the things here, Dennis." Her heart raced like a child in anticipation of a splendid gift for Christmas. She asked

Nathan, "Shall we go see how much there is and hire a wagon from the livery?"

"Yes. I'll get Nora to watch the desk, and we'll leave immediately." He climbed the stairs two at a time while she thanked Dennis and sent him on his way.

Her heart was glad. In all the weeks since her parents had died, this was the thing that held the greatest hope for her family. Michael and Sarah came home before Nora came to the desk, so she left the bell for any new arrivals to ring and told the children they could come along.

"Will I get a new bed?" Sarah held Nathan's hand as they walked to the train station. "And is there one for my doll?"

"Your pa and momma ordered these things special to make Green's Grand Hotel more grand than it's ever been."

Charlotte appreciated the way he spoke to the children. Sarah's hopes for something new weren't dashed by his explanation, but he gave her the truth. Most men dismissed her siblings as an inconvenience. In the beginning, Nathan had been so intent on the business of the hotel that she'd thought he'd be the same, but he'd endeared himself to her sister and brother. Sarah had been won over by the way he winked at her and asked for help in some project that made her feel essential to his plans. Michael had taken longer but, in the end, could often be found at the registration desk doing whatever chore Nathan assigned him.

Michael ran ahead of them and was sitting on one of the large crates when they arrived.

Charlotte was stunned at the number of crates. "Where will we put everything?"

"The drawings in your father's journal will show us." Nathan raised his eyebrows. "Seeing it all stacked here like this makes it seem an enormous task."

She didn't move from where she'd stopped when they rounded the corner of the train station and saw the shipment. "I wonder that no one told us about this before so late in the afternoon."

Nathan cupped her elbow and urged her forward. Sarah was still holding his other hand. "Let's have a look."

Michael stood up on the crate he'd chosen and held his arms out wide. "I'm taller than all of you." He climbed onto the crate behind it and stood higher still.

"Come down carefully, Michael. We can't have you getting hurt. There is too much work to be done." Charlotte shook her head. "I'm overwhelmed."

"Don't be." Nathan guided her along the platform to see how many crates were there. "I was able to contact all the extra help we need this afternoon. To a man, they were all willing to help on a moment's notice. We'll go to the livery and hire a wagon first. A couple of the men there will be great help. Then I'll stop in at the mercantile and the barbershop to get the word out to the others that the shipment has arrived."

And with that short list of things to do, Nathan took over and handled all the details of having the furnishings taken to the hotel. Most of the crates were taken to the livery to be stored while they worked on one wagonload at a time. They were back at the hotel in time for supper.

"Mrs. Atkins, it seems we're to be turned on end for the next many days. I had no idea the arrival of the furnishing would create such an upheaval." Charlotte accepted her plate of ham, mashed potatoes and green beans. A bowl of biscuits was placed in the center of the table.

"I'm sure we'll get it all done in time for the meeting of farmers that Mr. Thornhill is bringing next month. To be honest, I'm glad to see everything arrive so early. It'll give you and Mr. Taylor more time to get it all arranged to your liking." Mrs. Atkins asked if they needed anything else and went back into the kitchen.

"I wanna pray tonight." Sarah reached a hand out to Michael and Charlotte. The three of them bowed their heads while she offered thanks for all the new things they'd received today. "And thank you for school. Help me and Michael get as smart as Charlotte and Mr. Nathan so we can be the bosses when we get big."

"Amen." Michael snagged a biscuit and tore it in half. "Charlotte, I don't think I should go to school tomorrow. There's a lot of man work to do. I can help."

"Let me talk to Nathan first. That may be just the thing to do." Charlotte loved how they were all enthused. The shipment had arrived on the afternoon train. The same train that took their parents from them last month. Today it had brought back some of their joy. The shipment was a gift from their parents from beyond the end of their lives. Charlotte was grateful. She couldn't imagine if the hotel had been taken by the bank and there had been no good news to come of the trip their folks had made to Dallas.

Mrs. Atkins came to their table. "Miss Charlotte, would you like me to take a plate of supper to Mr. Taylor at the registration desk?"

Charlotte looked through the door and into the

lobby. Nathan sat at the desk alone. "Please bring him a plate here. I'll invite him to join me and the children. Make sure it's a healthy portion. He'll be needing his meals to match the amount of work he's facing."

"I'll get right on it." Mrs. Atkins smiled. "I'm grateful to you both for hiring my husband and son to help with the load of it. It'll be a nice boost to the savings we're working on to help buy more cattle for our place. And the things we'll be needing for our winter crops."

"You and Bertha are such a blessing to us here. We were glad to take them on for this job." Charlotte stood and rested her hands on Michael and Sarah's shoulders. "You two use your best manners. I'll be back in a moment."

Nathan looked up when Charlotte approached the desk. "Are you finished with your meal so soon?"

"No. We'd like for you to join us."

"I'll be fine here. Mrs. Atkins will bring me a plate of supper. All I have to do is ask."

"I asked her to bring it to our table." She grinned. "Please. I'm so excited, and you're the only person who understands why. This is a huge day for Green's Grand Hotel." She threw her arms out wide. "We'll be grand like we've never been grand before." She spun in a circle. "I had no idea it would be this amazing."

Nathan watched her twirl. A slight lift of one corner of his mouth was the sole reaction he gave to her jubilance. "I'll be right in."

She stopped still and lowered her head. "We'll be able to see the desk from the table." An earnest effort to be demure wasn't enough to hold back her joy, and she glided across the floor and back to the table as if she were dancing.

Supper went quickly, and Charlotte promised the children they would be allowed to stay home from school to help. They were entering the parlor when she made her decision. "But only for one day. Then you'll go back with the other children."

Nathan agreed. "It will be exciting to open the crates and put things away, but it is important that you learn all you can at school. Your sister will tell you that there is much more to running a hotel than working at the registration desk."

"Like you work at the desk, but you do other stuff, too?" Sarah cuddled her doll and looked up at him from inside the parlor.

He tugged on the long braid that hung over one shoulder. "Like that." He told her and Michael good night. "Make sure you go straight to sleep. You'll need to be rested for all the work we'll do tomorrow."

Charlotte got the kids tucked in for the night and went to look for Nathan. She found him in the restaurant on a ladder. The old curtains were in a pile on the floor near the kitchen door.

"I thought you'd make me wait on the curtains because the shipment came early." He jumped and almost fell when she spoke.

He clung to the top of the ladder with both arms. "I'd be glad of a warning the next time you catch me unawares." A tremor went through his shoulders.

"You were startled that badly?" she laughed. "If I'd known how easy that was, I'd have done it many times before tonight."

"So I'll thank God in my prayers tonight for the mercy that you didn't know."

Charlotte giggled then. A schoolgirl giggle that surprised and delighted her. First because she hadn't expected it, and second because she needed to feel joy again. "The season of mercy may have ended. You best be on your guard."

They worked together for the next hour in an effort to hang all the curtains that Opal Pennington had finished. Charlotte backed into the center of the room and studied their progress.

"It's lovely. I can't wait until tomorrow. The sun streaming in will be amazing."

Nathan descended the ladder and moved to stand by her. "You are right. The fabric was an excellent choice. The new decor will rival anything that is built in Gran Colina to compete with us."

Us? Nathan had invested himself into the hotel. He had every right to be proud.

"Do you think we'll be up and running under our new image before that kind of competition arrives in town?"

"I do. There's not building here that would suit. Anyone who wants to run a hotel will have to build before they can open. We'll have that much time to establish our reputation. The farmers who are booked here next month will give us plenty of exposure."

"With the furnishings arriving early, we'll be ahead of schedule for that. I'm so relieved."

She started to fold the old curtains, and he pulled the ladder away from the window. "I want to thank you for suggesting that we hire Mrs. Baxter. With her sharing the workload of the kitchen with Mrs. Atkins, I've barely had to do any of the baking."

"It was too much, Charlotte. I'm glad you came around on that point."

"Nora is doing well on the desk, too. I think we could promote her to a type of assistant as we grow." She folded another curtain.

He smiled at her and picked up the end of the curtain that had spilled onto the floor. He straightened it and walked toward her to fold the ends together. "You realize that you are talking about the future of the hotel in terms of we and us."

Charlotte dropped the corner of the curtain and bent to pick it up. Nathan's hand was there at the same time as hers. He held her hand in his gentle grasp. Time seemed to stop. They were so close. He was helpful and kind. A man who loved God and honored Him with his life. A man of integrity.

All that poured over her wounded soul in a healing goodness that confirmed her hope for brighter days. Days that no longer seemed so far away.

Nathan caressed her fingers with his and looked up to meet her eyes. Gone was the man who'd come to Gran Colina to take over her hotel. In front of her stood a man who'd worked side by side with her to fulfill her parents' dreams. He'd taken her siblings into his life and heart. And they had accepted him as part of their daily lives. She had promised herself that she'd learn the hotel business before she allowed herself to be distracted by any man.

Did she know enough to relax her guard? If the man didn't distract her—but he *attracted* her—she could keep her vow to care for Michael and Sarah and also have a life for herself that she'd given up on. Was it too much to hope for?

"Nathan, I can't tell you how much I appreciate all

you've done. All you are doing. Somewhere along the line I guess I started thinking of us as a team."

"Like a team of horses pulling a wagon?" He added a lopsided grin to his teasing words.

"Like a team of mules if you consider how stubborn we both are." She dropped her gaze to their hands. His grip swallowed her small hand. He was wise beyond his years and shared that wisdom with her every day.

"Yes. *Mules* is accurate." He tugged on her hand and took a step closer to her. The excitement of the day and the progress they'd made together in the room where they stood seeing it all come to life filled her head. She felt herself lean toward him ever so slightly. "We are a good team. Strong and determined."

"You've made a huge difference in everything here."

"I couldn't have done it without you. You stepped up into roles you knew nothing about and pulled the load of a prize mule." He winked at her. The same quick motion of closing one eye that he used to make Sarah smile, but it was different. It was slower and his gaze never left hers. It was as if he could see her with his eyes closed.

She knew if she closed her eyes, she could see every line of his face, every expression, hear every inflection in his voice. Yes, somewhere in the last month, she'd accepted Nathan as a part of her life.

Without a moment to consider the consequences, Charlotte followed her heart and raised up on her toes. She held his hand tighter and closed her eyes as she pressed her lips to his. The sweetness of the moment was more precious than any she'd ever imagined. No man had ever touched her heart like Nathan did. This, her first kiss, connected her to him with a power that startled and comforted her at the same time. She let her heels drop to the floor, and her eyes fluttered open. The look in his eyes matched the feelings in her heart.

And it settled her soul.

Charlotte dropped the curtain over the back of a nearby chair. "I'll finish this in the morning." She squeezed his hand and released it. "Good night, Nathan."

He lifted his hand and cupped her cheek. "Good night, Charlotte."

Her feet carried her from the room as though she floated.

When she closed her eyes to sleep that night, her mind confirmed her earlier thought that she'd see his image as clearly as if he stood before her. The peaceful slumber that overtook her was the best she'd ever known.

Nathan woke early on Tuesday. The shipment of furnishings should be on his mind. And it was. But Charlotte was in the forefront of his every waking thought. She'd been in his dreams. Her beauty and joy had filled the recesses of his mind for weeks. Longer if he dared to admit it to himself.

But after she kissed him last night, all other thoughts had fled.

Today would require his full attention. He and Charlotte would supervise every piece of furniture that was uncrated and placed in the hotel. He wasn't sure how she'd react to him this morning. Yesterday had been full of good news and unexpected surprises. Would she regret sharing her feelings with him? Nathan hoped not, but he would be cautious in how he approached her.

At the top of the landing, he checked his watch. There was just enough time for a quick breakfast. When he walked into the kitchen, Michael and Sarah were at the table with Charlotte.

Sarah bounced in her chair. "Are you ready, Mr. Nathan? I'm excited. Charlotte says there's lot of new things for all over the hotel. It's gonna be all fancy and new." She took a drink of her milk. "I like fancy."

"I am ready." He smiled at her. "What about you, Michael? Are you ready to work with me? I'm going to need a lot of help."

Michael nodded and took a big bite of a biscuit at the same time.

Nathan went to the stove and chatted with Mrs. Atkins while he loaded his plate from the bowls of fried potatoes, scrambled eggs and bacon. He added two biscuits to the top of the plate and returned to the table.

He stood across from Charlotte. "May I join you?" He waited for her to look up. A lovely shade of pink stained her cheeks. He was thrilled to know it was there because of him, but he wouldn't embarrass her. Mornings were his best time of day, but he took care to keep his tone and demeanor calm for her sake.

Charlotte nodded, and he sat down. "I'm glad we organized the crates at the livery last night. It will be easy to arrange one room at a time." He tore a biscuit into two pieces. "Three rooms of furnishings should fit on a wagon. Even with six men coming to help, the process could take the rest of the week."

"I've spoken to Nora and the other maid. They've stripped the linens from the first room and will be ready to make up the room as soon as the furnishings are in place. I thought it would be helpful if they worked quickly behind the men. They'll clean the other rooms while they wait on each of the newly furnished rooms to be ready for them."

"That's an excellent plan. I'll only be a few minutes." He picked up his coffee mug. "You'll see real changes by the end of the day, Charlotte. I hope you'll be pleased."

She met his gaze for a brief moment. "If the change of the curtains in the dining room is any indication, I'm sure I'll love it." Her mouth twitched as if fighting a smile before she looked away.

He could resist no longer. They couldn't speak openly because of the children, but he had to make some mention of the night before or he would never be able to concentrate on his work today. "So, you're happy with the changes that took place in the restaurant last evening?"

Charlotte darted her eyes in his direction, and the smile she'd been resisting made an appearance. "Very happy."

He nodded. "Good. I wanted you to be pleased." Nathan said a silent prayer of thanks for Charlotte's happiness.

He finished his breakfast, and they all went to work. The day passed quickly. He managed the crew of men who broke open the crates in the back of the wagon and hoisted the heavy furnishings up the stairs.

Charlotte handled the daily needs of the hotel. She made sure the maids were on task and took care of their departing and arriving guests. There was even time for her to step onto the porch and see almost every piece of furniture before it was carried into the hotel.

By late afternoon, the September sun had risen to a scorching heat, and the men they'd hired were almost done in.

Nathan called Charlotte and the children onto the porch when the men opened the final crate for the day.

Charlotte stepped onto the porch. "I only have a minute. There are a couple of things I need to help Nora with."

He smiled up at her from the back of the wagon. "I wanted you all to see what's in this last crate." He leaned close to the porch rail and spoke to the children. "It was important to your parents that you each have something special from their trip to Dallas."

"It won't make me sad?" Sarah backed up and clung to Charlotte's skirts.

"I promise it won't. This is something your parents wanted you to have. It's a gift from them to you. You'd never be sad about your momma and pa giving you a gift. It's like a big surprise." He hadn't known what to say, but that must have been the right thing. Charlotte mouthed her thanks to him over Sarah's head.

"A surprise! I love surprises!" Sarah danced on the porch with her doll.

"Good. The first surprise is for you." Nathan slid the lid off one end of the crate. "I was standing in the store with your momma and pa when your pa saw this bed. He wanted you to have it."

Sarah leaned over the rail of the porch and squealed her delight. "It's so pretty!" She jumped up and down and squealed again. "I love the flowers!"

Nathan reached out and lifted Sarah over the railing

and set her in the wagon. She rubbed her hand along the carved flowers on the corners of the headboard.

She turned to look up at him. "Will you put it in my room so I can sleep on it tonight?"

The joy in her eyes was contagious. It whisked away the fatigue of the long day. "I will."

He set her back on the porch. "Now it's Michael's turn."

Nathan pushed the wooden cover almost off the crate. Michael leaned forward and saw the corner of a writing desk. "Your pa told me you were a smart young man. He said he wanted you to have a desk so you could study in your room. He knew you'd work hard in school so you could be a fine hotelier when you're a man."

Michael's jaw dropped. "I don't know another boy with his own desk. Only bankers and agents and such got a desk." He squared his shoulders. "Mr. Nathan, I won't be able to help you with the rest of the crates you'll be bringing to the hotel. I've got to go to school tomorrow so the teacher can send me home some work to do on my new desk. I wanna make Pa proud."

Tears streamed down Charlotte's face, and she hugged Michael. "What lovely gifts you both have."

Nathan made a clicking noise with his tongue. "We'll have no tears, Miss Charlotte. Your momma picked out something nice for you." He slid the lid off the crate, and it banged against the side of the wagon.

In the far end of the large crate, he pointed to a cedar chest complete with carvings of grapes and vines on the corners.

Charlotte pulled a handkerchief from her skirt

pocket and wiped away her tears. "It's lovely. I've never seen anything so fine."

"Let's allow these gentlemen to carry these pieces into your rooms. Charlotte, will you please direct them?"

Once the final pieces were in place, Nathan sent the men away with a reminder to be earlier the following morning. Perhaps the heat wouldn't be as hard on them if they were able to do more work earlier in the day.

Charlotte walked into the lobby as the men were leaving. "Nathan, the children are overjoyed with their gifts. How wonderful that you were able to tell us the story behind each choice."

Nathan opened his notebook. He wanted to mark off the rooms that had been completed, and he needed a moment to compose his thoughts before he looked at Charlotte. She was standing beside him as she often did. But now that she'd revealed a glimpse of her soul to him, he was keenly aware of her every move. It would be difficult to turn to her and not reach out to touch her hair or her face. Even to hold her hand.

He put a pencil in the page of the notebook. He was able to turn to her and drink in the sight of her without closing the distance between them.

"Your parents were so excited that day. They'd taken their time to pick pieces for every room of the hotel. They knew the renovations would take up most of their funds, but they didn't want the three of you to feel as though the business was more important to them than you were. I am grateful that I could bring you those last few memories."

"The memories are as much of a treasure as the gifts." She smiled. This time there were no tears. It was good to see her remembering them without the horrible grief that had weighed on them all when he'd first come to Gran Colina.

He couldn't help himself. He reached for her hand. The softness of her skin against his was like dew on rose petals. The dew clung to the petals, but was light and enhanced the beauty of the flower without harming it. She was softness and sweetness. And joy and fun. All in a stubborn skin that protected her from harm.

"I'm glad."

She smiled at him and slid her hand from his. "I need to help the children. Michael is putting things in the drawer of his desk, and I promised Sarah I'd put her linens on her bed."

"What about you, Charlotte? Do you have anything to tuck into your cedar chest? Some treasure that only your heart knows perhaps."

"My treasure can't be seen or captured, and it's too big for a cedar chest." She took a step back. "I hope we'll see you at supper."

"You can count on it." He watched her close the door to her parlor and turned back to the registration desk. No amount of effort helped him remember what he had been doing before Charlotte came to talk to him.

Chapter Fourteen

"Hurry up, kids. We don't want to be late for church." Charlotte checked the picnic basket on the kitchen table one final time. Nathan had suggested they all return to the hotel and change out of their Sunday best following the service. Then they could head to the river for a picnic and enjoy the afternoon together.

Five minutes later Michael came into the parlor. "I'm ready. Can I go see if Mr. Nathan is ready to go?"

"Yes. I'll fetch Sarah, and we'll meet you in the lobby."

Sarah had dropped her doll behind her new bed and slid underneath to retrieve it. The result was a dusty dress and a recovered doll. It took Charlotte several minutes to help her change into a clean dress that matched the ribbons on her braids.

"Let's go." Charlotte took her by the hand and led her into the lobby.

Nathan was there with Michael. Mrs. Atkins was at the reception desk this morning. One of the changes in the hotel staffing that Charlotte liked the best was that several people alternated the duties on Sundays, so no one missed more than one service per month.

Charlotte let go of Sarah's hand and reminded Mrs. Atkins that they'd return for their picnic things and be gone for the rest of the day.

"Don't you worry about a thing, Miss Charlotte. Mrs. Baxter is in the kitchen, and we planned a simple lunch. It's simmering on the stove and will be tender and delicious by the time folks are back from church. I'm so grateful for the new bits and pieces your folks were kind enough to purchase. Preparing the meals is a lot easier than it was before."

"I'm glad Momma was there to choose things. Pa would never have known what to buy. I especially like the new pots and bowls. They're so big. It will really help when we're hosting the meetings like the one for Mr. Thornhill next month."

"You should have seen Mrs. Baxter when she was helping me this morning. She was making such a fuss over all the new things. It's made coming to work a pleasure." Mrs. Atkins laughed at her words. "Not that it wasn't before, but it's always nice to have new things." She smiled at Charlotte. "You all go and enjoy yourself. You've worked so hard, and it's past time you had some fun." Mrs. Atkins smiled at Charlotte and raised her eyebrows in Nathan's direction.

Was the woman hinting that she had noticed a change in Charlotte's relationship with Nathan? She hoped not. The feelings she had for him were new. She needed time to pray and ponder them before anyone else chimed in with their opinion.

She shooed the children out the door of the hotel

and stepped down to the street for the short walk to Gran Colina Church.

Nathan spoke softly from close behind her. "May I join you?"

She started and gasped. "I'm sorry. Of course. I was so distracted by Sarah being late that I'm a bit scattered this morning." Nathan walked in step beside her, and the kids walked ahead of them.

He leaned in to speak. "You look lovely this morning."

"Thank you." She lifted a gloved hand to adjust the bow that held her hat in place and peeked at him from under the brim. "I like that suit best of all the ones you wear."

Nathan smoothed the lapels of his coat. "Me, too." They neared the churchyard. "Would you like me to sit on the other side of the church today?"

"Do you want to?"

"No, but you made yourself very clear the last time we were here that Sarah was the one who invited me and not you."

She smirked when he leaned forward to look into her eyes. "You know that was a long time ago."

"Not so very long." He was going to force her to admit she wanted him near her. She understood. In his shoes, she'd do the same thing.

"Well, if you can't see that things have changed a bit since the last time we were in church together, I'll have to say an extra prayer for you today."

"So you want me to sit with you?" His eyes danced with teasing laughter.

"You may if you like." Charlotte quickened her pace and arrived at the door of the church several steps ahead of him. She settled the children into their usual bench and took a seat near the end of the row. Nathan came to stand by her.

"Miss Green, may I sit with you and the children this morning?" He spoke in a normal tone, and a hush fell on the room that had been filled with chatter.

Charlotte could feel the heat fill her face. Before the last few days, she'd have thought Nathan's words were meant to provoke her. Not anymore. She lifted her head and met his gaze. "You may, Mr. Taylor."

Cyrus and Ethel Busby occupied the bench in front of her. Cyrus glanced over his shoulder at Charlotte and leaned to whisper in his wife's ear. Ethel shushed him and put a hand against his cheek to turn him toward the front of the room.

Charlotte didn't see Cyrus's response. Her attention centered on Nathan and how much space he took up on the bench. She slid Sarah nearer to Michael and moved toward them, but was still so close to Nathan that she knew God would have to help her or she'd never remember a word of the sermon. How, in a matter of a few weeks, had he gone from being someone she didn't want to be in the room with to being someone who stood out in the midst of a room as if no one else was there?

The service began and everyone stood for the songs and sat for the sermon. Reverend Gillis preached a fervent message on caring for others. Michael and Sarah, warned that the picnic could be canceled if they misbehaved, sat still and quiet.

But Charlotte fidgeted. She toyed with the buttons on her lace gloves and tied her reticule more than once. She reached for the hymnbook, but Nathan captured her hand in his. In an instant her restlessness vanished. He rested the back of his hand on the seat between them and his long fingers closed around her hand. She sat on the bench her family had occupied for her entire life and allowed a man to hold her hand during a service. Some would call it scandalous. Charlotte thought it sweet. He didn't caress or attempt to distract her, but the security of his grasp offered comfort.

The words of the sermon broke through her former nervousness. When the service ended, she felt more refreshed in spirit than she had since her parents died.

Reverend Gillis prayed the closing prayer and everyone made their way out of the church. Rena came up to Charlotte.

"How are you doing?" Rena shifted her baby from her arms to rest against her shoulder.

"We're getting a bit better each day." Charlotte patted the baby's back. "Cordelia is growing."

"She is. Scott can't believe how quickly."

The sheriff joined them and took his daughter from Rena. "Come see your pa, little one." He tucked the baby into the crook of his arm and made funny sounds and faces at her.

Charlotte didn't want to be jealous of her friend's happy family, but a part of her had always wanted a husband and babies. It didn't seem like it was possible for her with the responsibility of the hotel and her siblings, but maybe God was doing something for her and Nathan. She hoped so.

After a short chat, Rena and Scott left her and the kids. Nathan joined them. "Are you ready?"

"I am!" Michael grinned. "I wanna get in the river. It's so hot I wanna go swimming."

"I don't know how to swim." Sarah put her hand in Nathan's and tugged. "Will you sit on the quilt with me and tell me a story? Pa always told the best stories."

Nathan nodded. "We best be on our way if we're going to do all the two of you have planned."

Charlotte followed Nathan and the kids back to the hotel. Michael and Sarah chatted with him the entire time. If they annoyed Nathan, he never showed it.

In short order they had all changed clothes and walked to the river. Charlotte and Sarah spread out the quilt and pulled their food from the basket while Nathan and Michael walked down to the edge of the water.

She let Sarah have a slice of bread while they waited on Nathan and Michael to join them.

"Charlotte, do you like Mr. Nathan?"

"He's a very nice man. Yes, I like him."

"I mean do you like him like I like Archie Sherman?"

Charlotte refused to smile at the sweet thought of Sarah being taken with the little boy who lived across the street from the hotel. "That all depends. How do you like Archie? Like a friend who plays tag at school during recess?"

"Like that." Sarah played with her doll. "But only I don't like when he tries to pull my hair."

Nathan and Michael walked up the hill and sat under the large tree with them. A gentle breeze stirred the oak leaves, and several translucent clouds floated across the blue skies. The combination was a welcome break from the scorching sun they'd endured for the last many months.

Nathan snagged a piece of bread from the basket on the quilt. "Who is pulling your hair?"

Michael answered for her. "Archie does it. He says he's only playing, but I told him not to do it anymore, or I'll have to punch him in the stomach."

Charlotte was surprised by Michael's protective defense of their sister. "Michael, you mustn't hit."

"Pa wouldn't let some boy hurt Sarah. He'd tan his hide." Michael took a slice of bread.

"He wouldn't allow someone to harm Sarah, but he wouldn't want you to fight."

Nathan spoke up again. "Sarah, did he hurt you?"

She spread her doll's skirt out on the quilt. "Not really. He said he's just playing. But I don't think it's fair. Boys don't have braids we can pull."

Nathan caught Charlotte's attention and wordlessly asked her permission to address the situation. She nodded. Listening to Nathan tell Sarah what to do with a boy who acted like Nathan had when they were schoolchildren would be interesting.

"If he's told you he's playing, and he's not hurting you, he may be telling you the truth. He may want to be your friend."

"Then he shouldn't pull my hair." Sarah laughed what she considered to be a silly notion.

"You're right." Nathan glanced at Charlotte. "But sometimes boys don't know that. You have to tell them."

"You mean just tell him to quit?" Michael didn't like this idea.

"Yes, but Sarah has to tell him."

"Okay. I'll tell him." Sarah picked up her bread.

"Can we eat the picnic now? I want more than just bread."

Charlotte helped Michael and Sarah with their food. "If you eat a good lunch, I made a treat for after."

"I like treats." Michael bit into his chicken leg.

"So do I." Nathan took another piece of bread.

"Then I think you'll all be pleased." Charlotte pulled a platter from the basket and unwrapped the towel that hid its contents. "I decided to put Momma's tea cakes back on the menu, so I made a big batch last night."

"I'm gonna eat all my food, 'cause I want two tea cakes." Michael took another bite of his chicken.

"Yummy!" Sarah was as eager as Michael.

The kids jumped up and ran to play in the deep grass along the water's edge.

"Don't try to swim before I get down there." Nathan leaned back on his elbows and watched them play.

"You don't have to take Michael swimming. He can go another day." Charlotte packed the remains of their meal into the basket.

"It'll be fun. I haven't been swimming in ages." He pointed to a bend in the river. "We used to come to this very spot and swim on summer afternoons."

"You have pleasant memories of your life in Gran Colina."

"I do. That's one reason I jumped at the opportunity to return."

Charlotte finished putting everything away and turned to him. "Were there other reasons?"

He nodded. "I wanted to better myself in my work, and I wanted a fresh start somewhere other than Dallas."

"Were there bad memories there?" Charlotte hoped he hadn't been unhappy.

"Losing my mother was the worst of it. But, in time, that part of me healed." He looked at his watch. "Would you and Sarah like to head back?"

It seemed there were other memories he didn't want to share. She supposed he was entitled to his private thoughts. She'd have to adjust her expectations of wanting to know everything about him with the reality that everyone had things they wanted to put behind them.

"Sure. Will you bring the quilt when you come? I can manage the basket, but Sarah would struggle with the quilt." She got to her feet and called to her sister that it was time to go.

"Leave it all here. Michael and I will take care of it." He stood and reached for her hand. It was the sort of thing he'd begun to do in the last week. "Thank you for a lovely afternoon." He released her and walked down to the river.

Charlotte and Sarah went back to the hotel at a pace that enabled the child to keep up. She fell across her bed without argument when they arrived home.

For the first time in a long time, Charlotte felt almost as carefree as Sarah. She wasn't, but the load she carried was lessened by Nathan's help. No one could have made her believe she would adapt to her new situation and learn so much in six short weeks. Maybe not short weeks. Some days seemed to go on forever and others, like today, were gone before she was ready to release them. The hard days were getting farther apart. It gave her hope for the future.

She was beginning to care for him, but was it wise?

She curled up in the corner of the settee to ponder her newfound emotions about Nathan and promptly fell asleep.

Nathan had Michael carry the quilt to the back porch so it could be cleaned the next day. He put the basket on the table in the kitchen and would have emptied it, but Mrs. Atkins and Mrs. Baxter insisted that they had caught up on their duties and needed something to do.

"Let's get you back to your residence. I'm thinking after a busy afternoon like we had, you'll be needing to rest."

"I'm a big boy. I don't need naps anymore." A giant yawn escaped him.

"I'm a man, and I like a good nap sometimes." Nathan put a hand on his shoulder. "Thank you for taking me swimming."

"We can go again whenever you want. Charlotte don't like to go. She says it gets her hair all wet. And Sarah don't know how."

"Maybe one day Charlotte can teach Sarah. We'll go again soon." Nathan waited while Michael entered the parlor, and then he went upstairs to his room.

Over the weeks he'd settled into the attic room. It was clean and large enough for all of his things. He sat at the table and opened his Bible. He had a lot to think and pray about.

Today was the most enjoyable day he'd had in years. The September heat didn't even dampen his pleasure. The picnic and the swim had been nice, but Charlotte's company had been his favorite thing about it.

Holding her hand in church while they listened to

the sermon together, sharing lunch with her and the kids, and coming home with the knowledge that she was here. Those were joys that couldn't be measured.

The future of the hotel was still uncertain in spite of their efforts. As a man he needed to make a good wage to provide for himself, but he'd rather live in an attic at Green's Grand Hotel than be away from Charlotte ever again.

Lord, let the work be enough to save the hotel for Charlotte and her siblings. It means so much to them. And to me.

The realization that he was falling in love with her hit him hard in the center of his chest.

Chapter Fifteen

On Monday morning, Charlotte nestled into the corner of the settee and savored her tea. When Nathan's familiar knock tapped a tune on the door to the lobby, she slipped her feet onto the floor and sat up straight. "Come in."

The door opened, and Nathan stuck his head into the room. His creased brow worried her. "You need to come to the desk."

"Is everything okay?" She put her cup on the table beside her.

His lips tightened, and a knot formed in her middle. He slipped into the parlor and pushed the door closed. He never shut the door when they were alone together. The children were in the kitchen, but it was still something he never did.

"I'm very concerned."

"What is it? The children haven't left for school yet." She stood and wrung her hands together. She saw no sign of Nathan's persistent confidence. He was always confident.

"Mr. Eaton is back."

"Why is that a bad thing? He stayed in a nice room and paid his bill. I'd think you'd be glad of guests like him."

"He's returned with the land agent. Something seems amiss to me."

Michael followed Sarah into the parlor. "We finished our breakfast, but Sarah only wants to play with her doll. I want to go to school early."

Nathan cast a glance over his shoulder. "We really need to deal with this matter now, Charlotte."

She tapped her finger on her cheek. "You may leave for school now. Both of you, gather your things. Then take Sarah with you. I need the two of you to be very good while I go into the lobby with Nathan. We have important business to discuss, and I won't be able to handle it like Pa would want if I have to see about the two of you. Can you do that for me?"

Michael glared at Nathan. "What's wrong?"

Nathan studied Michael for a moment as if deciding how much to tell the young boy. There couldn't be much to tell. Nathan had barely given her any details.

"There is nothing going on that you need to worry about. Charlotte can handle it."

Michael's glare intensified. "Are you sure?"

"Man to man, I promise." Nathan met Michael's stare with a calm and even manner. "I'll never lie to you."

Charlotte wanted to hug Nathan for treating Michael's concern with such seriousness. It was difficult for the little ones. Many adults tended to dismiss them. Nathan had taken to acknowledging their questions and answering with honesty. Kindness tempered his words, but he never belittled or ignored Michael or Sarah. The three of them had formed a strong bond.

The children headed off to finish their preparations for school, and Charlotte turned to Nathan. "Let's go see what Mr. Eaton and the land agent want."

Davis Conrad had been the land agent in Gran Colina for as long as Charlotte could remember. He stood next to Mr. Eaton on the opposite side of the registration desk and fidgeted. The man was never still.

"Mr. Eaton, Mr. Conrad." Charlotte greeted the two men. "How may I help you this morning?"

Mr. Conrad jumped in before Mr. Eaton could utter a word. "We're here to help you."

The front door opened, and Thomas Freeman entered. His smug expression didn't sit well with Charlotte. The knot in her stomach tightened.

Mr. Freeman approached the desk. "Ah, I see we're all here."

Charlotte was glad that Nathan stood beside her. He inched closer.

"Gentlemen, you seem to have Miss Green and me at a disadvantage."

Thomas Freeman stepped into the middle of the group. "I'm about to remedy that for you, little lady."

"Remedy what, Mr. Freeman?" She didn't like the arrogance of his statement.

Mr. Freeman pointed at Mr. Eaton. "Mr. Eaton here works for Turner Hotels."

"He does?" Charlotte spun to look at Nathan. Why hadn't he told her? "I was unaware, Mr. Eaton. Did you know Mr. Taylor in Dallas?" She held her hand out to indicate Nathan and watched the guest with a keen eye in search of any sign of recognition.

"No. I met him on the train when I came to town on my last visit."

Charlotte sensed something was afoot. Mischief? Omission of some important truth.

She wasn't one to dillydally. "Please, someone, do tell me what the nature of this visit is." She crossed her arms. Skepticism filled her every pore. She knew she wasn't going to like what she was about to hear.

"Allow me to explain." Mr. Eaton didn't move forward like Mr. Freeman had. It seemed the man who represented Turner Hotels felt no need to push. He'd stayed with them for almost two weeks, and not once had Charlotte felt him imposing himself on others. Did an ulterior motive guide his actions? "I was sent to Gran Colina by my employer for the purpose of determining whether or not this town would be a suitable place to establish one of our hotels. Mr. Turner was very specific in his request that I discover the profitability of the area based on the success of your particular establishment, Miss Green."

Nathan bowed up at the revelation. "Why would Mr. Turner send you to this specific hotel? He usually goes into a new town and builds on a vacant property. He did it time and again while I was in his employ. I have never known him to spy on the competition, unless he wanted—"

Charlotte looked at Nathan. "Wanted to what?"

Mr. Freeman broke his silence. "Unless he wanted to purchase the property. Mr. Turner prefers to go into a community and eliminate the competition." He looked across the lobby. "Even if that competition is really no competition at all."

Charlotte started to get the big picture. "Mr. Conrad, why are you a part of this meeting?"

"You know I do my best as land agent for Gran Colina. This is a perfect opportunity to promote growth in our fine community. A hotel that belongs to Turner Hotels will give Gran Colina an appeal like none we've known before. We may not ever achieve the success of a city the size of Dallas, but we'll be set for sure if we embrace businesses like Turner Hotels. It can change us forever to have them locate here."

"But the town doesn't own this property. I do."

Mr. Freeman raised his hand. "Well, Miss Green, if we're going to talk about ownership, the bank owns the largest portion of Green's Grand Hotel."

She felt the color drain from her face. "Are you saying you're considering selling my note to Turner Hotels?"

"It's not a consideration. I'm in negotiations with Turner Hotels to sell the entire property to them."

"You can't do that! It isn't right. You gave me your word, and we've made all these changes with the money Pa borrowed from you. We're going to be able to pay the note." Charlotte tried to keep from screeching, but her voice rose with every word.

Nathan put his hand on her arm. "Don't let's get ahead of ourselves here. Mr. Conrad, explain what you're saying."

"I'm saying that Mr. Eaton and I have arranged for the purchase by Turner Hotels of the land beside Green's Grand Hotel."

Charlotte leaned forward, and Nathan squeezed her

arm. She didn't know if he was supporting her or trying to keep her from standing up for herself and her siblings. "And you want to sell them my hotel?" She pointed at Mr. Freeman.

Mr. Eaton answered her. "That is the purpose of my return to Gran Colina." The man seemed oblivious to her outrage. At any moment she would make it plain to him and everyone else in the lobby. "I'm here to offer the full asking price that Mr. Freeman has quoted me. Also, because of the good impression you made on me during my stay here, Miss Green, I'm prepared to offer you this check." He slid a check across the desk for her to see. The amount was substantial. It was more money than she'd ever imagined having in her possession at one time.

But that money wouldn't provide for her and the children in the coming years. They would be fine for a while if she accepted, but their parents had planned for the coming generations.

She pushed the check back to him. "You underestimate the value of my establishment, Mr. Eaton."

"I assure you that this is more money than anyone else will ever give you for this place. And once there is a Turner Hotel next door, you won't be able to keep your doors open. No one will opt for a quaint inn when they can stay in the finest accommodations for less money. The only reason we want to purchase your property is to remodel it as the restaurant and meeting facilities for our new property. Of course, the staff will have to be brought up to the standards of a Turner Hotel."

Mr. Conrad looked at her. "It was my hope that you'd be open to keeping your hotel as a local business, Miss

Green. When you let your stubborn pride keep you from considering Junior's generous offer to court you, you gave me no choice but to see the benefits of the offer from Turner Hotels. You've shown your inability to make wise decisions for yourself and this business. A young woman like you should be married and caring for little ones—not trying to hold on to something she can't possibly understand. Consider this offer carefully. Mr. Eaton is telling you the truth. The money his company is willing to pay for the adjoining property will help Gran Colina make a great start on building the new structures the mayor and sheriff spoke of during the elections this year."

Charlotte's mind reeled with the way the land agent addressed her. He gave her no consideration for any business knowledge. She countered his argument. "The properties will help build and grow *my* business. The town hall for a start. I've spoken to the mayor about it." Nathan cleared his throat. "Mr. Taylor and I spoke to him weeks ago."

Mr. Conrad continued to spout off his reasons for agreeing with Mr. Eaton. "There will even be enough money to build the town square in the center of town. It'll be a fine gathering place for the people of Gran Colina." He spoke as if the entire project had been his idea.

Charlotte shook her head. "You are all mistaken if you think there is one scintilla of hope that I'll sell this place. I will not. Not to Turner Hotels, not to you, Mr. Freeman. Not to anyone. My name is on the sign. This is my father's legacy, and I will not let it go."

Mr. Eaton turned to Nathan as if her impassioned speech were pointless. "Mr. Turner is prepared to offer you a position in management at the Turner Hotel of Gran Colina. It will include a significant raise over the salary you enjoyed in your previous position with Turner Hotels." He handed an envelope to Nathan. "These are the details of his offer. You'll find that he's expressed his wishes to forget any past squabbles that contributed to your exit from his employ. He holds no grudge against you in regard to Miss Turner, who is now engaged to a prominent businessman in Dallas."

Charlotte's head was spinning. "Wait." She held up her hands. "Mr. Eaton, you are offering Mr. Taylor the run of my hotel?"

"Yes. But in reality, it will no longer be your hotel. We are offering him the job of running this establishment while we build our hotel next door. Then we will convert this building in accordance with our needs." He looked around at the new curtains. "I will say the place is improved, even if it's not up to the Turner standards of excellence."

She could listen to no more. "You may all go. There is nothing else to discuss. Every one of you must leave my hotel immediately."

Nathan tucked the envelope from Mr. Eaton into his pocket, and her heart sank. The closeness of their friendship crumbled with any imaginations that more could come from the meager beginnings they'd shared in recent days. The thought that it could all have been a ruse flashed across her mind. She tried to press it down. Not to entertain it. As angry as she was in this moment, she did not want to think she had misjudged Nathan's character to that extent. But the envelope in his pocket spoke of his intentions.

Thomas Freeman pointed his finger at her. "This is not your decision to make, Miss Green."

"Yes, it is. And I won't be bullied like a schoolgirl into whatever works for the lot of you." If they didn't leave, she might not be able to hold her tongue.

Mr. Conrad grumbled. "I don't have time to waste with a silly lass who has no business as a proprietor. Junior is better off without you. He deserves someone who'll appreciate him."

It took all her strength not to ask if Junior's value to a woman would ever include a work ethic.

The three men headed for the door.

"Just a moment." A sudden question came to Charlotte. "Mr. Eaton, you and Mr. Taylor arrived in Gran Colina on the same train. When were you hired to come here?"

His smug face made her angrier than she'd been in a long time, but she needed to know. "I have been in the employ of the Turner Family for many years. It is my job to assess their expansion into new towns."

"But when were you told to come to Gran Colina to target my hotel?"

He twisted his mouth in a thoughtful pose. "I'd say a couple of days before I arrived. I'd been working on a property near the coast in the south of Texas. A telegram came to my hotel there, and I journeyed straight to Gran Colina on completion of that assignment."

Charlotte turned to Nathan. "And you had no idea of any of this?"

"None." His face was open and his eyes clear, but could she trust him?

She was surrounded by men who wanted her property. At least the men from Gran Colina who'd come calling as suitors had wanted her, too. If she'd accepted the courtship of one of those men, she might not feel so alone at this moment.

"And you, Mr. Freeman. When did you offer to sell my hotel?"

He ran a finger under the collar of his shirt. "I don't recall the exact date. It was a recent development." He stiffened. "One reinforced by your stubbornness."

"You gave me six weeks. You stood in this lobby on the seventh day of last month. And told me to make the improvements my parents borrowed the money for. I have made those improvements and even accepted the help of Mr. Taylor—on your insistence. I will visit Sheriff Braden today and apprise him of your attempts to coerce me to leave this property. Do not underestimate my determination. You may hold the note my father signed, but you do not hold my future."

"We'll see who holds what, Miss Green. You are in over your head in this venture. I will not risk the soundness of my bank on your emotions and sentimentality." Mr. Freeman turned and led the other men out of the hotel.

Mr. Eaton stopped at the door. "Mr. Taylor, I'll need your answer by noon tomorrow. I had hoped to stay here, but I don't think it would be advisable given the circumstances. I shall expect to return and make this my temporary home when the purchase of the hotel is complete." He nodded at Charlotte. "Good day to you." And he left.

Charlotte ground her teeth and balled her hands into fists.

Nathan launched into a speech. "Charlotte, I had no idea of any of this."

Mrs. Atkins came out of the restaurant. "Miss Charlotte, can you make time to talk with me this morning? I'd like to finalize some of the menus for Mr. Thornhill's meeting."

Charlotte took a deep breath. And then another.

Mrs. Atkins looked at Nathan and then back at Charlotte. "Is anything wrong?"

"Everything is wrong, Mrs. Atkins. Everything that could possibly be wrong is wrong." Charlotte couldn't think. She didn't know what to do. But she needed to act fast.

"Is there anything I can do?" Concern filled Mrs. Atkins's face.

"Perhaps you could create a menu that you think will work. You've done an excellent job with everything else. I'll try to go over it with you in a day or so."

"I'll be glad to do that. Please let me know if there's anything else I can do for you."

"You can pray for me. I need God's help. And wisdom."

Mrs. Atkins reached out and grasped her hand. "I will. God promises to answer any time we ask for wisdom." She left Charlotte with Nathan.

He spoke as soon as Mrs. Atkins closed the restaurant door. "Let's put our heads together and see what we can do. I think you're right about going to the sheriff. There is probably a law about Mr. Freeman keeping his word to you. That gives us one week."

"No. It gives me one week." She pointed at his coat pocket. "You have until tomorrow to decide if you want to return to Turner Hotels. I will decide what to do about my hotel."

"Let me help you." He reached out as she passed him, but she dodged his attempt to stop her.

"I don't think so, Nathan. Not after the people you worked for when my parents were talking to you in Dallas have come here to buy the hotel you showed up to fix." She spun on her heel. "Were you in on Mr. Freeman's plan? Did the two of you enjoy a hearty laugh at how naive I am? It must have been fun to watch me go from distraught daughter to hopeful hotel owner, knowing the entire time that you'd end up with my hotel." Her mind reeled like a child lost in the middle of the floor at a spirited barn dance. She wasn't sure she'd ever trust anyone again.

"That's not true, Charlotte. I would never do that to you." Hurt filled his eyes.

It might not be fair, but it was a rational conclusion given what she'd learned today. Those men all knew how vulnerable she was, and they'd conspired together to take advantage of her.

"And you let me hope for things." She shook her head and took another step away from him. "I don't know what to think. I need to talk to the sheriff and consider all that's happened this morning."

"I'll watch the desk and make certain everything here runs as scheduled." He lowered his head to look into her eyes. "If you want me to."

"You may as well. If I can't stop this, you'll be running it all before long." She went into her rooms for her reticule and her father's journal. If there was any way to save her hotel, she had to find it. And find it quickly.

Nathan couldn't have been more surprised to learn that Mr. Eaton worked for the Turner family.

He looked at his watch. Charlotte had been gone for two hours. Would she fire him as soon as she returned? If her state of mind didn't change, he could be out of a job before the day ended.

He pored over his notes and tried to think of a solution. If he could find a way to keep Mr. Freeman from selling the hotel to Mr. Turner, then maybe Turner Hotels wouldn't buy the adjacent land. How could he persuade Mr. Freeman? The man had brought Nathan to Gran Colina under false pretenses. A man like that would be focused on his personal gain, and Nathan had nothing to offer.

Nathan was still at the desk that afternoon, absorbed in his work, when he felt a tug on the end of his suit coat and looked down to see Sarah.

"Why do you look so sad?" Sarah asked. Her blond curls and knitted brow were at odds with one another. Such cuteness shouldn't be marred by worry.

"I didn't mean to look sad." He went down on one knee in front of her and forced a smile. "Is that better?"

She dropped her head to one side and pulled her lips into her mouth. "I don't think so. Your eyes aren't smiling. Only your mouth." Her tiny hand came up to rest on his shoulder. "It's okay to be sad. But you shouldn't be sad all by yourself. Charlotte taught me that."

"Your sister is a good teacher." The smile he gave Sarah this time was genuine.

"That's better." She smiled back. "But you need to get someone to help you not be sad. Charlotte helped me. She could help you, too."

Sarah's kindness was just the thing he needed for his soul. In the last few weeks, he'd dared to imagine the possibility of a future with Charlotte and her siblings. Any inkling of hope had died with Mr. Eaton's return. No matter how he tried to convince Charlotte that he hadn't been in on some scheme to buy her hotel, she'd always wonder.

"You're very kind, Sarah. I think God may be the One to help me with this sadness."

"That's a good idea. Charlotte said God helped her to feel better in her heart." Sarah put her tiny hand over her heart. "She said sometimes it takes a long time, but Jesus can help you while you're waiting."

"Thank you." He stood as Michael joined them.

"We played tag during recess." He pointed over his shoulder at Sarah. "She played, too. She ain't bad for a girl."

Nathan tousled Michael's hair. "That sounds like a fun time."

He ushered them toward their residence. "Charlotte is out on some errands. Can you two take care of your homework until she gets back? It would be a big help to her."

"Can we have milk and cookies first?" Sarah asked. "You can come with us. Mrs. Baxter made fresh ones this morning."

"I can't leave the desk right now, but I'm sure if you go tell Mrs. Baxter that I sent you, she'd be happy to give you a snack."

Nathan caught Michael studying him. "What is it, Michael?"

"Is something happening? Charlotte is always here when we get home."

He wouldn't lie to the boy; nor would he tell more than a child needed to know. "Charlotte is very busy working on some business for the hotel. I'm sure she just lost track of time and will be home any minute. You go with Sarah and have cookies. I promise to send Charlotte to see you if she comes back before you finish eating."

Mrs. Atkins approached the registration desk. "Michael and Sarah just told me that Charlotte isn't here. Have you seen her since this morning? I've finished the menus, but I'm more concerned. Is she okay?"

"I pray so." He shrugged. "She hasn't returned from her errands."

Charlotte returned an hour later. She barely acknowledged him when she walked by the desk on the way into her parlor.

Nathan decided to break for something to eat. He'd forgone a meal at noon to keep working to find something that would help Charlotte keep the hotel. As much as he hated to do it, he put a sign on the desk for anyone who might happen by and went into the restaurant. Mrs. Atkins brought him a bowl of the stew she'd served for the lunch special.

He let her know Charlotte had returned and was with the children.

"Good. I worry about her. This hotel is quite a load for a young lady." She slid her hands into the pockets of her apron. "I hope I won't be wrong for saying so, but I don't think she'd have made it through the last weeks without your help."

"You're kind to think so, Mrs. Atkins. I'm not certain Charlotte would agree with you today, but I do appreciate you telling me."

Sheriff Braden entered the restaurant and lifted a hand in greeting to Nathan.

"Can I join you? I missed my lunch."

"Sure."

Nathan waited until Mrs. Atkins took the sheriff's order and returned to the kitchen. "Have you seen Charlotte?"

"Yes. And she is very upset."

"I was as surprised as she was when all those men arrived this morning."

"She isn't only upset with them." Scott Braden had moved to Gran Colina after Nathan had left town years ago with his family. He'd met the sheriff at church and a couple of times since his return, but Nathan didn't know Scott well. He'd witnessed the respect the townsfolk had for him. From the sternness of his tone, Nathan expected the man to be protective of Charlotte as his wife's best friend.

"She seemed unhappy with me when she left this morning, but I haven't done anything to deserve it." Once again he found himself in the middle of controversy with someone who held claim to ownership of his job. He should have learned from his experience with Viola Turner that trying to build anything other than a boss and employee relationship with a person whose name was on the sign outside could only bring him harm. Losing this job could hinder future opportunities. He thought about the envelope in his pocket. He hadn't opened it. Mr. Eaton had given Charlotte a reason to be suspicious of Nathan when he'd offered a job with Turner Hotels. The offer could very well be the sort of position he'd thought he would have when he arrived in Gran Colina. A lot had changed since that day. A lot about Green's Grand Hotel and about Charlotte Green. Nathan thought the biggest change had been in him. Having the best hotel in town and removing all hints of anything personal used to suit him.

Today, the strains of music from a windup box on a mantel in a small parlor soothed him more than he'd have imagined possible. Because that music played in a room filled with the people he'd come to love.

Helping Charlotte retain ownership was his best hope of attaining his dream of running a hotel. He hadn't read the offer from Mr. Turner, but he knew it wouldn't be as favorable to him as the way he and Charlotte worked together. She was his boss, but he was her teacher. The arrangement made them depend on one another. It had been the foundation of their blossoming relationship.

The sheriff accepted the plate Mrs. Atkins brought for him. She refilled Nathan's tea glass and went back to the kitchen.

Scott bowed his head in silent prayer and picked up his fork. "I do enjoy the roast here."

Nathan could wait no longer for any news of Charlotte's state of mind. "Can you tell me what you told Charlotte when she asked about the banker trying to sell the hotel before the end of the six weeks he promised her?"

"There's a good-faith expectancy among folk around here. Thomas Freeman gave his word." Scott took a long drink of his tea.

"She hoped for something like that to be a law. I heard him tell her how long he'd wait. She and I have been working as hard as two people can to get things in order."

"Mr. Freeman will likely say he's got the right to do as he pleases. It would be different if Charlotte had borrowed the money. Since it was her pa, and he put the hotel up for collateral, Mr. Freeman could make a good case for having the right to sell. He could argue that the bank could be exposed to financial risk if Charlotte doesn't make the payments in a timely manner."

Nathan pushed his plate to one side. The more the sheriff said, the less appetite Nathan had. "How do I deal with her?" He needed advice. "I know how to handle the hotel business. And I know how to deal with the people who want to buy the hotel. They're not the kind to accept her refusal. What I don't know is how to help her see that I'm on her side."

Scott studied him for a minute. "Are you? Really?"

"Of course I am. Why else would I stay here after she made it so plain she didn't need anyone's help? It's not easy to work with a woman who thinks your only goal is to take advantage of her and her family." He smiled at his memory of their first few days together. "Believe me, it took a fair amount of convincing for her to realize that wasn't true. My concern is that the men from this morning may have set her back to her previous opinions."

"She is a stubborn one." Scott chuckled. "I think that's why she and my Rena are such good friends. Those two are more determined than most people. Man or woman."

"So you know what I mean." Nathan pulled his plate back and decided he had best eat. He'd need all his strength to face Charlotte and the Turners' attempt to take over her property. Either obstacle would be a challenge. Both would require his utmost ability and the help of God. "I'll admit I thought I would be given full charge of the hotel when I arrived. In truth, Mr. Freeman made it out to me that he owned the place and had all authority to make the decision about my position here."

"You didn't count on a spunky young lady, did you?"

Nathan smiled at the thought of Charlotte. "With fire in her eyes." He nodded. "I knew Charlotte years ago. She intrigued me then."

"And now."

He shrugged. "I'd say the only thing that's different about her now is the fact that she's become more beautiful. I'm starting to understand that she is the most intriguing woman I'll ever know."

"But now she counts you as one of her enemies. That won't be easy to overcome. I don't envy you." Scott drained the last of the tea from his glass. "I will pray for you though. It'll likely take the help of the Almighty to find your way through this mess."

The sheriff left him with his thoughts. Thoughts that swirled around a beautiful lady and two young kids on their own in a world that threatened to swallow them up.

Nathan would help them. If it cost him his position at Green's Grand Hotel, so be it. If it kept him from a future with Turner Hotels, he didn't care. He'd do everything in his power, by the help of God, to erase the worry from Charlotte's brow. All he had to do was find a solution.

The peace that washed over him at the thought of helping Charlotte was followed by a jolt of surprise.

Why would he be willing to give up an unprecedented offer to return to the employ of Turner Hotels if it meant his future would be settled?

When had the security of Charlotte and her family become more important than his own?

The answers were no longer buried deep in his soul. They'd risen to the surface when the love he held for her filled his empty heart and spilled over like a flooded river.

Finding a way for Charlotte to keep the hotel was the right thing to do. The Bible was clear on matters concerning widows and orphans. These three orphans needed him.

The fact that he needed them wasn't something he would focus on today. Or maybe ever. Not if he didn't succeed.

Chapter Sixteen

Charlotte fastened the top button on her green dress. It was a glorious summer morning. She refused to let the challenges that lay ahead of her today keep her from appreciating the good things in her life. It boosted her spirits to wear her favorite dress. Memories of the day she and her mother had chosen the fabric pushed themselves into the front of her mind. They made her smile.

She could hear Sarah and Michael laughing in the parlor. It brought her great comfort that the children had healed to the point of laughter. Their days had settled to a somewhat normal routine.

Lord, please don't let them lose that childlike resilience. It was unimaginable to lose our folks. If we lose our home, too, I don't know what I'll do.

The reflection that stared back at her from the full-length mirror in the corner of her room wore every appearance of confidence. Only in her eyes did she see the doubt that warred in her gut.

Michael called to her through her bedroom door.

"Charlotte, Mr. Nathan is at the door. He wants to talk to you."

"I'll be out in a minute. Ask him to wait for me in the parlor." She smoothed her skirts and took a deep breath. She'd done her best to avoid Nathan after their encounter with Mr. Freeman, Mr. Eaton and the land agent yesterday. When their paths had crossed, they'd barely spoken or acknowledged each other. He'd probably come to tell her he would be accepting the offer to return to Turner Hotels. It was time to face him.

Knowing the day would be full, she'd asked Mrs. Atkins's daughter, Bertha, to see that the children had breakfast and made it to school on time. They were on their way to the restaurant kitchen when Charlotte entered the parlor.

Charlotte gestured to a chair near the fireplace. "Please have a seat, Nathan."

He looked as uncomfortable as she felt. The camaraderie they'd come to enjoy was gone. Awkward movements and avoided glances had taken its place.

Charlotte stood with her hands clasped in front of her to keep from wringing them together. She didn't want him to see how vulnerable she was at the moment. Maybe one day she'd be as strong as she'd been before her parents died, but today she longed for them to be here, guarding her from life's harsh realities.

"Charlotte, I'm so sorry—"

She held up one hand. "There's no need for you to apologize. You must do what you think is best for you." She lowered her hand. "Just as I must."

He seemed to be at a loss for words. Good.

Charlotte bristled at the effort it took to have this conversation. "I'm very busy, so if you have anything you need to say, please say it now. I don't have time to waste."

"Really? And exactly what are you going to be so busy doing?" A scowl replaced the lost look he'd worn a moment earlier.

"Saving my hotel from you and Turner Hotels. And Mr. Freeman and Mr. Conrad. And anyone else who thinks they can slither into Green's Grand Hotel and take it from me and my family."

"Slither in? Is that what you think I did?" He was on his feet now and stepped close to her. His chiseled features looked as if they were set in stone.

She jerked her chin up in a firm nod. "I do. All of you. I may be young, Nathan Taylor, but I'm not stupid. I'm fully prepared to run this place without you. You may go at your earliest convenience—and only return if the Turner's win. I warn you. I'll do everything in my power to keep that from happening. I've made an appointment with an attorney to insist that Mr. Freeman honor his word to me. You may expect to be summoned to his office any day. I pray you don't allow your eagerness to run this hotel to cloud your memory when he asks you to recall that discussion." She backed up a step, but he advanced as she did.

"You think I would lie?" He leaned in, and her breath caught in her throat. His blue eyes searched hers with a fierceness that warned her of his bridled emotions. She got no sense that he was trying to intimidate her, but that she'd wounded his pride.

"I don't know what to think anymore." She didn't. Two days ago, if he'd stood this close to her, the memory of their kiss would have flooded her mind. Even now, it pressed against the restraints of her determination to keep herself aloof from him.

"Well, think on this." He drew closer still, and the warmth of his gaze intensified. "I have never, in all the years I've known you, misled you. Not even as a young lad who didn't know how to share his new and mysterious feelings for a girl he thought he might fancy. My integrity is more important to me than an easy lie to gain control of a business. For some reason you've decided that I'm part of the group of men who were here yesterday and threatened your ownership of this establishment. Perhaps when all is said and done, you'll realize that I wasn't one of them. They caught me unawares, just as they did you." He gave the slightest shake of his head. "I'm going. I'll have my things out of the hotel within the hour."

He put a finger under her chin, and his eyes softened to the color of glowing blue embers. His touch was gentle. The fire that ran along her skin at the contact came in a rush. She leaned in without wanting to. It was as if her heart was in control of her reaction to him. The heart she knew she couldn't trust when it concerned men. Hadn't her mother warned her often enough that her choices lacked wisdom? There was a directness in his gaze that argued for her to see that he wasn't the man she'd all but accused him of being.

He caressed her cheek with his thumb. "Oh, Charlotte, you don't know what you're facing or how much you need my help. I wish I'd never caused you to doubt me when we were young. Maybe you'd trust me now. I pray God helps you. For your sake and for the children. If you decide you want my help, I'll be at my uncle's place." He dropped his hand. "Don't wait too long to make up your mind." He left her there, and the door to the lobby closed behind him.

After a long moment she drew in a deep breath and reached up to touch her face. The memory of his touch lingered on her skin. She dropped onto the settee and wondered if she'd just sent away the solution to her problems.

How could that be? He held the offer from Turner Hotels.

She twisted her hands together in her lap, hands that held nothing that could save her. She had nothing but her force of will.

Charlotte stood and headed into the lobby. By God's grace and help, she'd figure out a solution. Without a man. Of late, any contact she'd had with a man served only to confirm her mother's concerns.

An hour later, she watched Nathan walk out the front door of lobby. He turned and touched the brim of his hat before he disappeared from view.

A cold wind wrapped around her heart. The heat of the day did nothing to warm it.

On Sunday, Charlotte followed the children into the church for service. She was more fatigued than she'd been in the days and weeks after her parents' deaths when she'd had to bake and run the hotel alone. It wasn't a physical fatigue, but an emotional exhaustion that threatened to rend her heart in two.

The lawyer she'd engaged had made no promises of being able to solve her situation in a way that favored her. Mr. Freeman had returned to the hotel on Saturday and tried to convince her to stop struggling against her inevitable end.

If there was to be hope for her life, she knew it would come from God and the peace she always found in His house.

"Miss Charlotte, I heard about the dreadful mess with Mr. Freeman and Mr. Conrad." Cyrus Busby, the owner of the mercantile, made a clicking sound with his tongue. "What will you do when they take your hotel?"

The peace she'd longed for escaped her. "Mr. Busby, I have no intention of sitting idly by while anyone steals my hotel. As a local business owner, I'm sure you can understand the fervor I feel about this matter. Mr. Freeman cannot be allowed to violate his word to the good people of Gran Colina." Mrs. Gillis began to play the piano. "If you'll excuse me, I need to get the children settled for service." She nodded at Mr. Busby and guided the children to their customary bench.

More than once she caught the sympathetic glances of her fellow churchgoers. News of her dilemma must have reached everyone in town.

Reverend Gillis ended his sermon with a verse from the book of Romans. "'If it be possible, as much as lieth in you, live peaceably with all men.'" He closed his Bible. "I know sometimes the hardest thing for us to do is live in peace. It may feel impossible, but God wants us to do it if we can. Even if we have to stretch ourselves to make it happen."

Charlotte almost laughed aloud. *"...with all men."* God knew it would be difficult, and sometimes impossible to live at peace with men. She caught herself as the first sound of imminent laughter escaped her and turned the response into a cough. Nathan turned and met her gaze. His look told her he knew what caused her reaction.

The preacher dismissed the service a few minutes later, and Charlotte tried to make a hasty exit. She was on the bottom step outside the church when Sarah tripped and fell.

"Oh, baby, did you hurt yourself?" Charlotte helped her up and scanned her hands and elbows for scrapes.

"My doll's dress is dirty." Sarah's familiar pout appeared, and she held up the doll. "And her skirt is torn." Tears followed the pout, and so did the attention of everyone leaving the church.

Charlotte wrapped Sarah in a hug and tried to soothe her.

Someone came to stand beside them and cast a welcome shadow over them. Welcome—until she realized it was Nathan. She fumbled to stand and held Sarah's hand.

"Please, Charlotte, don't rush off on my account." He went down on one knee and reached out to Sarah. "I'm sorry about your doll. Will you show me?"

Charlotte marveled at how Sarah dropped the hand she was holding and went into the circle of Nathan's arm to let him inspect the damage.

"I think your sister can repair this." He fingered the torn hem of the doll's dress.

Sarah nodded. "She's good at fixing things."

Nathan looked up at Charlotte. "I want to be good at fixing things."

"You fixed up the hotel all pretty like Momma and Pa wanted." Sarah put her hand on his shoulder. It had become her method of keeping his attention when she talked to him. Charlotte still marveled that Nathan had forged such a strong bond with Michael and Sarah.

"Charlotte helped a lot with that." Nathan didn't take the credit he deserved for all he'd done.

Sarah looked up at Charlotte and then back to Nathan. "Charlotte was sad before, and you fixed her. I think you need to do that again 'cause she's all sad again. I can hear when she cries at night in her room."

"Sarah." Charlotte reached for her hand. "We need to go. I'll repair your doll after lunch."

"Thank you for showing me your doll." Nathan hugged Sarah. He stood and said, "Can we talk, Charlotte?"

A pang of fear hit her middle. "There is nothing to say, Nathan."

"Please—"

"Miss Green, I need to speak to you." Charlotte's lawyer, Garth Renfroe, interrupted them. "It's important that we speak as soon as possible."

Charlotte tried to calm herself. Mr. Renfroe would not have approached her on a matter of business on a Sunday unless it was serious.

"Will you meet me at the hotel in twenty minutes? That will give me time to take care of the children so we can speak in private."

While she spoke, Nathan backed away from her and headed in the direction of his uncle's home. Part of her wanted to go with him, and part of her never wanted to face him again. Not if it hurt this much to watch him leave.

Mr. Renfroe agreed to meet her, and she took the kids to Mrs. Atkins.

"I'm so sorry to intrude on you again. I had no

idea I'd be handling all the business of the hotel on my own." Michael and Sarah went to sit at the table.

"They'll be fine here with me and Bertha. You go tend to your meeting." Mrs. Atkins followed Charlotte to the door that led into the restaurant and lowered her voice. "I've heard rumors in town, Miss Charlotte. I want you to know that I'm praying for God to let you and those sweet children keep your home and this hotel."

"That's a great comfort to me."

Mrs. Atkins leaned in and whispered, "I do miss how much easier your life was when you had Mr. Taylor here to help."

Charlotte rested her hand on Mrs. Atkins's arm. "He's a hard worker."

"And such a nice young man." Mrs. Atkins grinned at her.

"He seemed to be, didn't he?" Charlotte left before Mrs. Atkins said anything else that could distract her from her determination to keep the hotel.

Mr. Renfroe arrived five minutes later, and Charlotte led him into her parlor. She left the door ajar and offered him a seat on the settee. She sat on a chair that afforded her a full view of the lobby.

"Miss Green, I want you to know that I've done everything I can within the confines of the law. I've interviewed everyone from the mayor to the sheriff and others who had contact or business with Mr. Freeman or Mr. Eaton."

"I thank you for your efforts."

"You won't thank me when you've heard my news."

Charlotte's heart began to weep. The words she dreaded filled her ears.

"The deadline that Mr. Freeman gave you is tomorrow. There is no law or evidence that can prevent him from taking possession of the hotel. You've told me how much money your father borrowed from the bank. When I spoke with Mr. Freeman, he confirmed to me that's the amount of the loan. Standard banking procedure gives the property to the bank in the event a mortgage goes unpaid."

"Did you speak to the land agent? Davis Conrad?"

"I did. I saw nothing amiss in the papers Mr. Eaton signed showing the intent of Turner Hotels to buy the adjoining land."

"So there's nothing I can do?"

"No, ma'am. I do hate it more than I can say. I knew your pa. He would never have wanted you to lose this place."

"Thank you for that. It helps a bit to know that people understood my father's ways."

"He and your mother were fine folks." Mr. Renfroe looked out the window by the fireplace. The poor man was as uncomfortable bringing her this news as she was receiving it.

"What is my next course of action? If we have to go, I want to know when and how. I'll have to prepare my brother and sister. And find somewhere to live. And means to support them."

"You'll have the money that's over the amount of the banknote. Mr. Freeman tried to say that you would be walking away with nothing. I convinced him that it wouldn't be in his best interest for me to take him before a judge who would read the case in another way entirely. A judge who might even give you the property. But in any regard, he'd ruin his reputation in town if he was seen to be stealing from a passel of young ones."

Charlotte leaned forward on her chair. "Could a judge do that? I'd be willing to plead my case before the judge. Surely a fair-minded judge would see it's only right for my family to keep what our father built for us."

"By law, the only thing owed to you will be the balance of the purchase amount after the loan and any unpaid interest is given to the bank. Mr. Freeman knew there was no chance we'd win a case like that. I was only trying to force his hand and prove that he couldn't take what you're rightfully owed. He relented to keep from smearing his name. That's the only reason."

"How long will I have to move out?" The words came from her, but she didn't recognize her voice anymore. The question made no sense. They couldn't move out. It was their home, the only place they'd ever lived. All their memories were here.

"Mr. Freeman has agreed to give you one month after the papers are signed by the Turners. That should happen in another week or two. I'll notify you as soon as I know for certain what day it will be."

"I see." She was numb. The pain had become so overwhelming that her mind and heart refused to feel it. She shook her head. There were things to be handled. "If Nathan taught me anything, it was to stay focused on the task at hand."

"A valuable lesson in business." Mr. Renfroe tugged at his collar. "I'm sorry to be speaking to you on a Sunday about all of this. It's just that Mr. Eaton came to my home this morning before church. He'd received a telegram from his employers and wanted to begin the process of shifting the business over as soon as possible."

"Am I obligated to do that before they sign the papers?"

"No, but I didn't want him to barge in on you and upset you. I thought you deserved to know."

"I think I'd like to keep him out of the hotel until it belongs to the Turners. I might even try to get myself somewhere to go at that time. I don't think I could bear to be here while they work at my desk and manage my workers. The children don't need that."

Mr. Renfroe nodded. "I'll let him know. I can handle all the communication with him. You won't have to deal with them at all." He took a breath and continued. "They want to keep all the reservations that are on the books for the foreseeable future. Word of Mr. Thornhill's meeting for farmers has spread through town. It seems the Turners would like to have that income to help pay for the purchase of the hotel."

"I see. The meeting that I booked will be used to buy my hotel. I've effectively lost my home, and the labor I did has made it possible. I've worked myself out of my job and home."

"It didn't start off that way, but that is the ultimate effect of things. I am sorry for you, Miss Green. Truly, I am."

"As am I." She needed to know the rest of the details. "Will you accept payment from the funds I'm to receive? Will that be paid to me when they sign?"

"I'll be waiving my fee, Miss Green. The Good Lord wouldn't want me to profit off the sorrow of orphans."

Orphans? The whole town saw them as orphans.

That's what they were. Somehow, until this moment, Charlotte hadn't thought of them like that. Without their hotel, they'd be orphans without a home.

"You're most gracious to offer, but I insist on paying for your services. I'll not raise Michael and Sarah to think of our family as an object of pity."

Nathan walked into Sheriff Braden's office on Monday morning. "Were you able to do anything to help Charlotte and her siblings?"

Scott stood behind his desk. He took off his hat and hung it on a peg on the wall. "Good morning, Nathan."

"Today is the day the six weeks are up. I don't have time for pleasantries."

"No." Scott sat on the corner of his desk. "Mr. Renfroe and I talked with the mayor and the land agent. Everyone's hands are tied. I can't say Mr. Conrad is sorry. He treats that job as the land agent like the county land belongs to him. He's happy to see a big company come to town."

"What will Charlotte do?"

"Mr. Renfroe has been over the details with her." He scratched his chin. "I don't think I oughta tell you her private business. Not since she asked you to leave."

Nathan slumped into the chair in front of Scott's desk. "All I wanted to do was help her."

"I think all she remembers now is you coming to town to take over her place."

"I didn't know it was hers. You know Mr. Freeman wasn't completely honest about the arrangements when he hired me."

"I know from experience in the last election that

he's been known to bend the truth in his direction if he thought it could help him."

Nathan sat up straight. "Do you think he might lie about something? Even if it broke the law?"

Scott shrugged. "I never caught him in anything so blatant. Can't say as I know the limits of his determination on things. He's been known to be a bit ruthless."

"Have you seen the loan papers that Charlotte's father signed?"

"No. I figured Charlotte had a copy in her father's things. And there'd be a copy at the bank."

Nathan shot to his feet. "Thank you, Sheriff! Thank you very much." He opened the door.

"For what?"

Nathan stopped at the door. "I'm not sure, but you may have just given me a clue as to how I can help Charlotte."

He went straight to Mr. Renfroe's office, but the man wasn't there yet. He scribbled a note on a page from his notebook and tucked it into the door frame. There was no time to waste on the day of the deadline.

His next stop was the bank. He marched up to the first desk inside the door. "I need to see Thomas Freeman. Right away."

The man at the desk rose from his chair. "Do you have an appointment?"

"I do not, but I will be seen. Now."

Mr. Freeman must have heard him, because the man came out of the office in the back of the bank where Nathan and Charlotte had signed papers on the accounts for the hotel.

"We don't have any business that I'm aware of, Mr. Taylor." The banker's arrogance grated on Nathan.

"I want to see the loan papers on the hotel. The ones signed by Mr. Green."

"You have no reason to see those papers."

"They are the foundation of your insistence that you can make all the decisions about the hotel. I want to read them."

"Those papers are private. I do not run a newspaper. The matters that are handled by my bank are not for the public to read."

Nathan recognized when he was being stonewalled. He had precious little time. He wouldn't waste it on Mr. Freeman, not if he had any hope of saving Green's Grand Hotel.

He left the bank without another word. Mr. Renfroe was on the sidewalk reading his note when Nathan arrived back at the lawyer's office.

"Mr. Renfroe, do you think I may be on to something?"

The man lifted one shoulder. "It bears consideration." He pushed the door open and waited for Nathan to enter. "Let's see what we can find out before Mr. Eaton arrives with another telegram."

An hour later, Nathan and Mr. Renfroe went into the hotel. Charlotte stood behind the desk.

It took every bit of his self-control to let Mr. Renfroe explain the purpose of their visit. "If you'll show me the papers your father signed with Mr. Freeman, we can see if there is anything there to help you." He looked to Nathan. "When I spoke to Mr. Freeman at the bank, my main concern was verifying that the loan existed, and he had the right to take possession of the hotel. I took him at his word. It would never have occurred to me to look for improprieties in the banknote itself. It's highly unlikely."

Charlotte held her hands out. "I don't know where to start." She pointed at Nathan. "You looked through all of the hotel journals when you first got here. And we both went through Pa's journal. I don't know where else something like that would be."

"Think, Charlotte. This could save the hotel for you." Nathan rapped the side of his fists against the edge of the registration desk.

"Why can't we look at the bank paperwork? Won't it be the same?" Charlotte spoke to Nathan. He was glad to see her trust in him flicker to life by this one action. If she thought him to be against her, she'd have addressed the lawyer.

"It's should be. But what if it isn't? Or what if there is something there to stop Mr. Freeman from selling the hotel? We can't know if we don't see the papers. And he refused to show them to me. He said the papers belong to the bank and your pa. Without your pa here, the bank is the only entity with the authority to view the papers."

Mr. Renfroe shook his head. "That refusal is all I needed to cause me to suspicion that something is awry here."

Charlotte rubbed her temples with the tips of her fingers. "I'm trying to think. Where would he put such a thing?"

"What about in the valise where you found the journal? When you found the journal, you left the valise on the bed. Have you been back into that room?"

"No." He knew she was thinking of her parents again. The soft word was referent for the memory, but lilted up in a note of hope as she opened the parlor door and went into her residence.

Nathan and Mr. Renfroe stepped into the parlor and waited while she turned the valise upside down again. She ran her hand inside along the edges of the bag. Nothing.

"Nathan, what am I going to do? If you're right, and I don't find the paper, I'll lose all of this for no reason." She stopped still. "If you're wrong, you'll be here with Mr. Eaton, running my hotel." The edge came back into her tone.

Mr. Renfroe lifted his hand. "I have an idea. The two of you can keep looking here. I'm going to see if I can persuade Mr. Freeman another way. Mr. Taylor, do you think Turner Hotels would be involved in a business deal if there was something that was perhaps unethical—or even unlawful?"

"No. I can say without hesitation that, in the five years I worked for them, I never saw anything that would give me cause to think they would do such a thing."

"Good. I'm going to see if that bit of information will motivate Mr. Freeman to let me see the loan. It wouldn't go well for him if I insisted that the Turners review the details to make certain they were taking lawful possession of the property. As Miss Green's lawyer, I'd have to insist on it." He grinned and left them.

Charlotte sat on the settee. "They really wouldn't take the hotel from me if they thought Mr. Freeman was trying to do some underhanded deal?"

"No. Mr. Turner is a stern businessman, but he didn't build his reputation on injustice."

She looked at him. For the first time since Mr. Eaton had announced the impending sale of the hotel, Charlotte looked at him. He'd watched her in the churchyard, but she had been closed off from him. "Why are you doing this, Nathan? Won't you risk your new job?"

"Charlotte, I didn't come here to take your family legacy from you." He sat on the edge of the settee beside her. "No matter what anyone tells you, not the fact that Mr. Eaton came to town at the same time I did, not the offer to run this place that he gave me last week—none of that means anything. I came here to build a life for myself. In a place where I'd been happy before."

She covered her face with her hands. Her muffled words tore at his heart. "What if we can't find the bank papers?"

"If we don't find them, we'll never know. Unless Mr. Renfroe has more success with Mr. Freeman than I think is possible."

She dropped her hands. "What about the journal? Did Pa mention where he put the banknote?"

"I don't remember anything like that, but we can look. Where is the journal?"

"I haven't seen it since you left. I don't know where you put it."

"Did you check the shelves in the registration desk?"

"Yes. I decided it was lost. I thought we'd accomplished everything Pa wanted to be done."

Nathan went into the lobby and searched the shelves. "Do you think one of the kids may have found it? Michael was fascinated by your father's handwriting. He'd sit and copy the pages when he was working with me." Nathan missed the little guy and the time they spent together at this desk.

"I'll check his room."

Nathan followed her. "Look in his desk. He may have fancied himself being like your father by working at the desk they bought for him."

She called out from his room. "I found it!" She rushed back into the parlor and began to flip through the pages. Her hands trembled, but when she'd skimmed the last page she shook her head. "Where else could it be?"

"Did your father have a lockbox of any kind? Somewhere he might keep extra money or important things."

"No, but mother does. It's under her shawls in her dresser." She was on her feet in an instant. She brought the box into the parlor and put it on the small table where they'd worked so many nights on the plans for the hotel. "It's got a lock, and I've never seen the key."

Nathan thought for a minute. "Did you tell me her reticule was in the box from the train?"

"Yes." She retrieved it and turned it inside out on the table. A pink ribbon was tied to the inside seam of the reticule. A tiny key was looped into the ribbon.

Charlotte fit the key into the lock and opened the box. The first thing on the top of the stack of papers inside was the loan from the bank. She darted a glance of pure joy in his direction before she held it up to read.

Nathan stepped beside her and read over her shoulder. They both murmured as they read the words. Halfway down the page, Charlotte pointed to a paragraph.

"That's it! That's what Mr. Renfroe needs to see."

He read the paragraph and nodded. "You're right! I can't promise it will work, but I think you just saved

Green's Grand Hotel from Thomas Freeman and Turner Hotels."

She turned toward him. They were so close that the scent of lavender on her hair dared him to breathe deeply.

"I didn't do it, Nathan." She tightened her fist around the paper and pushed her hand into his chest. "You did it."

He shook his head. "No. It's your hotel. You found the papers. This is your victory."

Nathan took a step away from her. He couldn't bear to be so close and not wrap her in his arms.

Mr. Renfroe came into the room. "I found Mr. Freeman at the bank. He is a stubborn man. I got nowhere with him."

Charlotte waved the paper back and forth. "We found it." Her face erupted in a smile. "There's a paragraph that no one has told us about. We need your advice, but we think it will save the hotel."

The lawyer read the paper and nodded. "This is it! I'll get the sheriff and head over to the bank now. Would the two of you like to come along?"

Charlotte squared her shoulders. "I'd like to meet you there. I have something to discuss with Mr. Taylor first."

"Fine. I'll be there within a half hour." Mr. Renfroe whistled a happy tune as he left them.

"Nathan, I need to tell you something."

"I understand. You're glad to have the hotel secure, but you're ready to be on your own. It's true. You've handled everything that's come up since you've been in charge. You don't need me anymore. Your training is far enough along for you to learn the rest as you go."

"That's not what I was going to say, but since you brought it up, I don't want to be your boss anymore."

Chapter Seventeen

"I see. Well, you told me from the beginning that you didn't want me here." Nathan was using his most businesslike voice. She hated the distance he so easily put between them with his tone.

Charlotte didn't know how to tell Nathan what was in her heart. She just knew it had to be said before he left. "That's how I felt the first day, but I thought we'd managed to put that behind us." Her heart remembered their kiss and the feel of her hand in his.

"You treated me like a hired hand from the moment Mr. Eaton showed up and tried to buy this place. How long do you think a man can go along with being treated like that?"

"I was upset. Losing my home and livelihood when I'm responsible for two small children is enough to upset a lady." She punched the air between them with her finger. "And you pocketed his offer like it was a lifeline."

"You had every right to be upset." He held his hands wide. "I was upset, too. I had you standing there accusing me of trying to steal your hotel, and Mr. Eaton offering me a way to make a living if you pushed me away."

"But you took him up on his offer, didn't you?"

Nathan reached into his jacket and pulled the envelope from his pocket. He handed it to her without a word. She turned it over in her hand.

"You never opened it."

"No."

"Why not?" The dead place in her chest started to quiver with resurrected life.

"I couldn't work for someone who would take all this from you." He looked around and shrugged his shoulders. "Even if you didn't want me around, I couldn't work against you."

"Are you sure you wouldn't rather work at a bigger hotel? I'm certain they'd take you back on in Dallas." She handed him the envelope. "I'm sorry. You probably can't forgive me. I wouldn't blame you if you didn't want to."

"Losing your trust was more than I could bear." He raised his brows. "I've learned something about myself since I came back to Gran Colina. I'd rather have a better quality hotel with you. It's a better place, because the people running it love it."

"Momma always said I needed help when it came to judging character. She said I wasn't serious enough to see people for who they are."

He tilted his head to one side and looked at her. "How old were you when she said that?"

"Fifteen or so the last time she said it, I guess."

"Would you allow yourself permission to grow?" He leaned a bit closer to her. "Like you did me. I'm not the same boy I was when I teased you. And you're not the same schoolgirl who needed her mother to guide her about people and associations."

"I hope you're right."

"Why?"

"Because I have made some decisions on my own that I want to work out like I imagine."

"What sort of decisions?"

"Oh, about people. And associations. I need to tell you about one of them." She reached for his hand.

"I'm listening."

"I don't want to be your boss anymore." She took a small step closer to him.

"You're going to keep to that decision after all we're talking about?"

"Yes. I'm determined not to be your boss anymore."

He took a step toward her. "Will you tell me what caused you reach this decision?"

She put her hands on his shoulders. "I don't think I should be your boss anymore because I fell in love with you."

He captured her hands with his. "But you weren't looking to fall in love."

"No. And you weren't, either."

"I wasn't."

"Did you?"

Nathan nodded and lowered his face toward hers. "I did." He told her how much with his kiss. No words could convey to her soul the power of the love they shared.

She pushed against his chest and leaned back to look into his face. "We're going to be late for our meeting at the bank if we don't leave now."

He dropped a light kiss on her cheek and another

on her forehead. "I will go with you to the bank, but, later, I want us to finish this conversation about the decisions you're making."

She smiled and stepped away from him. "I want to go by the school after we leave the bank so we can tell Michael and Sarah the news."

"The news about the hotel?"

She hooked her hand in the crook of his arm as they walked across the lobby. "After we tell them about us."

When Charlotte and Nathan entered the bank lobby, the sheriff motioned for them to follow him into Mr. Freeman's office. Mr. Renfroe waited for them there.

Mr. Freeman stood behind his desk. "I don't appreciate all of you interrupting my business. Mr. Eaton and the land agent will be here any minute to sign the papers for the transfer of the hotel."

Mr. Renfroe answered the banker. "That's why we're here."

"You told me that Miss Green didn't want to be here for the signing." The puzzled look Mr. Freeman wore deepened to annoyance.

Charlotte held up one hand. "I didn't want to come sign away my father's work or the livelihood he built for me and my siblings."

Mr. Freeman huffed out a breath. "Then I suggest you leave." He pointed toward the lobby. "The gentlemen have arrived to deal with the paperwork."

"We aren't leaving." Charlotte took Nathan's hand and enjoyed the comfort of his unspoken support when he gave her hand a reassuring squeeze. "Nor are you going to sign away my hotel."

"Miss Green, we've been over this." Mr. Freeman

turned to Scott Braden. "Sheriff, will you clear these people out of my office?"

"No."

"No?" He folded his arms across his chest. "Will someone please explain to me what is going on here?"

Mr. Renfroe pulled her father's copy of the banknote from the inside pocket of his suit and handed it to Charlotte. "I think you should handle this."

Nathan released her hand, and she took the note from the lawyer. "We found this in my mother's things."

Mr. Freeman's patience vanished. "What could your mother have possessed that would be of interest to me? I don't have time for sentimental letters or such."

"This is sentimental." Charlotte unfolded the banknote. "To me and my family." She held it up for everyone in the room to see. "I'd like to read the paragraph my father wrote in his own hand."

She cleared her throat and read aloud.

"This banknote is for the sole purpose of refurnishing and refurbishing Green's Grand Hotel. The furnishings are the only collateral. At no time will Green's Grand Hotel be seized in exchange for the obligations of this note. A grace period of six months will take effect immediately in the event the payments are ever in arrears."

She loved her father. He'd proved his love and determination to provide for her and her siblings by including these provisions.

Charlotte folded the banknote, and silence filled the room.

Nathan smiled at her and winked. She looped her hand into the crook of his elbow.

Mr. Freeman finally spoke. "That clause was added by your father. It isn't in keeping with bank policy."

"Was it written before you signed the document?" Mr. Renfroe asked.

"Think carefully before you answer, Mr. Freeman. As sheriff, I'm prepared to insist on seeing the bank's copy of the note."

"May I add to what you've read, Miss Green?" At her nod, Mr. Renfroe continued, "We are prepared to accept that this provision wasn't your idea and that you didn't want such an exception to become public knowledge. For the sake of the bank's reputation in regard to their business practices and fairness, of course."

Mr. Freeman opened his mouth to speak, but Mr. Renfroe held up his hand to stop him. "I'm not finished. Miss Green deserves an apology from you for the sorrow this situation has added to her grieving family. In exchange for that apology and your assurances that the banknote will be honored by the bank and transferred to Miss Green with the same provisions her father previously arranged, we will keep the matters that have been discussed here today in confidence. Should you violate any of the conditions I'm offering, we will have no obligation to protect your privacy and will seek immediate remedy by taking this information in its entirety before a judge in open court. Is that satisfactory to all parties?"

Charlotte was pleased with how quickly and proficiently her lawyer took the situation in hand. "I am willing to abide by those conditions."

Mr. Freeman stared at the floor. "I accept your offer."

"Good. I'll draw up the papers and present them for

all parties to sign later this afternoon." Mr. Renfroe pointed at Mr. Freeman. "As soon as you offer your sincere apologies to Miss Green."

The banker lifted his head. "I apologize to you, Miss Green, for any and all harm I've caused your family."

She watched the color fade from the banker's face. "In good Christian faith, I accept, Mr. Freeman. And I trust that we will have no problems in the future."

Mr. Freeman nodded. "You have my full assurance."

Charlotte turned to Scott Braden. "Sheriff, if you and Mr. Renfroe can handle the details, I'd like to accompany Mr. Taylor to the school. We need to talk to Michael and Sarah about all that has transpired today."

On their way through the bank lobby, Mr. Eaton put out a hand to stop Nathan. "Are you certain you won't reconsider our offer to return to the employ of Turner Hotels? We're about to sign the papers to purchase Green's Grand Hotel and the adjoining land. This will be your last opportunity to work with us."

"My mind is made up." Nathan pulled his elbow closer to his side and covered Charlotte's hand with his. "Now, if you'll excuse me, I have pressing matters to attend."

When they stepped out of the bank into the sunshine of the day, Nathan turned toward her. "You were amazing. Have I told you that I love you?"

She shook her head. "You did give me every indication, but you never actually spoke the words."

He put his hands on her shoulders and slid them down to capture her elbows. "Let me rectify that omission immediately." He leaned very close.

Suddenly shy of him, her heart pounded so that she thought he might hear it. "Nathan, we are in the street. People will see."

"I don't see anyone but you." He took a small step closer. "I love you, Charlotte Green."

"I'm very glad." She got lost in the depths of his blue eyes. "I love you, too."

He took her face in his hands. "I love you and your family."

"That's a good thing, because I know Sarah loves you." She laughed and lifted her hands to rest on his shoulders. "And, as long as you promise that Michael can have the run of the hotel one day, I'm sure he'll come to love you, too."

Then Nathan kissed her. In the middle of the street where anyone who wanted to could see.

And she didn't care. She didn't even think Momma would object after all they'd been through together.

Epilogue

Three weeks later, Charlotte went into her parents' room. She folded the clothes that she'd left in a heap on their bed. She'd have Opal alter her mother's dresses to fit her. Nathan was taller than her father, so she'd offered his things to Revered Gillis. Mrs. Gillis had promised to collect them this afternoon.

Nathan's knock sounded on the parlor door.

She stepped into the hallway. "Come in. I'm in my parents' room."

"Won't you come into the parlor and greet me?" He winked when she cast a glance over her shoulder at him.

"Let me finish this first. It will only take another minute or two."

"Only a minute. I have to go to the meeting Mayor Livingston is having about the new town hall."

Charlotte picked up her mother's blue skirt. Charlotte had loved to see her wear it. The color was lovely with her cream blouse. As she folded it to add to the stack of other things to be altered, she felt something in the pocket. She reached in and found her mother's small notebook. It was the one she used for recipe ideas and notes about the hotel. She must have taken it on the trip to record things she saw in Dallas.

Charlotte carried the book into the parlor. "Look what I found in my mother's pocket." She held up the book for Nathan to see. "It's the notebook she used for work things."

"What a great thing to find. Maybe she wrote down things you'd like to implement here. Now that the farmers' meeting is behind us—and a great success it was—we need to begin planning the next phase of improvements. It won't take many meetings like the one last week for the bank loan to be paid in full."

They were ahead of schedule on the payments. "I look forward to that day, though I am satisfied with the way Mr. Renfroe arranged things."

She turned the pages of the notebook and smiled at her mother's neat handwriting. There were new recipes and a couple of notes on how to help the maids do their jobs with more efficiency. Tucked into the very back was a small envelope. Charlotte looked at the front of it and tears began to flow down her cheeks.

Nathan was at her side in an instant. "What is it?"

"A letter to me. She must have decided not to post it. She probably thought she'd arrive home before the letter did."

Nathan urged her to sit on the settee and read it.

She slid her finger under the edge of the envelope and lifted it. The letter inside was only one page, but Charlotte knew no matter what the content she would always treasure it as the last words from her mother.

My dear Charlotte,

Your father and I didn't share the purpose of our trip as we wanted it to be a surprise for you. You've grown into such a lovely young woman, and we are honored to be your parents. The financial future of the hotel is more important than ever as you have reached adulthood, and your siblings will be grown before we're ready for them to be.

I promise to share all the details of our trip with you over the next few weeks, but there is one item of a personal nature that I want to share immediately.

Your father and I have encountered Nathan Taylor in Dallas. You'll remember him as the young man who tormented you in school before he and his parents moved away from Gran Colina.

We have spent a good deal of time with him and found him to be a man of good character. After we finish the changes we want to make to the hotel, your father wants to contact Nathan and ask him to help us run the hotel. He has a vast knowledge of the workings of the hotel business, but it's more than that. There is something about this young man that your father and I approve.

In fact, God has not given my heart reason to pause over this young man as He did with so many others who offered to call on you.

And I daresay you might even find him handsome.

I will tell you more about the reasons for our approval when we are together again.

*I love you, so. Thank you, our darling girl, for
caring for Michael and Sarah in our absence.
The three of you hold our hearts in yours. We
thank God for all of you when we pray.*
Momma

Charlotte wept tears of joy at this wonderful gift
from her mother. It was greater than anything she
could have asked for.

She read it again. Aloud this time for Nathan's benefit.

He sat beside her on the settee and, when she finished the letter, he dried her tears with his handkerchief.

"I'm amazed at this." Nathan hadn't realized how
much Charlotte's parents had thought of him and his
future. Especially in regard to Charlotte.

"She never approved of anyone. Not once." Charlotte shook her head. "This is God's way of letting me
know how they felt about you."

"Charlotte, I've waited for the right time to talk to
you about something important. I didn't know what
would be proper and fitting given the fact that your
parents aren't here for me to seek their counsel."

Her heart raced. The joy of this moment was overwhelming, and she thought God was about to bless her
beyond her dreams.

Nathan took her hands in his. "Given the approval
that I've just received from your parents—" He cleared
his throat. "Charlotte, will you do me the honor of becoming my bride?"

The tears flowed new and fresh. "Yes." She threw
her arms around his neck. "Yes!"

Michael and Sarah came into the parlor. The day had passed so quickly that Charlotte didn't realize it was time for the children to return from school. She unwound her arms from Nathan's neck and rested her hands in her lap.

Michael frowned. "What are you screaming about, Charlotte? You never scream."

Charlotte looked to Nathan. "Shall we tell them?"

He nodded his agreement. "I'm still in awe."

"What is it?" Michael wasn't so angry anymore, but neither was he patient.

Nathan put his arm around Charlotte's shoulders.

Charlotte knew her excitement was more than the kids ever saw in her. "Nathan and I are getting married!"

Sarah squealed with Charlotte. "I love weddings!" She ran and hugged them both.

"Do I have to dress up in my Sunday clothes for the wedding?" Michael scratched his head. "Because if I do, I think you should get married on Sunday so I don't have to wear them an extra day."

Nathan laughed. "We might be able to do that, Michael."

Sarah leaned over to Nathan and whispered in her loudest whispering tone. "Are you gonna kiss her now?"

"Sarah!" Charlotte was shocked at her question.

"I'm only asking 'cause Nathan said you should only be kissed when you want to be kissed."

Nathan nodded. "I did say that."

Charlotte laughed.

"Don't you wanna be kissed?" Sarah tugged on her hand. "Momma and Pa were married, and they kissed. Momma said Pa kissed her because it made her happy."

She looked at Nathan. "If you want to make her happy, you have to kiss her."

Out of the mouths of babes.

Charlotte leaned toward Nathan, and he kissed her in a sweet way that made Sarah clap for joy.

Momma was right. Nathan's kiss did make her happy.

* * * * *

If you enjoyed A Ready-Made Texas Family, *look for these other Love Inspired Historical titles by Angel Moore:*

Conveniently Wed
The Marriage Bargain
The Rightful Heir
Husband by Arrangement

Find more great reads at
www.LoveInspired.com.

Dear Reader,

Grief is always eased in the presence of love.

Charlotte's responsibilities seem unmanageable for someone so young, but she's a determined soul. And it shows as she overcomes one obstacle after another. Nathan's help is a godsend. Together they create a life and home that will serve their family for generations to come.

God does the same for His children. I can't count the times I've been at my wit's end only to be rescued by God's provision—or intervention. When the battles seem the heaviest and our pain is raw, He brings comfort and grace.

Thank you for taking the time to read *A Ready-Made Texas Family*. The lessons of grief are real and personal. I didn't know that I'd lose my beloved sister, Lisa, weeks after I turned the book over to my editor. I can say from experience that the hope of heaven eases the pain of loss and enables us to look to the eternal future.

I'd love to hear from you. You can reach me through my website at www.angelmoorebooks.com, where you'll find links to all my books, the latest news, and ways to connect with me on social media. You can also sign up for my newsletter on the home page.

May God bless you with the strength, wisdom, and determination to overcome everything life brings your way.

Angel Moore

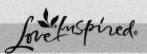
"I wanted to talk to you about a project I'm getting started on. I'm opening a bakery."

"You are?" Annie couldn't keep the surprise out of her voice.

"Ja," Caleb said. "I stopped by to see if you'd be interested in working for me."

"You want to hire me? To work in your bakery?"

"I've had some success selling bread and baked goods at the farmers market in Salem. Having a shop will allow me to sell year-round, but I can't be there every day and do my work at the farm. My sister, Miriam, told me you'd do a *gut* job for me."

"It sounds intriguing," Annie said. "What would you expect me to do?"

"Tend the shop and handle customers. There would be some light cleaning. I may need you to help with baking sometimes."

"Ja, I'd be interested in the job."

"Then it's yours. If you've got time now, I'll give you a tour of the bakery, and we can talk more about what I'd need you to do."

"*Gut.*" The wind buffeted her, almost knocking her from her feet.

She mumbled that she needed to let her twin, Leanna, know where she was going. He wrapped his arms around himself as another blast of wind struck them.

"Hurry…anna…" The wind swallowed the rest of his words as she rushed toward the house.

She halted in midstep.

Anna?

Had Caleb thought he was talking to her twin? She'd clear everything up on their way to the bakery. She wanted the job. It was an answer to so many prayers, for God to let her find a way to help her sister be happy again, happy as Leanna had been before the man she loved married someone else without telling her.

Leanna was attracted to Caleb, and he'd be a fine match for her. Outgoing where her twin was quiet. A well-respected, handsome man whose *gut* looks would be the perfect foil for her twin's. But Leanna would be too shy to let Caleb know she was interested in him. That was where Annie could help.

As she was rushing to the house, she reminded herself of one vital thing. She must be careful not to let her own attraction to Caleb grow while they worked together.

That might be the hardest part of the job.

Don't miss
The Amish Bachelor's Baby *by Jo Ann Brown,*
available March 2019 wherever
Harlequin® Love Inspired books and ebooks are sold.

www.LoveInspired.com

LIHEXP00521